D0610097

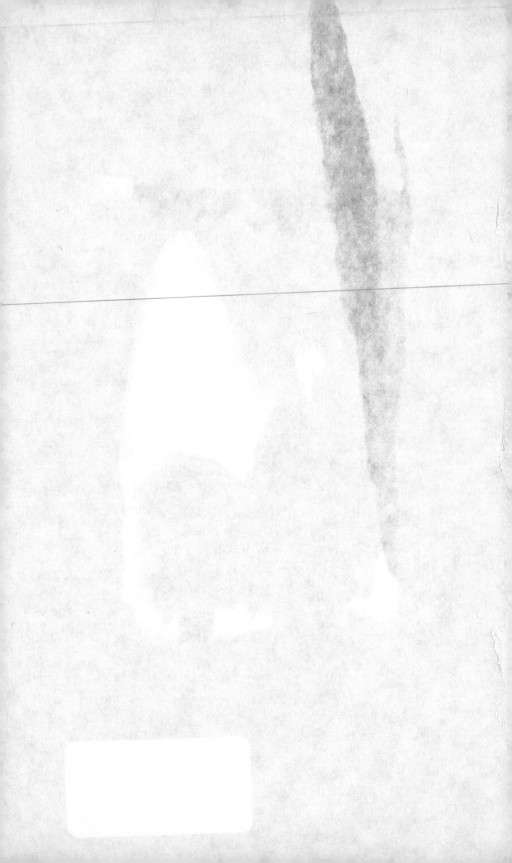

No Trust

No Text

No Trust

LESLIE ESDAILE BANKS

KENSINGTON PUBLISHING CORP.
http://www.kensingtonbooks.com

DAFINA BOOKS are published by

Kensington Publishing Corp.
850 Third Avenue
New York, NY 10022

Copyright © 2007 by Leslie Esdaile Banks

All rights reserved. No part of this book may be reproduced in any form or by any means without the prior written consent of the Publisher, excepting brief quotes used in reviews.

All Kensington titles, imprints and distributed lines are available at special quantity discounts for bulk purchases for sales promotion, premiums, fund-raising, educational or institutional use.

Special book excerpts or customized printings can also be created to fit specific needs. For details, write or phone the office of the Kensington Special Sales Manager: Kensington Publishing Corp., 850 Third Avenue, New York, NY 10022. Attn. Special Sales Department. Phone: 1-800-221-2647.

Dafina Books and the Dafina logo Reg. U.S. Pat. & TM Off.

ISBN-13: 978-0-7582-1332-7
ISBN-10: 0-7582-1332-8

First Kensington Trade Paperback Printing: September 2007
10 9 8 7 6 5 4 3 2 1

Printed in the United States of America

LANCASHIRE COUNTY LIBRARY	
10660226 ʃ	
HJ	31/10/2007
F	£8.99

This book is dedicated to my mother, Helen, and my father, William, for all their tireless community devotion. While on this side of heaven they never got to see all their dreams come true, I hope they can rest easy knowing that the baton got passed and picked up. Some of us still have the flame. Much love!

SOUTH LANCASHIRE LIBRARIES

SUH
11/07

Acknowledgments

I would like to thank the fine folks at Kensington Publishing who got behind this four book project, and my new editor, Selena James (also my very first editor, Monica Harris), for making sure that this last book neatly tied up the adventures of Laura Caldwell and James Carter. Thank you so much!

Chapter 1

Maui, Hawaii

Jamal dropped the keys to his Hummer on the dresser, pulled his cell phone out of his pocket, and clicked it off. It was amazing what a couple million dollars could do for a brother. God bless his cousin Laura! If this was how the other half lived, then he better understood his cousin's philosophy: get rich or die trying. Membership most definitely had its privileges. If he had it his way, except for a few quick annual visits to see his father, he'd never go home to North Central Philly again. It was cold, nothing but concrete jungle and hassle. This was paradise.

Jamal looked at Safia and the way she sprawled out on the bed for him. *Damn,* she was fine. He didn't care that she felt more comfortable at her house rather than at the plush environs of the hotel. Whatever she wanted was cool, as long as it made her get nasty like this. So what that her joint had just a few pieces of rented furniture.

This female was *all that*... Hawaiian, she had gorgeous, silky, chocolate brown hair hanging way down her back and dusting her ass, skin like caramel, a pretty face, man-made tits, legs longer than his, and a cute little belly ring. Yeah, a brother could get used to this. Even though the rap career never took off and he'd gotten caught up doing a short bid for possession, he was now living the life—and it was all about the now.

Watching her watch him, anticipation added to the throb that was making his stomach clench. Jamal yanked his white Phat Farm T-shirt over his head, pleased with Safia's reaction. That's right, he wasn't the skinny, lanky kid anymore. A personal trainer, eating properly with time to work on his build had changed that, too. The correct bank digits in the seven figures could definitely change a man's life, just like it put two rocks of ice in his earlobes.

He kicked off his Air Force 1 sneakers, stripped off his white walking shorts and boxers, and smiled. He couldn't believe it— she'd actually licked her lips and closed her eyes and then slid her hand between her legs. *For him.*

He walked forward, balls aching. It had been so long since he'd gotten any, given all the bullshit that was always going down in the family—always on the run, always somebody shooting at 'em, and he didn't have any real cash before.

Safia pulled herself up to kneel in front of him, as he approached the edge of the bed, and looked up with a sultry smile. He was trying to act cool, as though females did this to him every day, but it was something that he'd experienced only once. Sad but true, it was in the backseat of his boy's ride, performed by some fat chickenhead with a bad weave who was trying to get some product for free. But it definitely wasn't anything he'd ever had done by a female so fine that she looked like she'd stepped out of a Luda video.

Her intention was clear, though, as she kissed each newly created brick in his abdomen on her way down. Just knowing what she was about to do made his dick jump and begin to leak pre-cum.

His palms roved over the butter-soft lobes that he'd been craving to touch since he first saw her in the club . . . the way they jiggled in her halter, and now they were in his hands, their tiny brown nipples biting into his palms as she pressed them hard against his touch and moaned. He could see her round, luscious ass beginning to tighten and release in a promised dance. Feeling like he was about to pass out, he closed his eyes for a moment and held his breath, determined to chill. But when she pulled the head of his rod into her wet, lovely mouth, the sensation made his body buckle.

"Oh, shit . . ."

His voice had come out in a strangled rush as she drew him in slowly all the way to the hilt, then caressed the lobes of his ass with satin palms. He looked down, breathing hard; she didn't even gag, just took it all like a pro. Dazed for a second, he wasn't sure what to do with his hands, and definitely didn't want to interrupt her flow by trying to touch her awe-inspiring breasts while she worked.

Eventually, his hands found her hair and his fingers reveled in the silky texture. It was real; there was no glue to snag his fingers. She was real, not an image on cable to beat off to at night. Her big, beautiful eyes held his as her tongue worked in a swirl each time she pulled back, and then she finally gripped his base with both hands in a way that let him know she was about to get serious.

They shared a still glance for a moment, both breathing hard. She smiled a sexy half smile and lowered her head to his body again. This time there was no way to be cool, no way to fight against the rhythm she set. He was panting, sweating, and thrusting out of control. Then she suddenly stopped, threatening to give him an aneurism.

The immediate loss of contact with her warm, tight, sucking motion made it seem like all the air collapsed out of his lungs, pulling his stomach and nuts up into his chest. For a few futile seconds he couldn't stop moving and was thrusting nothing but air.

"Don't you want to finish off inside me?" she murmured against his stomach.

Truthfully, at this point, it really didn't matter, but he told her what she wanted to hear. "Yeah, baby," he croaked. "Find the latex."

He'd just have to make it up to her next round. In his heart he knew that in a few hard strokes he'd be finished. He watched her lean over, get a condom off the nightstand, and open it. The moment she began to sheath him he winced from the needles of pleasure that were stabbing his shaft. He couldn't help it. When she sprawled back against the bed, he instantly blanketed her, clumsily finding her opening and entering her hard. She cried out and her nails dug into his shoulders. He didn't care; he was practically swooning from the sensation of being inside her, feeling her heavy breasts cushioning his chest, feeling her satin-smooth legs wrap around his waist, her ass in his hands putting a hump in his back.

Oh, *shit*, he was gonna get it and get it good—would make it up to her later at the mall. She smelled so damned good, and her tight pussy was putting starlights behind his lids, the harder he pumped. Her soft hands were caressing his cornrows, gliding over his scalp. She was thrashing and murmuring to him in a language he didn't know, and he didn't care as long as she kept swirling her hips in that snap-jerk motion that put tears in his eyes.

He came so hard and so fast that he almost swallowed his tongue. She was still moving beneath him, trying to get hers, but he couldn't help it, he was too far gone.

"It's still hard, baby," he said after a moment, gasping. Sweat was rolling down his sides and back and he kissed her forehead as she held him tighter. "Let me put a new one on so we don't have no accident, feel me?" He kissed her slowly and then traced her pout with the pad of his thumb. "You just so fine I couldn't help it . . . but trust me, I'ma make sure you get yours, too. Aw'ight?"

She nodded and closed her eyes, brushing his mouth with a kiss. He really felt bad when he held the rim of the condom and pulled out and she gasped, her expression agonized like she had been right there but just missed busting a nut. Although he'd initially had no intention of going downtown on a babe he technically just met . . . this one was fine enough and definitely sweet enough to make him forget all his self-imposed rules of booty chasing.

Jamal rolled over and stood with effort. "I'll be right back." He watched her roll over and offer him a sad smile as he crossed the room to head for the bathroom.

Yeah, this one stood a very good chance of being *the one*. She was sweet, didn't argue, didn't ask for much, was off da meter in bed. She could dance and liked to party, but wasn't a bona fide hoochie. He could get used to having a quality woman like that on his arm on a permanent tip, no doubt. When he got back to bed, he was gonna do her right. Then, maybe he'd take her somewhere real nice when he got back from Philly, like take her shopping, treat her to a real expensive dinner, maybe they could check out a flick.

He dropped the used condom in the toilet and flushed it, and then grabbed a towel to clean up any semen residue that could get her pregnant.

But a loud noise made him freeze and stare in the mirror, too paralyzed for a second to even turn around. It sounded like the front door had come off the hinges, and the heavy footsteps running down the hall were worse than a raid by po-po. Then, all of a sudden, the biggest, burliest, blackest, dreadlock wearing motherfucker he'd ever seen in his life crossed by the half-cracked open bathroom door as a spooky flash in the mirror, and headed for the bedroom bellowing Safia's name in a Jamaican accent.

"Wha' you tink, I'm crazy? You wif 'im in me house and expect wha, woman? Where 'im at! I'll blow him ass away gulley, you fuck 'im den, hear!"

"I don't know what you're talking about!" Safia shrieked. "Just because you helped me with rent a few times doesn't mean you live here, Terrence! I was getting dressed for work and, and—"

"Bitch, you got an open box of condoms on de dresser! You ass is wet, and you smell like sex! You tink—"

"'Cause I missed you, baby . . . I was hoping you'd come over, but you came in here accusing me!"

A closet door banged open. A search was obviously on.

"I told you wasn't nobody here."

"Den whose motherfucking Hummer is in da driveway, and who keys and cell phone is dis, huh? You wear a shirt dis big, love? You now wearing size fourteen Air Force 1's? Don' fuck wit me, Safia! You too gorgeous to hit, but I'll bust a cap in his ass!"

"I don't want you to go back to jail, baby—let him go," she wailed.

Jamal's mind processed everything in hundredths of micro-seconds—he was naked; a big, crazy-ass Jamaican was gonna cap him for fucking his woman. His car keys, cell phone, wallet, and everything else were in there with a madman. Safia would be all right—this was her man. Chivalry was dead, and he wasn't trying to be. *He was out.*

Towel in hand, Jamal dove through the bungalow window. He hit the ground with a thud and was up in a flash. Neighborhood dogs barked. Driveway gravel cut into his feet. But a hollering Jamaican was now hanging out the bathroom window, too big to get through it as quickly as he had. Gunshot report put every in-stinct from the old streets of Philly into Jamal's legs as his Hummer windshield took a 9-millimeter shell. Jamal moved like a zigzag blur, dodging bullets, ducking low, moving forward like greased lightning. God heard his prayers. The crazy Jamaican bastard had left his Jeep running.

"I'll kill you . . . touch me Jeep after touching me woman, bitch, and you a dead mon!"

More gunfire rang out as Jamal jumped into the Jeep's driver's seat and shifted into reverse, burning rubber against blacktop, and jumping as the side-view mirror exploded off the vehicle.

"Where is your brother?" Laura groaned, plopping down on the couch. "If he doesn't come on, he's gonna be late for the air-port, and we all promised your father we'd come home together for a visit this time."

"I know," Najira said. "You know how Jamal is." She looked over at Steve. "You think we should just leave the suitcase he packed and all his travel docs here at Laura and James's house, or take them back to his apartment?"

Steve raked his fingers through his blonde buzz cut and began to pace, growing agitated. His face was red and his mouth had become a tight line. "Why does your brother always pull this shit, huh? He brings his bags over here, says he's just gonna make a quick run, and then disappears for two hours."

"It's not my fault, Steve," Najira said, growing peevish. "I've been blowing up his cell all afternoon and he's not answering!"

James leaned against the wall with a thud, folding his arms over his chest. "Why don't we give him a few more minutes? Worst case, since he's not answering his cell, we can leave a voice mail on there and at his apartment. He's got a key to everybody's place, so you can tell him where his gear is and then he can catch the next available flight home. Case closed. No need for us all to get bent."

Grumbles of dissension wafted through the spacious living room of his and Laura's beachside bungalow. James watched Steve sulk away to go find a beer, which wasn't a half bad idea. Najira plopped her short, curvy self down on an overstuffed portion of the ivory leather sectional and flung her rust-toned dreadlocks over her shoulders with disgust. His wife did what she always did—Laura paced.

For a moment all he could do was watch her smooth her hands down her wheat-colored linen slacks as she stood. When Laura was pissed off she was often at her most sensual; his Scorpio woman had a way of turning quiet outrage into an art form. Her dark, moody eyes smoldered, and her normally lush mouth was set in a kissable pout, resolute. There was a slight tinge of rose hue beginning to creep into her caramel complexion that was very reminiscent of a sexual flush. Then she raked her long, graceful fingers through her short, silky onyx curls, leaving a just-tousled-in-bed look that he adored.

James rubbed his palm over his close-cropped hair, and then his newly clean-shaven jaw. He had to get his mind out of the gutter, but last night and this morning had really put a strain on his libido. All his wife had wanted to do was cuddle and talk.

He stared at her unashamed as she took in slow, cleansing breaths, her full breasts rising and falling beneath the linen shell she wore, and each slow, sauntering stride she took between the door and the window was like watching poetry in motion. Her regal height that made her fit so perfectly against him, her long legs, the mesmerizing sway of her hips, and the distinctive curve of her gorgeous ass. God, he loved that woman, and should have insisted on a little attention before this huge family affair. But how could he? She'd just wanted to be held when her uncle Akhan had called. The old man was cryptic as usual and refused to discuss anything on the telephone, but had insisted that the whole family come home immediately.

James had to admit, as he stared at his wife, that part of him was really pissed off and wanted to just yell to the old neighborhood street warrior that *the man* wasn't behind every goddamned corner. But then again, Akhan didn't get to be almost ninety without knowing something. It was just the brother's timing. Why did the call have to come after he and Steve had been away for almost a week deep-sea fishing?

Glimpsing his old partner from the force, who was guzzling a beer, James was sure that Steve quietly shared the same lack-of-nookie blues. If Laura Caldwell-Carter was concerned, then her young, high-strung cousin, Najira, had to have been a basket case last night—which meant that neither he nor Steve got lucky when they came home.

A whole week, and now they'd be traveling back to Philly not knowing what conditions they'd meet, since Akhan had gone conspiracy-theory-cryptic on them . . . which could mean even more emotional drama that would make his wife disinterested.

James sighed and made a mental note to remind himself to kick Steve's ass the next time he wanted to do some guys-only shit. He didn't care whether it cleared his partner's head so that Steve could decide to pop the question to Najira or not. Before long, Najira was gonna be showing, so it was pretty much a done deal. Akhan would probably try to shoot Steve's crazy ass if he didn't marry Jira. Maybe that's why Akhan had called for a family meeting—to get a clear sense of what was gonna be up. Who knew? But both Steve and Najira were sweating bullets about the visit, so Jamal being late was just plain ole fucked up.

Growing weary and philosophical, James pushed off the wall, needing to get Laura out of his sight. Hankering for what he couldn't have for the foreseeable future was just making him ornery. He headed for the kitchen and opened the fridge. Steve didn't say a word and just handed him a beer. The two nodded. After years of working together on the force before they'd retired, some things were simply done by telepathy.

Still, the disappearance of Jamal didn't sit right. James popped the top off a Heineken and turned it up to his mouth. Everything in his dormant cop senses told him that something was wrong. True, Jamal was prone to get lost in a good card game, might go AWOL smoking weed or chasing tail, but he wouldn't blow off going home to see his father. Those two were tight, and Akhan was getting up there in years.

The old man had suffered and survived World War I, Great Depression, World War II, Jim Crow, civil rights, marches, water hoses, and dogs; fled lynching states and the system, survived the mean streets of Kingston and then Philly, raised two sets of kids and outlived two different wives; had taken a bullet, had struck the deal of life with old man Donald Haines, and had probably done more in each decade of his life than most folks did in their entire lives. So, no, Jamal wouldn't blow off a flight home, even if Akhan had called a war council meeting. Of that he was sure.

The sound of a vehicle screeching into the driveway confirmed James's suspicions. He relaxed. Yeah, Jamal was running late, got caught up, and had driven like a bat out of hell to get there on time. Now, maybe everyone could relax. James and Steve shared a smirk and gave each other a fist pound. They both watched their women's shoulders drop by two inches and polished off their beers, silently sharing the same thought about Jamal's probable whereabouts.

But when Jamal burst through the unlocked deck screen door, eyes wild, naked except for a towel, hands shaking, nobody moved much less blinked. Jamal was a splash of fast-moving mahogany against the expansive sand-hued interior of the beachfront mansion. The sight was surreal and seemed as though one of their huge African sculptures in the living room had suddenly sprung to life in a disoriented whirl.

"Oh, shit, oh, shit, I ain't have my keys and that big motherfucker was on my ass—but I gotta get him back his Jeep some kinda way 'cause I'm not going down for grand theft auto over no bullshit—honest to God, I ain't know she had a man! Damn, this is fucked up—he shot my Hummer windshield, man. Probably fucked it up—my wallet and shit is at her crib, my cell, my license, my gear—I can't believe this shit! Her ass was too fine to be that fucking crazy, yo! Oh, my God, his ass was as big as James, like six five and shit, but built like he was on the prison yard bench pressing two-fifty for ten years and shit! He shot at my ass with a nine, unloaded what had to be a whole fuckin' clip in broad-ass daylight, yo!"

For a moment no one said a word as Jamal clutched his towel and closed his eyes.

"Damn," he murmured, slowly calming down. "She was sooo fine, too."

Najira was on her feet; Laura sat down slowly in a chair. "You mean to tell me that Daddy called with some important family business and you was getting *your swerve on* and that's why we are all waiting on you?"

"Najira, are you out of your fucking mind!" Jamal shouted, his voice cracking from stress. "Did you hear what I was saying? I was shot at, girl, I was—"

"About to get a mud hole stomped in your narrow ass," James said with a sigh and then couldn't fight the smirk.

Steve glanced at James with a grin. "You got an extra nine-millimeter in the house?"

"You know me, dog," James said, chuckling. "Never leave home without it."

"Shall we get this guy his wallet and keys back, maybe his Hummer in a fair trade for the Jeep?" Steve peered out the window. "Damn, this is just like old times. Bullet holes in the back panel, no side view mirror—"

"The crazy motherfucker shot it off!" Jamal hollered. "I told you, his ass wasn't playing."

"Y'all ain't going over there!" Najira shrieked. "You heard Jamal. This is some crazy domestic drama with a wild-ass Jamaican."

"Since this guy knows where you live, and your key ring has all of ours on it, I'll have the locks changed on all the doors and push back the flight," Laura said through her teeth, giving Jamal the evil eye. "Then, I will call your *father* and explain *why* we have to be delayed. I cannot believe you sometimes."

"Baby, that's cold," James said, trying to soothe her. "Don't go there . . . just tell your uncle something came up. That's the man's business. Okay?"

Laura glared at James and let out a breath of frustration. "All right, fine. He doesn't need this ghetto mess on his soul anyway, at his age." She then turned her narrowed gaze on Jamal. "But I suggest you plan on breaking your lease, a hefty expense for the lesson, and that you stay out of whatever clubs she frequents with her man, and that you get a new cell phone and find a new place really close to your backup—James and Steve. Serves your short-sighted, booty-dazed behind right."

"She was drop-dead *fine*, Laura," Jamal said quietly, humiliation singeing his voice. "Hawaiian, and shit."

Laura lifted her chin and walked toward the telephone, ignoring him.

"What dat mean?" Najira yelled, looking as though she was about to stomp her feet.

"Jamal, man, I feel you, but lemme get you some sweats and a T-shirt, man," James said, trying hard not to smile and remembering being Jamal's age once. Yeah, in his twenties, maybe even his thirties, he would have taken a bullet for some really exquisite tail.

"It's cool," Jamal said, his voice weary. "I can just take whatever from my suitcase—but, man, I need a shower."

"You *feel* him?" Laura echoed, her hands going to her hips. "Oh, now Hawaiian women are worth a nine-millimeter slug in your ass, huh? Men!"

"Or worth blowing off a trip home to see you elderly father." Najira cocked her head to the side and hotly foided her arms over her petite bosom.

"Baby, I didn't mean it like that."

Laura and Najira sucked their teeth in a unified click.

James let his breath out hard as he glanced at Laura, whose eyes burned with an open threat. The direction of the conversation had the potential to get real ugly real fast. He could feel his wife whipping herself up into what could become a sudden tirade, and Lord knew the woman held a grudge like nobody's business. He glanced at Steve, who shrugged and left him hanging.

Trying to forestall any further issues, James held up his hands in front of his chest and spoke as calmly and as rationally as possible under the circumstances. "I was just saying that I understood that if the brother was saying goodbye to his new lady and it got intense, time has a way of slipping by. We *all* know how that kinda thing can happen, so let's not act like we don't." Satisfied that both Najira and Laura looked away, and that Steve was now studying the ceiling, James pressed his point. "And if the woman didn't come clean with Jamal and she got him in a position, you know—hey."

Steve shook his head and chuckled. "How big is this sonofabitch we've gotta do a vehicle trade with?"

"Huge," Jamal said, looking much improved by the male support in the room.

"Now my man and our cousin's husband could go get shot behind your booty chasing. Just great." Najira flopped back down on the sofa and folded her arms over her bosom again. "You didn't even think about that, did you?"

"Hey, people," Jamal said, looking around the room. "I don't want anybody to get hurt. It's not even worth it. I can just leave off his Jeep somewhere, call her, tell her where it is, you know . . . and—"

"We'll do this the old-fashioned way," James said calmly. "Real smooth. Local cops know we used to be one of them—old school respect, and since we occasionally do some PI work to help them out, we have a few lightweight markers that we can call in."

"Man, Philly never looked so good to me," Jamal said, raking his fingers down the oiled parts in his scalp between his corn-rows, remembering how Safia had touched him there. "I can't wait to go home for a few. Fuck all this beach and warm weather and palm trees and shit. I'll take the concrete and frostbite of home any damned day over this madcap bullshit."

"If I'm reading my partner right," Steve said with a grin, "we'll have the boys in blue go by your lady's joint, if they haven't al-ready from the gunshots, give the chick and her man the Jeep keys, and go in with the cops to get yours, plus get your wallet, cell, and clothes. Whatever's missing, you're just gonna have to suck it up and call your credit card companies to reissue."

"Right," James agreed. "No doubt all your cash will be gone, too, not to mention whatever was of value in your Hummer—"

"Oh, maaaan . . . all my CDs . . ."

"Yeah, but you're alive," James said, shaking his head, "and it's a good thing you never took off your Rolex. But this doesn't need to make it to an episode of *Cops.*"

"No doubt," Jamal said with a sigh. "No fucking doubt."

Chapter
2

As expected, the street was crawling with cops by the time James and Steve pulled up to the far end of Safia's block. Jamal told them what to expect and where to go, but seeing it firsthand was deep. White chalk circles outlined shell casings, neighbors were in driveways, and crime scene tape separated off sections of evidence—like Jamal's Hummer. James and Steve groaned in unison.

"Damn!" James hit the steering wheel. It was easy enough to simply leave the Jamaican's Jeep parked across the street from the precinct with the keys in it. An anonymous tip would have the vehicle immediately impounded, but at least not listed as stolen. This way if the brother had any priors or outstanding warrants, the authorities could settle it. The problem was that now Jamal, with his old history coming back to bite him in the ass, would have to explain a bid for possession and what now seemed like a drug dispute carried out into the streets. Nobody would believe it was over some poontang.

Steve just shook his head. "It wasn't supposed to go down like this, partner. Dude was supposed to find his Hummer in parts unknown, stripped to the axle, and then put in a nice insurance claim and walk." He raked his fingers through his hair. "What's wrong with the criminal element today, huh? I ask ya?"

"Maaaan . . ." James let out a weary breath. "Common sense dictated that the girl was supposed to get Jamal's wallet and cell, you know. Any woman living with a crazy, off-the-hook type should know that. Then we could buzz by—"

"Or the big SOB was supposed to take it, just like the Hummer, and Jamal could say that he'd left his wallet in the glove compartment while at the beach, along with his phone."

"Cancel out the credit cards, get a new driver's license—" James said, nodding, his eyes keened on the police activity down the block.

"And never come up on radar," Steve said, finishing James's sentence.

"Correct."

"Now what?"

James looked at Steve. "A family visit might be a long way off, all because of this nonsense, man. You know the drill. Jamal has gotta sit for questioning, gotta get him an attorney. They'll wanna know if he fired shots back, what allegedly caused a potentially deadly outburst in the community, yada, yada, yada."

"We ain't got that many markers here in Maui, dude," Steve said, rubbing his palms down his face. "And the likelihood of the girl clearing Jamal to implicate Lurch is slim and none."

"Would you?" James said with disgust, getting out of the car.

"Hell, no," Steve said with a smirk. "From the description Jamal gave, in prison I'd be his bitch."

James just shook his head and began walking.

"The plan?" Steve said, catching up to James's long strides.

"They may take a statement from the chick, or they might haul her in, but if they just take a statement, we can possibly get in close, let her know we're Jamal's fam, and see if she was able to stash his keys, his phone, whatever." James gave Steve a sideways glance. "Hopefully, she'll be smart and play the distraught victim. I just don't want that big SOB to have Jamal's government."

"Man, it's bad enough the cops got his tags and can run all that through DMV—but to have some deranged bastard out there with his address, all his numbers, keys . . . *shit.*" James rubbed his palms down his face and he and Steve joined in the large crowd that was held back from the house.

"I hope it was worth it," Steve muttered, his gaze roving the crowd.

James motioned for Steve to look across the street with a terse nod of his chin. "Looks like it might have been."

Steve released a low whistle. "The broad looks like a Vegas showgirl."

"Uh-huh. Which tells me this thing could be a to-the-death grudge match for our Jamaican friend. That's a trophy if ever I saw one."

"You know, partner, something about all of this just ain't sitting right with me, ya know?"

James pounded Steve's fist as he watched the pretty young woman go back into the house, and then he pulled out the pre-paid cell phone they always used when they didn't want the call tracked. "You go talk to any of the guys who might give us a break for old time's sake. I'll call the girl."

Steve nodded and walked away as James entered the number Jamal had given him, pushed send, and waited. On the third ring, she picked up. James walked away from the crowd.

"Hello, Safia. This is Jamal's family," James said crisply when the call connected. "I know you've been through a lot, and I'm glad to see you're all right. Jamal is okay, too."

"Ohmigod," Safia said quickly. "I thought he might be dead. I really didn't have anything to do with—"

"It's cool, it's cool," James said, reassuring her. "I just want to get back his phone and wallet, keys, anything that the police might have missed or your boyfriend didn't take."

"I have all that stuff," she said quietly. "I didn't give it to the cops. When he went out the window after Jamal, I just hid every-thing, 'cause I know how things can get all misunderstood. None of his money is missing, either. I swear. He never came back, just shot after Jamal and then one of his boys picked him up and they went looking out."

James closed his eyes. The girl clearly misunderstood. He didn't give a rat's ass about money or credit cards, it was keeping Jamal's ass out of jail for parole violations, and most assuredly out of harm's way. Retaliation was eminent. If they had just taken the car so it wasn't the only piece of evidence at the scene!

"All right. Thanks. But listen—the block is real hot right now, and there's no way I can get in there to get it from you right now. Let things die down for a couple of hours, just put everything in a shopping bag and in a few, a take-out food delivery driver will come to your door—me—and you can decline the mis-delivered food. We'll swap bags, and that will be that. Cool?"

"Okay," she said quietly. "I can do that. Just tell Jamal that I love him."

"Yeah, okay," James muttered, and then hung up.

Fifty possibilities tore at his brain as he walked to find Steve. If he'd been thinking, they could have taken the tags off the Jamaican's vehicle and put it on Jamal's vehicle—ripped off the VIN . . . He shook the thought. Major evidence tampering could land them all in the state pen. He flipped his phone open and called Laura.

"Drive by the precinct for me, baby, and get the tags on the Jeep. If it's legit, I wanna run a DMV search real quick. I wanna know more than I know now."

He heard his wife suck her teeth before answering.

"Okay, done. It's bad, isn't it, though?"

"Yeah."

"I knew it." She hung up.

Steve walked back from the crime scene tape barrier shaking his head. "I don't understand it, dude. Babes never functioned like that for me."

In no mood for a game of twenty questions, he held Steve in a hard glare. "What'd you find out, man?"

"She doesn't know his full name—can you freakin' believe it? All she was able to tell the cops is his name was Terrence B, or Big T or some crazy shit, but had been balling the guy for almost a year." Steve threw up his hands as they walked back to James's 4X4. "I thought you had to *communicate* with women, *share*," he said, growing sarcastic.

James cracked a smile. "Maybe Terrence has a soft side and is in touch with his inner child?"

"More like dropped so much dirty cash on her and laid so much pipe there wasn't much to talk about."

"Don't hate," James said, smiling as they piled into his vehicle.

"I know the Darwinian theories of survival of the fittest, Holmes. I'm not hatin'. Just don't seem right, though."

"Life ain't fair. The primate with the biggest dick and biggest wad of cash wins. I told Jamal it was time to evolve outta that Neanderthal shit, but did Junior listen? No."

"So now he's out there like Barney Rubble on *The Flintstones*, running from a troglodyte."

James began to chuckle as he turned on the engine and pulled away from the curb. Even though the situation was deadly, it was so ludicrous that he needed the old police humor to keep him going. Steve chuckled with him.

"This is beyond fucked up, partner."

James just nodded. "You know what this means, though?"

"Yeah," Steve said with a weary sigh. "The ladies have to go find out what's up with Akhan, and me and you have to stay here and babysit Jamal, keep the cops and some lunatic off his ass."

"Yeah. Pretty much."

"What!" Laura shrieked as James and Steve recounted the story.

James held out the bag of Jamal's personal effects, handing everything off to Jamal. "Sooner or later they're gonna come looking for you to question you, so my advice is that we get you an attorney right now and me and Steve security-escort you to the precinct."

Jamal put both hands on top of his head. "Oh, man . . ."

"All this over some booty, Jamal?" Najira folded her arms and glared at him.

"Took the words right out of my mouth." Laura straightened and picked up her suitcase. "I guess it would be too much to ask for me and Najira to get a ride to the airport?"

Neither Laura nor Najira really spoke during the entire flight, at least nothing beyond the perfunctory. What was there to say, really? Jamal had screwed up again. This was déjà vu for Najira; it seemed her brother always got in trouble just on the brink of some family event. Laura could tell that Najira was seething just as much as her heart was breaking; she'd wanted to move forward with her wedding plans with Steve and now this.

Deeply contemplative, Laura simply squeezed Najira's hand and then sought the limousine window for her thoughts. This was eerily familiar for her as well. It seemed as though she was always going in and cleaning up after family disasters. Only this time she wasn't sure that her contacts reached as far as Maui. If her cousin had gotten in trouble in Philly, no problem. She could have greased enough skids to get him sprung, especially since she was sure that he wasn't involved in a drug scenario. . . . At least she prayed that was the case.

The blustery Philadelphia cold made her clasp her camel-hair coat tighter and reinforce the snug fit of the belt tie. Why did she always have to come home to drama in the fall, she wondered, as the driver retrieved her Louis Vuitton luggage to give to the bellman at the Ritz Carlton. Najira looked like she was about to pass out. The strain, the long flight, and the late arrival in Philadelphia were taking an obvious toll. Laura touched her cousin's back as the bellman began to push the cart inside the plush establishment, and that's when she saw the first tear fall.

"It's gonna be all right," she murmured, pulling Najira into a hug. "Hasn't it always been?"

Najira released a weary sigh and nodded, then slipped out of

Laura's embrace. "It's just not how I envisioned coming back here," she admitted quietly. "Without Steve."

All Laura could do was nod, having no remedy for what ailed a pregnant woman too blue and too tired to rationalize with. Instead she opted for the tried and true, avoidance.

"How about if you just go on up, take a long soak, order some room service, and get some sleep. Tomorrow morning we'll go see your father. I'll call him to let him know we got in safely and that you're beat."

Laura watched Najira's shoulders slump as though someone had taken the weight of the world off them.

"You don't mind?" Najira said quietly.

Laura just squeezed her hand as they entered the hotel.

Restless energy threaded through Laura as she entered her hotel room. First call would be to let James know they'd arrived safely, then she'd have to contact her Uncle Akhan. But before she got a chance to even take off her coat, her phone vibrated loudly inside her amber Coach bag.

Annoyed by the intrusion on her thoughts, she let out a quick sigh and rushed to get the offending device, then smiled.

"You're stalking me now?" she said playfully, and then began taking off her coat. Simply hearing James's voice had a way of pouring liquid balm over her raw nerves.

"I figured you all arrived okay, since Steve was on the phone trying to calm his fiancée." James's easy baritone filled the receiver and the comforting sound of it made Laura sit down on the bed and relax.

"I could just pop Jamal upside his big head," Laura said, smiling and falling back onto the fluffy duvet. She closed her eyes, listening to the sound of James's vehicle hitting driveway gravel.

"Me and Steve already did that like fifty times," James said, chuckling. "I think he slapped his own forehead a few times, too. But don't worry, baby, I won't hurt him too bad for putting a cramp in my style."

She chuckled softly against the cell phone and released a little sigh, suddenly realizing just how much she missed her husband. James had a way of making her feel like a giddy schoolgirl.

"You'd better stop all that heavy breathing," he teased. "I can't start anything, not with Jamal bouncing off the walls and our attorney on the way to the house."

"Aw . . . not even a little phone sex?"

James laughed hard. "Woman, you ain't right. Get off the telephone so I don't shoot your cousin."

"Good-night, baby. I miss you. Thank you for always taking care of things."

She kissed the receiver and heard him let out a slow exhale, and smiled.

"I'll call you later . . . probably real late."

She laughed softly. "I was kinda hoping you'd say that. I love you. Bye."

"I love you, too, baby . . . but I really gotta go."

They both laughed and hung up. She rolled over on her stomach and shook her head with a groan. The phone in her palm buzzed in a high-vibration whine that ran through her, making her shiver and giggle with mischief. She clicked the Razr panel open without looking at the display.

"Yes . . ." she drawled out low and sexy.

"Wow," an unexpected male voice said. "And here I was expecting voice mail."

Laura's eyes snapped open and she immediately rolled over, sat up, and then stood. "Joey?" A cold chill ran through her but she forced her voice to remain steady.

"Yeah, babe," he crooned, his voice dipping to a seductive octave. "If I had known I'd get such a warm welcome, I'da come to Philly instead of staying down at the casino. Guess I hedged my bets wrong, huh?"

She chuckled and tried to keep the sound from being brittle. If a mobster like Joey Scapolini knew she was in Philly and had been watching her, that could not be a good sign.

"Since you called, I take it that you were hoping we could get

together while I was in town?" Laura slowly walked over to her
luggage and began rooting in it for a strapless little black dress.

"So . . . uh, where's the Mister?"

She smiled. So Joey wanted to play bullshit games. Okay, she
could play, too. "I left him home this time," she murmured.

There was a pause.

"Good. Because what we need to discuss . . . should be between
business partners. Spouses are sorta on a need-to-know basis.
Capice?"

"Yeah, Joey," she said as sexily as she could given the circumstances. "See you in a coupla hours?"

"Want me to send a limo for ya, hon? I keep a driver in South
Philly who's only, like, fifteen minutes from The Ritz."

She froze. A dozen thoughts ran through her mind. Maybe
she'd move Najira and her luggage quietly down to the Hyatt, but
not check out of The Ritz.

"No, hon," she crooned. In order to get Joey to open up, she
had to lean on the old chemistry that had always been between
them. "Don't go to all that trouble. You know I like to drive to
clear my head . . . long flight, husband on my case. I need the
head room. I'll be there in a couple hours." Oh well, James would
have done no less if an old Mob babe had info he needed. It was
part of the game.

"All right, babe. See you soon."

The call disconnected and Laura was instant motion. So the
big Philadelphia crime families, by way of their heir apparent,
Joey Scapolini, were watching her. This had to be a part of what
her Uncle Akhan was calling about. Yet, if she moved Najira now,
called Akhan, and alerted her husband, all hell would break loose.
Her family would freak, and she might tip off the other side that
she was wary.

Right now Joey probably felt like they could bargain, which was
a good place to be. He wanted something from her, so he wasn't
going to kill her just yet—otherwise she would have already been
dead. His not-too-subtle hint about her whereabouts was a veiled
threat. So she couldn't just flee; how did one outrun the Mafia,

anyway? That was like trying to outrun a tiger in a flat-out fifty-yard dash—never happen. There'd be no way to understand what demands were being put on the table, what new contracts they wanted in on, unless she played along.

Laura raked through her suitcase, found her black push-up bra, stilettos, silk stockings, garter, and thong, and then dashed into the bathroom to quickly shower. Calling James ahead of time was definitely out of the question; sometimes there were things that required the femme fatale touch of détente.

Every conceivable combination of events pummeled her brain as she stepped into the shower and the water beat against her body. When she and Scapolini first entered into their unholy alliance, she was bent on revenge and was bringing down Philadelphia's black bourgeoisie crime families. She needed him, he needed her. Scapolini didn't mind; it was more contract money for him in construction deals by way of the late great Donald Haines. Same thing when those families tried to retaliate. She and the now dearly departed Haines, in a triumvirate with her shrewd uncle, had been able to break Scapolini off a hefty slice of the new Pennsylvania casino charters and building contracts for much-needed protection. That kept things in harmonious balance.

The only problem now was she wasn't bent on revenge, and had been out of the financial shell game for what felt like years now. She thought she'd finally put the past and all the crimes that went with it behind her. Wrong. As she lathered and rinsed her body clean, she tried to clear her mind to think of any stone she could have left unturned but drew a blank. When the whole debacle went down with the Micholi Foundation, with greedy senators and Main Line land barons trying to push the Russian Mob into rebuilding contracts in post-Katrina New Orleans for personal, skimming gain, she and Akhan had worked it out so that Scapolini and his boys got the waste management contracts. That was by far the largest and most lucrative aspect of the clean-up efforts down there. Xavier Mortgage Company, the firm that Haines and Akhan had built decades ago, was left unmolested.

Laura let out a hard breath as she turned off the water and stepped out of the tub. The choice had always been simple; when it came to hefty contracts, the Mob always got a slice of the pie and one had to pay the freight or die. So what the fuck did Joey Scapolini want at this juncture? To date, they were even.

Chapter
3

Laura tucked her cell phone and keys into her beaded clutch, grabbed her black raw silk wrap, and headed out of the room. She quietly hurried past Najira's room and released her breath when she got to the elevator bay.

First order of business was to catch a cab over to the private lot that kept her black Jag primed and waiting, and then she'd head over to her and James's penthouse condo at 2400 Lofts to get the small, pearl-handle Lady Derringer that her uncle had given her after the last family debacle. She looked at her clutch in disdain as she impatiently waited for the elevator to come. For a visit with Scapolini she would have preferred the heavier Glock nine-millimeter James had brought her, or her father's old .357 peace-keeper. But neither would fit in her purse.

In one lithe motion, Laura opened her car door and swung her legs out to stand, not waiting for the eager valets. She calmly dropped her keys into an outstretched male hand, ignoring the appreciative glance he gave her and accepted an orange ticket from him.

The intense glare of casino lights practically gave her a head-ache as she strolled into the lobby with fluid grace and kept her

gaze roving, looking for Scapolini's head enforcer, Tony Rapuzzio—
a tall, somewhat handsome, no-neck brunette who wore a constant leer that made her so desperately want to slap his face. She
hated having to drive all the way to Atlantic City, and she just
hoped that Scapolini would have his pit bull on a short choker
chain, or else she'd have to shoot the dumb bastard. Plus the constant ringing of slot machines was making her temples throb.

The moment they both spied each other, they smiled. Rapuzzio
gave her a slight nod of recognition; she fought the urge to give
him the finger and smiled demurely. The huge bodyguard cut a
swath through the casino crowd with ease and was at Laura's side
within moments.

"Long time no see, Laura," Rapuzzio said with a lopsided grin,
ushering her through the VIP section toward the employee-only
area by touching the small of her back.

So now the SOB wanted to make small talk? Laura smiled. "It's
been too long, Tony."

"You need to come down more often . . . like this," he said, his
eyes roving over her body. "Maybe we could comp you a room?"

She knew what he meant—like this without James. Only in his
wildest wet dreams.

"I'll have to take that under serious consideration, Tony," she
murmured, looking him up and down with a half smile. "How's
Joey doing?"

At that, Scapolini's henchman guffawed and straightened the
knot in his tie as though it were choking him.

"You know Joey is always Joey—doing good as ever."

Laura nodded as they waited for an elevator. "I wouldn't expect any less."

Tony Rapuzzio looked off into the distance, staring at nothing,
and then fixed his gaze on the numbers as the elevator came. She
knew he'd back off once she'd mentioned Scapolini. The macho-
guy test to see if she was down for whatever was over. Rapuzzio
might be a little thick, but the man wasn't crazy. How would that
seem for him to get caught trying to tap the same ass that his boss
Scapolini so badly wanted?

Laura fought not to shake her head as they walked down the long, ornate corridor that led to the VIP suites. She watched Rapuzzio insert the card key and then swing the door open with a flourish for her to enter first. She gave him an acknowledging sideways glance with a sexy smile that seemed to make him stand a little taller. But she knew that wouldn't mean jack shit if things didn't go down right.

Joey Scapolini stood and opened his arms with a drink in one hand. "Laura . . . looking fabulous as always."

"You, too, Tone," she said, sweeping over to him to give him a hug.

He held her out from him a bit and looked her up and down. "Man, the sun and surf did you real good, babe."

"Thanks," she said with a wicked smile. "Now what's a girl gotta do to get a drink around here?"

"Looking like you do, there's about fifty ways I could answer that question."

"You're gonna get me in trouble, Joey." She offered him her most dashing grin, which he seemed to accept in good nature as she pecked his cheek with a kiss.

He laughed and let her go, motioning to Rapuzzio. "Where's my manners? Bring the lady some champagne or something, will ya?"

She laughed and sat down on the huge white leather chair that faced an obscenely massive white leather sectional sofa within the outrageously white-on-white room, taking great care to cross her long legs just so. Theirs was an old, familiar dance of flirting and testing, but neither was so foolish as to believe that it would change the outcome of their business negotiations. It was simply a warm-up to the eventual sparring match.

With great amusement she watched Joey's gaze slide up her thigh to follow the side slit in the dress, knowing that the bit of lace peeking through at the tops of her stockings told him that she was wearing a garter belt and probably scant else beyond that.

Joey sat down heavily and rolled his short rocks glass between his palms, staring at her. It was clear from his troubled gaze that he was trying to figure out where to begin the conversation, so she waited. She studied his Hollywood handsome face and his tight, wiry build beneath the designer suit, her gaze finally glimpsing his well-manicured hands and the heavy gold Rolex watch and thick gold bracelet that ensconced his wrists. Hands of a killer. Her gaze met Joey's intense, dark gaze. But never so foolish as to do the work himself.

Joey looked up when Rapuzzio handed Laura a champagne flute, and his eyes seemed to demand privacy. Rapuzzio immediately read the request, as theirs was also a long-standing dance of spoken and unspoken cues.

"I think I'll go check out the casino floor, Boss," Rapuzzio said. "Unless you need anything?"

"No, Tone. I'm good. Thanks."

"Sure thing, Joey," he said and then gave a very respectful nod to Laura. "Good to see you down here with family, Laura."

"Good to see you, too, Tony. Thanks for the champagne."

She watched him leave and then returned her gaze to Scapolini, feeling a wire of tension weave its way between each vertebra. "So, that leaves you and me."

He set his drink down carefully on the large, kidney-shaped coffee table and watched her take a leisurely sip of her champagne. "You know I love you, Laura—been crazy about you since the first day I saw you—so what I'm about to say, I don't want you to take the wrong way, okay?" He let out a hard breath as though the words were giving him an ulcer. "Me and you go way back, have done a lot of deals together and have made a lot of money together, and the one thing Joey Scapolini never does is renege on a deal."

His preamble was making her nervous. What deal was he about to renege on? She set her champagne flute down with care, her eyes never leaving his.

"I know you're good people, Joey. Your word is your bond. So what's happened?"

He rubbed his palms down his face. "You ain't making this any easier for me, you know that?"

She reached over and gently touched his leg. "Talk to me, Joey," she said in a low murmur, the tone that was designed to siphon a male confession.

He finally leaned forward and collected her hands within his. "Laura, it's like this. Old Haines ain't around anymore to make sure those of us from the old friends and family network get what's due 'em, ya know?"

Joey let her hands fall away and then sat back against the butter-soft leather. "The waste management contracts were having technical difficulties. People looking into so-called improprieties and such. Not that it's your fault in any way, but we already took a beating with lost revenues down in the Gulf from our casinos that had to be rebuilt, same thing in the Caribbean with all the storms."

Suddenly he stood and walked over to the wet bar at the far side of the suite and refreshed his drink. "Laura, some of the family ain't willing to be patient to rebuild. They heard some things on the news when that Alan Moyer sonofabitch went down that maybe they shouldn't have heard. Now with the added pressures coming from competitors . . . now it's getting complicated. This is such bullshit. Sometimes I hate this part of the business."

He looked over his shoulder at her and she held his gaze knowing exactly what he meant. They'd heard about Xavier Mortgage sitting on primo real estate down in the Gulf. They held lien to mortgages issued years before those properties were thought to be worth anything. She and her uncle could easily foreclose on all those post-Katrina unpaid debts to sell off land parcels to the Mob—at dirt cheap prices so they could build their casinos in devastated areas. But that would mean selling houses out from under poor people who'd already been through enough. She knew her uncle—he'd rather die first. She knew herself—she'd rather put the bastards who were attempting to force her hand in their graves.

Laura forced her voice and her expression to remain eerily

serene. "Joey, what pressures? Who's on your ass? You know I've got your back, the same way you've always had mine." She waited, practically holding her breath. If she could go after his competitors, perhaps, it might temporarily deflect him from forcing her hand—forcing her to kill him. She so didn't want it to have to come to that. And it seemed they were both in the same position. She could tell he didn't want to whack her either. Thus, a stalemate.

Joey picked up the bottle of champagne and brought it to the seating area with his tumbler of Scotch. "Laura," he said quietly, setting his glass down and slowly extracting hers from her hand to refill it. He brought the neck of the champagne bottle to the tilted side of her flute and watched the bubbly pour into it. "Fucking Jamaicans are gonna make a run for that area, okay— but you didn't hear that from me." He kept his gaze on the translucent fluid, seeming almost mesmerized by the thousands of tiny bubbles within it. "You don't have enough juice to go after them, kiddo. I love your style, and you're the only woman I know crazy enough with enough brass balls to try something so wild." He handed her back her glass and then tipped his against the side of it as he sat. "*Salud.*"

"*Salud,*" she murmured, staring at him over the rim of her glass. "Joey, you know I'm insane. So why don't you let me be the judge of how far I'll go to protect what's mine?"

He smiled, but this time it wasn't a tight smile or even a false one. The erotic pull within it was unmistakable. "So when are you gonna leave that big burly motherfucker and finally hook up with me?"

They both smiled.

"When you leave your wife and four kids."

"I'm Catholic—we don't do that," he said, chuckling. "But you make it tempting."

"Why don't we do the common enemy together, like old times, Joey?"

He leaned forward and took a healthy swig of his drink. "I respect the hell outta ya, Laura. You know that? In all seriousness."

He stared at her, his gaze searching her face. "You're the only babe I know who can come into my suite, talk dirty to me, give me a hard-on, and leave without so much as a kiss and I feel like I still wanna pay you."

Again, they both laughed as he swept up one hand and kissed her knuckles.

"Let me talk to my uncle," she said softly, now stroking his hand. "His resources go long and deep. And I see no reason for anyone from the outside to take what, by rights, should stay within U.S. hands."

"Yeah, lovely U.S. hands at that," he murmured thickly and gazed at her intently. "You sure I can't coax you to stay? He'll never know."

"Your wife is such a sweet lady, Joey. I respect your family—just as you've always respected mine. I wouldn't want to do that to her."

He nodded and reluctantly dropped her hand with a sigh, and then smiled. "I was thinking more on the lines of doing me—but I understand your position." They both laughed as he flopped back against the leather upholstery. "It's part of what I like about you. You're a very complicated woman—will blow an SOB away, but then would never think of hurting his wife. Sorta like old Sicilian style, ya know. Gotta love it."

"How much time do I have to try to find a way to get to these Jamaicans?"

"You're really gonna do it, aren't ya?"

She shrugged. "Yeah. Why not? We know some people in the State Department," she added, as a bluff.

"How's a week?"

"Tight timeframe, Joey. Damn."

"I need to be able to tell the family something definite by the next meeting."

She looked off in the distance through the large row of windows that seemed to kiss the night sky. "Do you at least know where we should start digging? Who's the main target?"

Joey shook his head. "We don't know their organization so good—that's the problem. We don't know who to hit, who to go after. All we know is they might start leaning on your uncle, to get him to turn over some primo land. If they get their hands on the land, first, the revenues that come off of any casinos they build will make them stronger so they can funnel that cash into their other operations. Those operations directly challenge our off-the-books lines of business. Need I say more?"

For the first time since they'd begun playing this game over the years, Laura allowed her eyes to fill with tears for theatrical effect. She wanted Joey Scapolini so shook when she left his suite that she'd be assured of having the full week to work without interference from the Italians. But allowing tears to build wasn't a difficult thing at all. They were not tears of fear or even sorrow, but pure rage. Fuck whoever thought they would kill Akhan and leave her sole heir to Xavier Mortgage.

"See, babe," Joey said in a gentle voice. "I didn't want you to get yourself all worked up. That's why I'd asked you to come down here. Me and you could cut a deal to take all this off your shoulders. I'd buy the land from you and your uncle for a reasonable price—fair—seriously—and then whoever was gonna start any bullshit would have to come see me. Wouldn't that be easier . . . in the long run, I'm saying?"

She looked at Joey through glittering tears and then swallowed hard as they burned away. "That's why I love you so much, Joey," she lied. "You'd do that even for me." Partners, hell. She and Joey had an odd alliance, one where they both knew they'd ice each other as quick as look at each other, even though they were friends. Twisted. But effective.

"I would, baby. You don't have to be afraid, okay?"

She set down her champagne flute with a shaking hand—again, not from fear but pure rage. However, she kept her voice calm, stroking his male ego. "I can't let you do that, Joey. You've done too much. If there's anybody in the world we'd sell to, it's you, and you know that." She stood, forcing his eyes to follow her as she wrapped her arms about her waist and walked to the window. What she was saying was pure bull, but she needed him to believe her to buy a little time. "If anything happens to my uncle, anything that isn't from natural causes, there's a fail-safe in the will document to make sure the land liens cannot be sold for less than triple the current market value. Haines made sure that was in there because of potential shit like this." She drew a shuddering breath. "And, Joey, you oughta know me well enough by now to know that, when I find these fuckers who are plotting on my elderly uncle, I'll cut their balls off—one way or another." She studied her manicure as she spoke.

Laura looked at Joey hard hoping he read between the lines. She wanted him to see the pure venom in her eyes now, wanted him to know that she would not be trifled with under any circumstances, and wanted him to breathe a sigh of relief that they were on friendly terms.

"You have an organization; so do I. Mine is smaller, a little less formal in structure, but very effective." She eyed him. "Mine don't work off shares of blind trusts and real estate deals," she added, bluffing. "For a few thousand dollars they'll go in buck wild, and will risk doing a hit—you know the streets, Joey. Very crazy, very unpredictable. You can't keep even a head of state secure from all those people in service positions, now can you?"

He took a nervous sip of his drink and forced a chuckle. "That's my girl. Crazy as a fuckin' bedbug."

She nodded. "Um-hmm. So, do let the family know that I'll protect their interests by not selling to any goddamned Jamaicans, and don't have a problem going down there to address the problem on foreign soil."

Joey spit out his drink. "You're going to Jamaica?"

"One can only assume the head man isn't here where he could get whacked. Last I heard, there wasn't extradition courtesy between there and the U.S. Besides, their forensics down there suck."

He wiped his mouth with the back of his Armani jacket sleeve, nodded, and stood. "I gotta hand it to ya, Laura. You're crazier than I thought. But don't go getting your lovely ass whacked, because you'll make me slobber like an asshole over your coffin. That would put a strain on my marriage, not to mention it might disrespect that lucky SOB you call your husband."

He pulled her into a light embrace. "You have a week, babe. Then, if we can't bring it to resolution . . . you know what we gotta do."

Tony Rapuzzio left the main casino vault with ten thousand dollars cash in his breast pocket. No one said a word, none of the counters made eye contact; he was Scapolini's main man and above reproach. To question him was to accuse him; to accuse him was to die.

Tony flipped open his cell phone and pushed speed dial.

"Yo, Safia. You alone?"

"Yeah," she said, sounding afraid. "Can I go back to Vegas now?"

"Yeah, that would be your best bet. I got your cash, will have it wired to you in a little bit. You done good." He paused. "Lose that bastard, Terrence, though. He played his role, give him his cut, and don't fuck him. I swear to you, Safia, I'll come looking for you if you screw around on me."

"Why would I do something like that, baby?" she said, sounding shocked. "I can't believe you'd actually say something like that, Tony!"

"Relax. I'm just protecting my investment. I bought the tits, your fucking clothes, your car, your condo, whatever, and got you the job in Vegas—so I don't want no moolies all over you, got it?"

"I swear," she said on a long sigh. "I haven't fucked anyone else but you. Now—satisfied?"

"Yeah . . . okay. Because, otherwise, I swear I'll kill ya."

"You absolutely sure I can't comp your room tonight?" Joey asked, walking Laura down the hall to the elevators.

Her phone vibrated in her purse and she smiled as he looked at her clutch. "My husband, no doubt."

"Then you should answer it so he doesn't get suspicious."

The phone continued to buzz, but it was the challenge in

Joey's eyes that had her in a stranglehold. She opened her purse with a smirk and kept him from seeing the gun as she extracted her cell phone. Holding intense eye contact with Joey, she decided to play with his mind to help seal the deal.

"Hey," she murmured as soon as she connected to James.

"Hey, yourself," James said in a deep baritone that caressed her ear. "Are you in bed yet?"

She and Joey continued to stare at each other.

"No, I was restless and went down to the lobby for a drink."

Joey chuckled quietly as the elevator button dinged.

"I was just getting on the elevator . . . so we might lose reception, but I'll call you when I get to my room—okay baby? But first I need to check on Najira to make sure she's feeling better, so it might be a little bit before I can hit you back, but you *know* I want to talk to you before I go to bed and—"

Joey held the elevator door and blew her a kiss. She clicked off the phone to disconnect the call to James.

"You sure you don't wanna have a brief, torrid affair?"

She held up the cell and wagged it at him. "Gotta run, love . . . and have to figure out a way to make it sound like I'm not on Route 42 for an hour and a half back to Philly." She brushed his mouth with a kiss. "Your word as your bond, I have at least a week?"

"Yeah," Joey murmured, his gaze raking her one last time. "How can I say no to that?"

Chapter
4

Doing close to eighty-five mph, she prayed there'd be no highway cops to pull her over. She had to get back to the hotel before James got suspicious. He'd wig if he knew she'd gone into a Mob negotiation without some type of backup, and then really go off the hook if she told him why she didn't particularly need that level of security around Joey. Whether she'd slept with Scapolini or not, James Carter was an old-fashioned kinda guy.

Laura let her breath out hard and backed down on the speedometer as she approached the Ben Franklin Bridge. All she had to do was get through the desolate tollbooth and make a short run from there through Center City, and she would make it up to James as best she could. She forced herself to slow the Jag to a gentle rolling stop as she entered the valet area of the hotel, took two deep breaths and got out.

The lobby was serene and quiet as she passed through the ornate, gold-leaf edged environs. Guilt roiled in her stomach as she depressed the elevator key. Half of her wanted to just blurt everything out to James; the other half of her knew he'd blow a head gasket. More important, she never wanted him to believe she was playing him again.

Again . . . damn. Laura closed her eyes briefly as she stepped into the vacant elevator. If he caught wind of this, that's just how he'd take it—as though she was reverting like a bad relaxer and going back to her old roots. But this was so different from before. Back then, she didn't know him, didn't trust him, and had been on a mission.

She fished in her clutch and let out her breath hard, suddenly realizing how hard it was sometimes to function as part of a two-some. Especially when things turned deadly. And in that instant she knew why, no therapy required. She sat down heavily on the edge of the bed and slowly slipped off her stilettos. No one was allowed to ever die again on her watch. People she loved as much as she loved James sometimes had to be kept in the dark for their own good. Death didn't frighten her; living as a hostage to the whims of the powerful did. That's what she told herself as she stared at the cell phone in her palm.

But the only thing that truly terrorized her was when she'd thought someone close to her might be harmed . . . which was why she'd fight tooth and nail to uncover who was threatening her family, and, yes, would go so far as to eliminate them without losing any sleep over it—if it came to that. Before, everything had been clean, crisp, and very antiseptic money ruses effected on paper. Transactions. However, if they'd brought in muscle, then, like the true Scorpio she was, she'd find the man who made the decisions and . . . hey. It was them or her people; she chose hers.

Laura depressed the send button and shrugged out of her wrap. Suddenly she felt weary to the bone, but would try to lighten her voice for James. He answered after two rings, but his voice sounded thick with sleep. She smiled and closed her eyes as she slipped the back zipper down on her dress with one hand.

"Hey, baby . . . did I wake you?" she murmured.

"No . . . well, maybe a little." His mellow voice contained a smile. "How's Jira?"

She almost hesitated. "Fine. Resting peacefully, finally."

James yawned. "Good. I was getting worried."

"I know," Laura cooed, climbing into bed in her underwear. "You in bed?"

"Just slid between the sheets," she said softly, beginning to initiate a delicious conversation that would be sure to make him forget her whereabouts. "I miss you."

"I miss you, too, baby," he murmured. "A lot is going on, though."

Laura sank against the pillows. There was no way in the world she'd so easily slide into nighttime phone play when he'd told her earlier that a lawyer had been at the house to see about Jamal, with Jamal's sister supposedly in near histrionics about that, blah, blah, blah. She was busted.

Shifting gears quickly, Laura turned the scenario back on James and fought smiling at their old dance. "I just thought you'd be too tired to talk about all that tonight. But now that you've mentioned it . . . how did it go?"

He chuckled. "You might as well come clean, Laura. I know you."

"You do. True. But tell me about Jamal, first."

"The fact that the boy fell out of the window naked and flashed the whole block waving a white towel around in the air like a lunatic while he was being shot at gives him plenty of witnesses to spare. Once the news vans got there, the same people who will never show up to court were all over the microphones talking about how they thought the naked dude was gonna get killed and how he didn't have a weapon, and then he jumped in a Jeep and took off—the same Jeep that was later returned to a precinct. So, we took your boy in to see the captain, who after a bit of bullshit negotiations back and forth, bought Jamal's alibi. Clearly it was some boyfriend-girlfriend madness, and the only person in real trouble is the guy who was blasting nine-millimeter shells up and down the block."

Laura let out a sigh of relief and then chuckled. "You know, this doesn't make any kinda sense."

"You're stalling," James said in a low, sexy tone.

"Okay, okay, I didn't go see Najira," she snapped, becoming peevish even though he'd made her laugh.

"I know."

"How do you know?" She sat up in bed and folded her arms.

"You're slipping," James said, laughing.

His confident tone irked her.

"How?"

"Because Najira was so upset that during the time you were supposed to be in her room comforting her, she was on the house line with Jamal getting the play-by-play so Jira could calm their father's nerves. Of course Jamal asked that Najira relay that to you—*once you woke up in the morning.*"

Laura simply shook her head and closed her eyes, and then unfolded her arms. "Aw . . . maaan."

"So," James said, mirth sliding from his tone. "Where were you?"

"Trying to handle some business that suddenly came up."

She heard her husband let out an exasperated breath.

"James, isn't marriage supposed to be about trust?"

There was dead silence on the line.

"All right. I can't discuss it over the telephone, but I was doing some digging while here in Philly . . . and we might have to go down to the Caribbean. I need to talk to my uncle first, though."

"I'm just going to say this to you one time, Laura. You know how much I love you, right?"

"Yeah, I do—same here," she said quietly.

"Then why would you go to the only place that would give me a heart attack to know you went alone? Those boys in Jersey play real hardball, and you know that."

She nodded, even though he couldn't see her, because it was the truth. "That's why I didn't want to worry you, baby."

"That's the only reason I'm not pissed off enough to want to wring your neck."

She paused, understanding that it took great effort for him to say that and to maintain a calm position. "They called me, or I wouldn't have looked them up alone like that. I'm not crazy. That would be like poking a stick into a hornet's nest. You don't bother them, they don't bother you. Been that way for years."

It was his turn to fall quiet.

"That's not good, them calling you," James finally said. "That means they'd been tailing your movements."

"Yeah. That's why I want you and Steve to stay alert," she said, her voice tight and her tone filled with very real concern. "I don't know if we should all just convene and stay close, or spread out."

"How bad, baby?"

She raked her fingers through her hair. "I have a week to make some significant changes in some paperwork."

"Since Jamal is clear to fly, we'll be on the next thing smoking with Steve. We'll meet you in Philly."

"Good . . . because I miss you, James."

James held the receiver tighter and nodded with his eyes closed. That would be as close as it came to Laura admitting that she was afraid. That made him scared for her. "I miss you, too, baby," he said quietly. "Keep your cell on, I'll let you know what flight. We'll work on the logistics once I get there, okay?"

He practically held his breath hoping that she'd read between the lines. It was about getting lost fast, and moving without being tracked. The moment they hit Philly, Laura and Najira had to be skillfully moved out of The Ritz-Carlton, and it all had to be a sweet shell game. However, the beauty was that both he and Laura had connections that went long and deep in Philadelphia, so that wouldn't necessarily present a problem.

"I know, okay," she finally said, as though thinking in lock step with him.

"Why don't you get some rest? Call me in the morning after your meeting."

"I love you."

"Love you, too, baby. Bye."

James leaned his head back against the headboard and let out a long, angry breath. If they knew Laura's movements, then that could only mean that they'd been under surveillance—their house could be bugged, phones tapped, whatever. He cringed at the thought of how close the threat was, and how even the most intimate aspects of his life with Laura might have gotten captured on tape. One slipup, one little act of inobservance and he might have been on the phone talking crazy trash to his wife, and both of them could have gotten popped.

He stood and walked through the house in his boxers, headed to the refrigerator for a beer with a gun in his hand, repeatedly telling himself to relax. Laura said they had a week to meet whatever deadline or terms. He just wished he knew what the fuck was going on!

Regardless, the sense of utter violation swept through him, further stoking his outrage. The surveillance job had to have been done while he and Steve were gone. That was the only opportunity—Laura and Najira might have been out together for the day, and all it would take was a pro to get in and out while no one was home . . . something that rarely happened. Their schedules were always too erratic and they had a solid housekeeper to be there while they were out together. Then, again, they could have just tailed her.

Nah, deep surveillance was the only way. James mentally reworked the puzzle until he thought his brain would bleed. Laura would have spotted a tail, easily. She had a mind like a steel trap and eyes like a hawk. He, Steve, and Jamal would have to stripsearch both houses . . . then, again, what was the point? They were out as of the first available flight tomorrow, and they'd have to go through that whole rigmarole again when they got back, anyway.

James opened the long neck bottle and turned it up to his mouth. This time, if they'd threatened his woman, then fuck all the nice, neat paper transaction shit Laura liked to use to hang a bastard out to dry. This was primal, visceral, something that had to be addressed the old-fashioned way—his family versus theirs.

Joey Scapolini fought the cringe of betrayal toward the people he'd hired that crept along his spine. He listened to the recording, quietly making a tent before his mouth as he leaned his elbows on his desk. Laura hadn't lied, which meant members of his own organization had.

He nodded as it ended. "I told you she was a straight shooter." His gaze was hard and narrow as he peered at Mike Caluzo, Syd Balifoni, and Art Costanza. "I told her the deal, she's gonna go talk to her old uncle and do the paperwork changes . . . if she can't get those Jamaican motherfuckers to leave sleeping dogs lie."

The three men who sat before him shared nervous glances.

"You tell your uncle down in Vegas, Big Caluzo, that I gave the chick my word," Joey said, standing and pointing at Mike. "I told her nothing would go down for that long, and it ain't like one week will make a difference."

Mike Caluzo held up both of his meaty hands in front of his flabby chest and his thick jowls shook in protest as he spoke. "Hey, Joey, relax. It ain't my call. I'll relay the message, sure thing—just like I always do."

"Don't fuck with me, Mike, I'm serious." Joey pointed at Mike Caluzo.

"Hey, I'm not pulling your chain, Joey. You know me and Sulli go way back to Catholic school tagetha from the old neighborhood, so I hope they make this neat and tidy so the family doesn't have any problem, too."

"You was in school with the moolie cop's partner, Sullivan? Steve Sullivan?" Syd gave Mike a look of shock. "Damn. Go figure. Small fuckin' world."

"Ex cop," Mike corrected, glaring at Syd Balifoni's gaunt smirk.

"Yeah, but once a cop, always a cop, and always in their network," Art Costanza said coolly.

"Like we ain't? Like we ain't got cops?" Joey paced over to the bar and poured himself another Scotch on the rocks. "So Caluzo got a friend who's helped us like we've helped him. One hand washes the other, one hand scratches the itch and so forth— what's your fucking point, Art?"

Art Costanza studied his manicure calmly. "What truly worries me is this black chick you're going out on a limb for." He glanced around at the others before looking at Joey Scapolini directly. "We all know the family is nervous. We know what she's got access to. Jamaicans or not, what the fuck difference does it make, huh? There's some who say make her give it up anyway. Regardless." He let out a hard exhale when Joey threw back his drink and winced. "Joey, we've been family for a long time—tight cousins. Don't let a piece of ass get you—"

"You threatening me?" Joey said, incredulous, and drawing his nine-millimeter before Art could take another breath.

"Of course not, Joey, man, shit—put the gun away." Art's eyes remained riveted to Joey's. "I'm just telling you what different branches of the family have been talking about. That's all."

Joey begrudgingly stashed the gun back in the waistband of his suit pants, and spoke to the threesome before him with a scowl. "Why not just take it?" Joey said releasing a tight, angry chuckle. "Don't you think if we could have we would have?"

The shower didn't help wake her; she'd already been up for hours. Sleep was a luxury her nervous system couldn't tolerate now. Rushing around the hotel room, Laura pulled an ivory-toned, heavy cable-knit sweater over her head and fluffed her short haircut by finger-combing it quickly, and then yanked on her black jeans, intermittently rooting for her black Prada shoe boots. Dressed in minutes, she transferred everything from the beaded clutch she'd had the night prior into a huge Coach barrel purse, checking the gun twice, before smearing on a glaze of apricot lip gloss and heading out the door.

She stood at Najira's door waiting impatiently, and then groaned when Najira answered, still half dressed.

"You know how your father is," Laura snapped, her nerves too raw to soften her brittle tone. "If he said meet him at eight, he means eight."

"I know and good morning to you, too," Najira grumbled. "But this isn't exactly my best time of day, all right."

Too exasperated to deal with Najira's morning sickness, Laura let out a rush of breath. "I'll be in the lobby having a cup of coffee. Ten minutes, Najira, or I'm leaving. I mean it."

They both shared a scowl, both also knowing that Laura wasn't above leaving her younger cousin. In fact, she was notorious for doing that when people were late.

Najira squared her shoulders. "I'll be down in a minute. Gimme a break, okay? Don't start your shit this morning, Laura."

"Ten minutes," Laura repeated, and then turned on her heel and strode down the luxurious hall.

A loud bang was Najira's reply, but Laura didn't even start when the door slammed. It wasn't about Najira's morning queasiness, or her attitude. They had to get to Akhan, figure out how much he knew of what was going on, and come up with a plan. Hell, if Najira was feeling nauseous by just getting up in the morning, she'd probably vomit once she learned what was going down.

Laura stepped into the elevator and thrust her shoulders back and chin up, forcing confidence into her bearing as she depressed the lobby button. Part of her knew that she was being a royal bitch this morning, but the part of her that frightened her—the soft interior—knew that fear was at the root of it. She'd die if anything happened to Najira or the baby. Laura closed her eyes remembering being pregnant ever so briefly for James . . . but the running, the gun battle, maybe it was stress or simply age, had taken the one chance the two of them had to create life. That's why Najira had to pull her shit together—things could get hectic before the calm, and she had to be alert, move swiftly, and stay on her toes. She couldn't lag. That was a sure way to get killed.

It was the same reason she wasn't trying to contact her sisters this week. She quickly said a little prayer of thanks that they were in Chicago and Florida, and had always been far enough away to seem like there was no tight familial connection. No one needed to know where they were or how close they were; it was bad enough that Najira, Steve, her uncle, Jamal, and James were at risk. But if the Mob went after her sisters and their children, she knew that she would lose her mind.

Almost cringing at the thought, Laura found the lobby coffee service and took her time at the ornate silver decanters. Just the smell of fresh brewed coffee was beginning to soothe her. Being freaked out was unacceptable as well as hazardous.

Uncle Akhan would have a plan, a way to get in and out of the country with false IDs, and most likely could set up some counterbalancing weights to go against the Philly Mob, if it came to that. But that was the problem. She didn't want it to come to that at all.

Calmly taking a seat in an overstuffed Queen Anne–styled chair, Laura sipped her coffee black and allowed her mind to sharpen to a razor's edge. Who were these Jamaicans who had rattled Joey Scapolini's cage so seriously that he was ready to bum rush her for Xavier's assets in the Gulf? She peered over the edge of her cup and spied Najira.

Only time would tell.

Chapter
5

"I thought you went to bed early and stayed in all night? When did you go get the Jag?" Najira asked as she and Laura waited outside The Ritz-Carlton lobby for the valet to exit the vehicle. Najira boxed her arms and stood in a heavy shearling coat and suede pants, waiting for a reasonable answer.

"Last night while you were asleep," Laura said flatly, keeping her eyes on the approaching young man as she fished in her black leather bomber jacket pocket for the ticket. She tipped the valet and then turned abruptly to stare Najira down for asking too many tough questions.

"The bullshit is starting again, isn't it?" Najira asked calmly, before walking away from Laura.

For a moment, Laura couldn't answer. All she could do was watch Najira get in on the passenger's side as she slid into the driver's seat. Once both women had buckled their seat belts and the door lock clicked, Laura briefly glimpsed Najira as she depressed the accelerator to clear the curb.

"Yeah, girl. It has." Beyond that, Laura knew there wasn't any further information she could give that would help.

* * *

A gunmetal gray sky leaked sunshine in slow increments as Laura and Najira drove along the Girard Avenue Bridge to meet Akhan. With the zoo behind them and a slate-hued river beneath them, Laura kept her eyes steady for the familiar left turn that would plunge them into the park on one side and dilapidated old mansions on the other.

For years their dance had been so familiar. Akhan, as he wanted to be referred to, refused the traditional titles of Uncle or even Dad, being so distrustful of *the man* that he saw a conspiracy around every corner. In her earlier years she would have thought the old man crazy. Now she knew that all his precautions were warranted.

Never talk in the house, never, *ever* talk on the telephone. The entire family had lived through wire taps, surveillance and everything in between. They all knew the deal: Meet out in the world in a different location each time. If it was something really serious, wash your clothes, first, to ensure a bug got ruined. And always, most assuredly, speak in code. This had been their life. She wondered what it must have been like living with him. No wonder Najira and Jamal's mother left under the pressure, just to breathe. Yet, still, Laura loved her uncle for all his eccentric and totally justified ways.

Najira didn't even question her when they parked two blocks from the previously agreed upon location. Damp leaves from the early morning's rain clung to Laura's boots as she stepped out of the vehicle, her eyes scanning the horizon for any sign of her uncle.

Today, the brightly hued foliage refused to do its fall dance of swirling, colorful majesty. Everything seemed heavy, weighed down, and a cutting chill clung to the dampness. She could see her breath.

"I shoulda brought a newspaper," Najira complained, hunched down in her coat. "I hate days like this."

"Yeah, so do I," Laura muttered, not talking about the weather, but rather the chill that ran through her bones. In the distance she could see her uncle slowly progressing toward them, but she lightly touched Najira's arm to forestall her running to greet him.

"Oh, yeah," Najira said with a heavy sigh. "I forgot. We just happened to bump into him." She shook her head and glimpsed Laura from a sideways glance. "This is so stupid. I swear he's getting worse the older he gets!"

Laura said calmly, "If I had all that he does on his shoulders, then, yeah, I'd be wily, too."

Najira gave her a direct gaze for the first time since they'd arrived. "Laura, what's going down?"

"The casinos are in it. Need I say more?"

Laura watched her cousin blanch. Suddenly she wished that she could have spared the young woman information. But there was no way to do that. Sooner or later, Steve and James had to know—and Laura knew in her soul that the two older ex-cops weren't about to let it all ride. So she began walking.

"*Hotep*," her uncle said calmly, embracing his daughter as the threesome met up.

Najira held onto him, grasping his faded army fatigue jacket as she slid into the hug, and simply laid her head on his shoulder. "Daddy, what did you do?"

The old man stroked Najira's hair and pressed her head against him, his eyes holding Laura's as he spoke. "This time it wasn't me. Just fate catching up with things."

Slowly extracting himself from Najira's embrace, Akhan went to Laura and held her face for a moment, placing a kiss on each cheek before hugging her. They stood that way for what seemed like a long while before he released her to take up Najira's hand. New worry threaded through Laura as they walked at a leisurely pace. Her uncle's embrace wasn't what it used to be, nor was his complexion. The embrace was limp like the damp leaves on the ground; gone was the vibrant swirl of energy he usually wrought. His normal ruddy skin tone was sallow. His eyes were somewhat cloudy. It was clear the old man was tired, exhausted of this life.

Unshed tears stung Laura's eyes. It seemed like just yesterday he could swing her up to his shoulders and was the strongest man in the world next to her daddy. Now she was his protector.

Knowing his routine, Najira and Laura walked alongside their elderly loved one in silence, waiting for the great Akhan to make the first statement or proclamation of what would be. And true to form he kept his eyes scanning the park, ignoring the junkies and homeless as would-be predators, his concern was always something more dangerous than what lurked in his neighborhood. However, Laura and Najira kept an eye out for all of it.

Neither age nor obvious fatigue kept Akhan from holding his back straight, his head high, a crocheted red, black, and green cap fitting snugly against his bald head. His worn brown corduroy pants offered gentle friction sounds as they made their way deeper into the park, and his old leather sandals created soft shuffles against the leaves while his thick white socks winked at the vivid colors.

A junkie stared at them and staggered forward with his hand dug deep in his grimy blue windbreaker pocket. Najira froze and stopped walking. Laura sighed and gently swept her hand over her barrel purse at the same time Akhan patted his coat pocket. Laura stared at the man unfazed, knowing what he thought— dressed like she and Najira were, add in the fly-ass car, and she was either a mule, a prostitute, or a dealer's woman. But women like that came into the hood packing heat.

Standing her ground told him she was no tourist and the subtle motion across her purse was as much warning as he'd get before she blew his filthy ass away. High or not, he seemed to understand the whole silent conversation. The junkie grinned a snaggle-toothed grin, his eyes darting around cautiously.

"My bad," the wisp of a man said, putting the shank back in his pocket. "Can't be too careful around here. I was just looking for a light."

"I don't smoke," Akhan said evenly. "Only my nine does."

The junkie slid back into the thicket of trees. Laura contemplated the gunmetal gray sky.

"That's why I'm going to Jamaica," Akhan announced with a defeated sigh.

He and Laura shared a look, she knowing that he wasn't talking about the junkie, but something else. . . . Laura set her mind to her uncle's cryptic puzzle. Did he mean predators, leeches, or was it the drugs themselves, the wares she was sure the Jamaicans peddled, just like the Mafia?

"Daddy, that's the best thing you ever said to me," Najira murmured, standing in close enough to hug him again. "I know you have a rep, and believe in the community and all . . . but I worry about you up in a house here all alone. You should go where it's beautiful and peaceful and pretty and warm. We can cover it."

Laura and Akhan shared a knowing gaze.

"Why not the Caymans," Laura said coolly, "or even come back with us to Maui?" She was pressing the old man for an answer and he knew it; she could tell by the amused expression in his eyes, and also knew he refused to be baited in front of Najira. Frustration claimed her. "At least where there's family," she added, trying to corner him into a partial explanation.

Akhan smiled at her and dug in his jacket pocket to produce a ticket. "Because I have family there, it's non-refundable, and my flight leaves today."

"Today," Laura stated flatly, her gaze now holding him hostage.

"Today? Is that what you wanted to tell us—you're moving there for good?" Shocked but ecstatic, Najira smiled widely and threw her arms around his neck, laughing. "We were so worried!"

Again, Laura and her uncle's eyes met and she could see the silent plea in them to be cool, not to tip off Najira. If he wanted that from her, given what was at stake, then he would have to speak to her in code. She leveled her gaze at him and saw his slide away in compromise.

"Yes," Laura said, her voice strained as she eyed her uncle. "We were worried."

"You're gonna stay with Brother B at his place?" Najira asked brightly, oblivious to the undercurrent.

"Either there or maybe I'll take an apartment in Kingston . . .

or I might go up to Montego Bay to the resort area. But I'll be with Braithwaite until I decide."

Okay, fine. He was giving her locations, too; a rough map outline of where he believed the problem to be.

"Then we'll help you move," Laura said, no nonsense in her tone.

He smiled a droll little smile and dug in his pocket. "No need." He handed Laura a safety deposit box key. "All my important papers have been moved, as you might have guessed, and I gave the young warriors in the neighborhood a lot of things that might help their lives. They'll clean out and watch the property like soldiers while I'm gone. The universe is efficient and one must make provisions." He sighed. "Plus, at my age, what do I need?"

The smile that had been on Najira's face began to fade. "Daddy, what's wrong?" she whispered.

Slowly, with a loving caress, he touched Najira's face. "And my children—most of them—have done well and don't need anything from me," he said, not answering her question as he spoke to Laura. He returned his gentle gaze to Najira. "I am so proud of you and approve of all your choices. Tell your brother that for me, too. The art and the house that I have, use it for my grandbabies, all right, sweetheart? Be at peace, this is the cycle of life."

"Oh, my God, Daddy," Najira murmured, her eyes filling. "You're sick, aren't you?"

Laura could feel the muscles in her body tense. For the first time in her life she couldn't tell if her uncle was using his statements as metaphor or truth. But the look in his eyes as he stared at his daughter confirmed her worst fears.

"I've been sick and tired of being sick and tired for a long time," the elderly man admitted, and then linked his arms around both women's waists to begin walking them back toward Laura's car.

Najira halted and hugged him. "Just tell me."

"My prostate."

Laura swallowed hard, fully understanding what her uncle meant to do—sacrifice himself so the next generation could live. It was a half truth, but the whole truth. If the old man was dying, then he had nothing to lose. She covered her mouth with her hand, willing herself not to cry.

"What did the doctors say?" Najira asked quietly, her voice breaking.

Akhan held his daughter back and lifted her chin with a gnarled, arthritic finger. "You go ahead and let James walk you down that aisle," he said with a sad smile. "He's my designee. I will watch from wherever old dogs like me go—back with the ancestors. *Ashe?*"

Tears spilled down Najira's pretty face and Laura fought hard to blink hers back. She watched her young cousin avidly shake her head no, fully understanding that at Najira's age, being philosophical about life and death and its unrelenting cycle was too much to ask.

"No," Najira argued, her voice becoming strident and loud. "I want you to be here! We'll find doctors! There are new treatments, I—"

"Shush, baby," Akhan murmured, pulling his now sobbing daughter into his arms. "It's all right. You mustn't upset the new life within you. This is why I don't want you to come to Jamaica." He looked up at Laura again with a more urgent plea in his eyes.

This time Laura nodded, but Najira broke her father's hold.

"You know about the baby?" Najira whirled on Laura, but her father caught her before she could launch into unfounded accusations.

"There was no betrayal of your trust. I have eyes," he said with a smile, calming his distraught child. "That is why I needed to see you before I left. Were Steve here I would have told him he had my blessing and to protect you at all costs. I wanted James here to tell him to walk in my stead, should you marry. I wanted Jamal here to let him know not to carry the weight of the past on his shoulders—as his father I am proud and he is a strong young soldier. He should make something good with his life, now that he has his second chance. A man rarely gets that. So he should marry well, and always stand by his brother-in-law's side to help protect his sister and her children."

He turned to Laura and slowly went to her to cup her cheek

with a weathered hand. "And I wanted my dear niece to know how much of a true warrior she has been—my young queen with so much on her shoulders. For her, my soul is indebted, for her my heart weeps and my prayers go up with incense to the ancestors. I have left offerings on altars for her. I love you all."

Emotion closed Laura's throat and momentarily blocked her protests as she simply hugged her uncle. "Isn't there anything I can do?" she whispered. "*Anything?*"

He shook his head as she released him. "Not this time. It's gone too far."

They stared at each other, knowing he had transitioned the conversation from the true state of his health to that of the external threat.

"How long did the doctors give you?" Najira asked, her voice choked.

"Not long," her father replied with a sigh, glimpsing her, but returning his gaze to Laura.

Laura nodded. "When did you first learn of your condition?"

"Shortly after I came back from the extended vacation with you all in Maui." He shrugged. "That's when they let me know."

Again Laura nodded and lifted her chin, clear now that her uncle was speaking to her in code. Oddly, she understood why. It was somehow easier for a daughter to accept the death of her father from natural causes than to think of his demise from a bullet. Why that was the case, she wasn't sure.

It was so clear that the latter choice that Akhan had made was swifter and kinder than any bestial chemotherapy and horrific decline. If Najira knew anything about the street warrior standing in the park with them, she should have known that her father had the level of pride that would only allow him to leave this life on his own terms—and that would not be as a frail old man.

"All right," Najira said, rubbing her palms down her tear-streaked face. "Then we fight this together."

Laura smiled sadly as she stared at Akhan. "It's in her DNA, Uncle," she said softly. "She will not stand by and see you pass without action." She set her shoulders hard. "Nor will I." She allowed her message to sink in and didn't speak until he nodded his assent.

"I didn't expect you would," he said with a weary expulsion of breath. "You are a Scorpio."

"Ashe," Laura said through her teeth. "And I will sting the frog and drown us both before I allow anything to happen to my family without redress."

Laura clamped her lips shut tightly, knowing that she may have gone too far, but then relaxed a little as Najira nodded, oblivious to her meaning.

"I want to see those doctors," Najira stated. "I want to know what they said, what treatments they—"

"The ones here are inconsequential," Akhan said, landing a steadying hand on Najira's shoulder. "I'm going to the naturalists in Jamaica." He looked at Laura. "Those in the bush."

Laura raked her fingers through her hair, her nerves filleted. "How can you trust—"

"That's the thing," he said, cutting her off. "This time, there is no trust. Do you understand me?" He captured both Najira and Laura's gazes in one, his eyes glaring a warning. "If you do not understand me, then overstand me. Don't fight me on this. I have known of my condition for a very long time. My decision is final—to die in the islands."

"Then the whole family is coming," Najira said, folding her arms. "I'll marry there, and we have enough resources to stay there, until . . ." She lifted her chin. "That's my choice, Daddy. To be with you till the end and I don't care what you say, you hear me?"

"I do and I said I don't want the worriment on your head to possibly harm the baby," he said, his voice escalating as obvious panic swept through him.

"Is there any surgery that can be done here, anything that could help from this end before you go to Jamaica?" Laura asked, trying to intercede and help her uncle's cause with Najira. She respected his desire to keep her out of the line of fire in a foreign country, but then again, where was safe?

"No," he said, calmly. "It's too far gone. Besides, they would have to take my manhood." Akhan straightened his back, his gaze now angry and blazing with untold indignities as it ricocheted from Laura to Najira and back. "Even at my age, why should I allow them to take that from me? That is death, in and of itself." He stared at his daughter. "Would you want that for me—to live as a eunuch because you couldn't stand weeping at my honorable death, child?"

"Oh, Daddy . . ." Najira turned away. "I just . . ."

"She just needs time to allow it to all sink in," Laura said softly, trying to rein in everyone's emotions. "Give her a moment."

"*Ashe,*" Akhan said. "But you hear me, Laura. Yes?"

"Yes," Laura said in a gentle tone. "But you hear me?"

He nodded.

"Together, we can possibly take preemptive measures, is what I believe Najira is saying—standing as one bundle of sticks unbroken." Laura leaned heavily on the old African proverb to get through to her stubborn uncle. "They have extracted one old stick from the bundle and will break it over their knee. But we have many sticks in our bundle."

She watched her uncle grapple with that truth, knowing that he would have to also understand the implication—he might get one or two of them, but they'd still come for his progeny and her.

"I will allow you, as the one with power of attorney, to see my doctors, Laura." He lifted his chin. "You are adept in such matters."

Najira's eyes widened at the affront. "But I'm your daughter!"

"And you are pregnant and to be married," her father stated flatly. "Give me the peace of mind of knowing at least that you are happy, child. Do not be so stubborn—you take so much after me! Don't you trust Laura to handle things as always?"

He and Najira both smiled and then chuckled, and then finally hugged.

"I'm going to need a full itinerary," Laura said with a weary but grateful sigh. "I'll handle things and will see if I can get us on a flight today or tomorrow to tail you . . . because I don't suspect you'd cancel your ticket and wait to go with us?"

"No," her uncle said with a wry grin. "Things are already in motion over there. Doctors are already waiting to see me."

Laura reached out and gripped his hand as a renewed sense of panic washed through her. "Then I *must* talk to you before you get on that flight."

He nodded and began walking toward Laura's car. "In the airport," her uncle said with a sly grin. "We can eat. Najira can rest as we stroll . . . I'll explain what I know. Just promise me you will not change my paperwork for anyone under any circumstances—because that will undo my whole life."

Laura squeezed his hand as they strolled across the street. *"Ashe."*

James leaned his head back against the seat and listened to the dull roar of the airplane engine. A hundred thoughts besieged his mind at once. The coincidences were too eerie to shake. The Rent-A-Center furniture. The girl's house had been rented for only a week, and now she'd skipped town. The Jeep was a rental, belonging to one Terrence Braithwaite. The last name gave him the chills. Braithwaite was a family name. Please, God, no. *Don't let it be family,* he quietly prayed. He glimpsed Jamal from a sidelong glance.

"Tell me something, brother," James murmured, his mind still working on the information they'd gleaned that morning. "How long did you know this chick?"

Jamal smiled and shrugged, leaning in to whisper to James.

"Don't answer that," James said, already knowing it couldn't have been more than twenty-four to forty-eight hours. He cut a glare at Jamal and then glimpsed Steve, who was snoring.

"Yeah, that long—long enough for a booty call," Jamal said with a smirk.

"Well, check it out," James said, leaning in to speak into Jamal's ear. "The Jamaican mother who was about to pop you was a

Braithwaite." He sat back and watched the revelation spread horror across Jamal's face.

"Could be coincidence," Jamal said, swallowing hard. "Like, that name could be like Jones is here, ya mean."

James nodded. "Could be. But if not . . ."

"Oh, shit . . . I've gotta talk to my old man, ask him the family names from over there—from his first set of kids. Like, I'm not believing this."

"What's not to believe?" James said flatly. "Regular blood would fight over a raggedy-ass, run-down row house in North Central. You think step-siblings would be above a brawl for it all over the millions in real estate your old man amassed with his old partner, Donald Haines?" He leaned forward, his nose almost touching Jamal's. "We've got five hours in the air in front of us. I want you to think about all this long and hard, because you might have been set up, man. Even I don't know what all was in your father's will—only Laura knows the full story. But the part of it that she leaked to her reporter buddy, Rick, when that other shit was going down with the Micholi Foundation and the Russians trying to move on the Gulf might have been enough to send the Braithwaite side of your family sniffing."

"Damn," Jamal whispered. "You think Safia tried to set me up? Get me shot by my own half brother and shit?"

"How much is land down there worth?" James said with a shrug. "All I know is your father is damned near ninety, and if he doesn't have any next of kin—like you and Najira . . . or maybe even Laura," James said more slowly as that reality sank in, "then who else would it go to? Charity?" He shook his head. "Not. Unless the old man had long-standing reasons to cut them out of the will."

"But shit," Jamal said, his voice a hiss through his teeth. "If Pops got all that, and the cash increased over the years as property values went up, then all of us would be phat-paid. Why they gotta do an old man like that or even come after us?"

"Some people ain't into sharing," James said without blinking in a low, ominous tone. Besides, you and Najira were closer to

Akhan. He left them and Jamaica almost thirty years ago, before both of you all were born. So, suffice to say that something probably went down, and maybe they aren't feeling so secure about the relationship." James flopped back against the seat and rubbed his palms down his face to chase away the fatigue. "An educated guess would say that he'd break them off a little, but would leave the lion's share with his second family—you and Najira."

"That shit is so grimy," Jamal said between his teeth. "It ain't even about what Pops mighta left any of us, J. If they ever got to know him, they'd love that old man for who he is." Jamal swallowed hard and shook his head, his eyes glassy with unshed tears of sudden rage. "If I find out they set me up . . . if they do anything to Jira or Pop, or even try to come for Laura . . ."

"I feel you," James said. "I just needed to know where you were at with this thing—and you best fill Steve in, too, because to get to Najira they've gotta come through him."

Jamal pounded James's fist. "By any means necessary."

"My point, exactly."

Jamal sent his gaze out of the window. "Damn, man. There just ain't no fuckin' trust."

Chapter
6

Oddly, she felt better, now that the partial truth was out. The fact that her uncle was traveling with only a small backpack, however, told her all she needed to know—he didn't intend to come back. Akhan was going to go after the threat and go out guns blazing. Probably the only person he trusted, Brother B, his old common-law brother-in-law over there, would supply him with ammo and transportation. Laura held his hand tightly as Najira walked up to the airport's food court and left them for a moment to choose Chinese food.

"Promise me you'll wait for twenty-four hours until I get there," she said into his ear through her teeth.

"If opportunity—"

"No," she said firmly in a low tone, and then stared at him. "Joey Scapolini contacted me. You could upset the apple cart. We need to set the balls in motion together, as one, so we're not bumping into each other." It was partially the truth, partially a bluff, but she needed him to wait so she wouldn't come to Jamaica to simply fly his casket home. The last thing they needed was for Akhan to be murdered.

She released her uncle's hand once he'd nodded.

"*Ashe,*" he murmured. "So the cancer has spread farther than I'd thought."

"Tell me where it first grew," Laura urged, watching Najira inch forward in the food line as she walked her uncle toward some tables to sit down. She had to get answers quickly, for soon he'd have to go through the security lines and neither she nor Najira had a ticket to follow him there.

He sat on the plastic and metal chair with a thud across from her, his gaze distant and sad as he watched his daughter place her food order. "My old life has come back to haunt me," he said quietly. "My sons from my first union. I left them there and refused to support their business endeavors when they turned away from the revolution and went for self."

She stared at him, watching years of pain enter his aged eyes and each line of his weathered, almond-hued face, somehow knowing that revealing this truth was carving out a part of his soul. Laura covered his hands with her own. "Uncle, I'm so, so sorry."

"As am I, dear child," he whispered. "I gave their mother all my love, and when she died, I promised her I would raise them to be fine soldiers. It was a time of revolution in the world. A time of revolution in Jamaica. We thought with enough weapons and money things would change. She believed in the revolution, like I did. Brother B, he too, believed. My brother-in-law had hopes, just like I did. We all had hopes, and then came the drugs. How did that happen, Laura?" His elderly gaze searched her face. "They used Malcolm's words, 'By any means necessary,' desecrated his overstanding on it . . . turned the philosophies back on us from the front lines, the ones who fought the system, saying that we were outdated, we didn't understand . . . that we had to finance a war—but they weren't financing anything but cars and lush homes and *themselves.*"

She watched him swallow hard and her heart wrenched as huge tears filled his eyes. What could she tell him? There simply were no words.

"When *the man* takes your son, he has won the next generation of your struggle," Akhan said quietly. "When you take your own wayward son, then you have cut out the rotten root of the tree so that the rest of it can overstand."

Laura squeezed his hands and closed her eyes, and then bent to bring his thick, ancient knuckles to her lips. With profound sorrow she sat in silence with her mentor, waiting for Najira to bring her father a meal to the table, and knowing that killing his Jamaican-born sons would put him in his grave. That was why he wasn't coming home again, even if he survived the cancer or the shootout.

"Let me and James do it," she murmured against his fists, tears of empathy flowing down her cheeks with her eyes still closed. "I'll back Scapolini off Najira and Jamal. Just let me work something out so that you don't have this on your soul—not with you being so close to the ancestors. *Please.*"

"You have a plan?' he murmured, bringing her hands to his mouth for a gentle, grazing kiss, "as your way has never been outright brutality, Laura, but a severe noose to bind up the enemy. My only fear is, this time, the only way may be through the barrel of a gun."

"Yes," she lied without blinking. "I have a plan. Don't do anything, and they can't kill you or any of us while you're there until they know for sure how the will is set. All they can do is threaten us, send us warning messages, until they figure out what's actually in the paperwork and how you've woven it together. Do that for me." Her eyes searched his face until it found compliance. "Just trust me."

"All right," he whispered as Najira approached with their lunch. "You're the only one that I do. And in this," he warned, "I suggest you do said same."

It felt so good to be in James's arms again that she just stood in his big, bear-like embrace, breathing him in and feeling him fill up her insides with warmth. There was something about the sheer mass of the man that brought comfort, as did the way his huge hands flattened against her back before his fingers threaded through her hair. They stood that way in the airport for what felt like a long time, connected, one flesh, just simply thankful to be alive.

"So, you ain't got no love for family now?" Jamal complained as Najira hid her face in the folds of Steve's puff coat and Laura practically collapsed against James's chest. "Where's Pops?"

Najira lifted her head and slowly extracted herself from Steve's hold. "There's so much I need to tell you, Jamal. C'mon . . . let's not do it out here in public."

James looked down at Laura as she turned her face up to him and could immediately tell something had gone very wrong.

"He's not . . . nobody—"

"No, no, it's all right," Laura said quickly, finally going to Jamal to hug him with Najira. "Baby, listen, your father is sick. He wanted to go to where he has a dear friend . . . to Brother B."

"He went to Jamaica! Oh, hell no—"

"Shush!" Laura and Najira hissed in unison.

"We need to get somewhere we can talk," James said evenly. "Laura, the Jag has to stay in the airport garage. I'll call in some favors on the force and have the cap tow it and rake it for a bug. Me, Jamal, and Steve already bought new luggage and went through our clothes."

Laura closed her eyes. "The suitcases . . ."

James nodded. "Yeah. A wire tap is easy—so they knew what flights you'd be on, and what better way to tail you than with something in your suitcase. That's gotta be how they knew. So, let's rent a car, stop at the Coach store in town, switch out yours and Najira's old luggage for new, run a tab at The Ritz, and change hotels on the sly. Whoever we give the bags to in the hotel, some homeboy who will be glad to take them, will have those bastards that tapped you chasing around to every beauty shop, barber shop, and bar that boosts hot gear—finally ending at a house in the hood where some sister has new LV luggage. They'll figure it out after a while, and won't shoot up some house. That wouldn't be worth their while and would definitely draw attention that they don't want."

* * *

"*Hotep*, Brother B," Akhan said quietly, embracing his long-time friend once he cleared Customs.

The gaunt, shorter man held Akhan away from him, his gaze sad and searching with worry etching deeper lines in his dark brown face. "My friend, you are not well."

"No," Akhan admitted as he hoisted up his backpack on his shoulder. "But, then, how could I be?"

Brother B nodded and the choppy movement caused his crocheted cap filled with silvery-gray locks to bounce. "These are some strange days and times, mon . . . perhaps the last days and times."

The two said nothing as they walked through the throng and out into the stark heat and humidity that made everything around Kingston's bustling Norman Manley International Airport feel heavier.

"We gwan haf to go up to the house in the hills," Brother B said quietly, before they reached his ancient station wagon. "Need help to get what we need, but don't trust to speak in me house or car."

Akhan nodded. "I think we should send them on a chase when we speak."

"A roundabout, *irie*," Brother B said with a hard smile, and the two fell silent as they entered his car.

Akhan kept his gaze out the window, his heart breaking in increments as the car struggled through the congested streets and finally broke away to move up the majestic, jewel green mountainside. He sat back calmly mopping perspiration from his brow, remembering the Jamaica that was lost to him forever with the death of his first wife. Tears of regret filled his eyes as the memory of each baby boy being born took root in his soul. The streets took them here no less than the streets almost swallowed Jamal.

Poverty was poverty no matter where one was in the world. Truth was an unrelenting taskmaster. Back then, he'd been so idealistic as to believe he could go to a homeland, a beautiful paradise lost and live off the land without intervention of *the man*.

But *the man* had conquered the globe worldwide. His friends who had expatriated to Brazil in the sixties had written home of this heartbreak . . . so had those who'd settled in Accra, Ghana, Nigeria, Liberia, it didn't matter. The effects of colonialism had made the people sick for hundreds of years and the devastation remained. Old sugar plantations now harvested cocaine, weed, whatever, or simply brought in tourists. Akhan closed his eyes against the lush foliage, fighting the nausea and exhaustion the heat pummeled against his being, vowing to fight to the bitter end.

"You all right, mon?" Brother B asked, his voice laden with concern. "You need some water—we can stop on the roadside?"

"No," Akhan wheezed. "How are your boys?" He didn't look at Brother B, but began their banter of code, hoping that his friend would sound natural once they arrived at the house in the bush.

"Terrence and Hector are like dey been since smelling themselves," Brother B said and then spit out the window.

"Mine, too." Akhan sighed and then fell silent for the rest of the steep, scenic climb up the mountain.

After two hours of narrow, rutted roads and breathtaking but perilous views of sheer drops without guardrails, Brother B turned off the main road to his acreage hidden in the dense thicket of bush. He brought the wheezing station wagon to a coughing, sputtering halt, and then opened the heavy door with effort.

Akhan sat quietly in agony, sweating, breathing deeply, almost too overcome by the sudden temperature change to move. In a labored, elderly gait, Brother B came to his side of the vehicle and opened the door, helping his friend out with tears in his eyes.

"It's hot, mon, but cooler in de hills," Brother B announced. "We have someting cool, put some water on our faces, and rest."

Akhan held onto his friend and inched up the back door steps, understanding why Braithwaite could never secure his long, L-shaped barrack of a home against surveillance or invasion. They had been so very, very idealistic to believe the revolution would not be televised. Renewed sadness claimed him as his friend helped him remove his jacket and helped him to sit. He leaned against the Formica table catching his breath as Brother B brought first cool water and then sought ginger beer to help settle his stomach.

"We should get some canned goods from de basement once we've rested, as old men, and head to Montego Bay. Tings are expensive dere, but I know your sons would want to see you. Mine have mansions—estates—in de North of Kingston in Constant Springs, but dey are not home and might not like me to visit unannounced—even if I'm dere father."

Picking up on the ruse, Akhan brought his cool ginger beer to his lips to open his throat. He remembered digging out the secret room and stashing weapons behind the shelf of canned goods in readiness, and also remembered how by that time their sons had abandoned the cause for their own ambitions before they knew about the room.

"How old are the cans?" Akhan asked, forcing a chuckle, hoping that Brother B had updated the selection of guns.

"Don't worry, mon," Brother B said with a smile. "You won't get botulism from dented cans, mon." He mouthed the words Uzi and automatics, and held up nine fingers to denote nine millimeters.

"Good," Akhan said in a casual tone. "I don't want to be a burden on Daoud or Hakim. In fact, I came here to explain my will to them, old friend," Akhan said in an extra loud voice for whoever was listening in. "They were first and eldest, so now that I'm sick, I need to explain the responsibilities—the white media machine misrepresented the facts and might have made them think wrongly about my intentions. Plus, I need to tell them about the very little bit I left my second set of children, and why I had their cousin, Laura, as my executrix. But there's more land down there in the Gulf than they realized."

Brother B nodded and pursed his lips, outrage clearly in his eyes. "Good. And this other problem, mon, what of dat?"

Akhan sighed. "Italians went after their cousin Laura, my brother. She came to warn me that they were after me to try to kidnap me and her to make me sign the papers over to them, and threatened to kill Jamal and Najira. That's why I have to go to Montego Bay as soon as possible to see my sons."

"All right," Brother B said, fetching a cool drink for himself. "We'll rest, and I'll fix us a little supper. Then, before it gets dark, we'll head back down the mountain, maybe stay in town, and tomorrow early we can drive the five to six hours to Montego Bay." Pure hurt took up residence in Brother B's eyes. "Maybe I can leave a message with my sons, even though we rarely speak . . . but since this is a family matter . . ."

"*Ashe.*" Akhan closed his eyes hoping that all the twists and turns of his story would set one group of predators against the other while buying his intimate family some time. It stabbed his soul that Daoud and Hakim, as well as their cousins Terrence and Hector, were no longer what he would consider his own blood. He'd sent them to the best universities to learn how *the man* operated. His sons were to take a page from *The Spook Who Sat by the Door*, but instead of embracing the revolution, they desecrated it with drug money. The new decade of me-generation children had obviously corrupted his house.

Something had gone so terribly, terribly wrong that he and his old buddy of decades would be couriering heavy artillery down a mountainside, not to meet some revolutionary threat, but to execute their own gang-entrenched sons before they stole the lives of their siblings and robbed the people of their land. A single tear spilled over the edges of his tired eyes, and Brother B simply walked over and laid a hand on Akhan's shoulder, his face also wet with tears.

"I know this is hard, mon—not what we ever dreamed." Brother B's voice broke into a harsh rasp. "We are finally old men and it's time to lay down de weary load."

It was all in their eyes, each person explaining some but not all of the threat to Najira. Without even needing to discuss it, they were all very clear that there'd be no telling Najira about her father's role in any of this. Not after what had happened before when the girl had been on the verge of an emotional collapse.

Add a pregnancy to that, and who knew the outcome. Obviously no one wanted to be responsible. Besides, Akhan wouldn't have it any other way.

Yet, they had to tell Najira something plausible. The maneuvering of suitcases and hotels had been the tip-off; there was no way to avoid it, especially when Steve later blurted out that the bug James located in Laura's carry-on bag liner looked like a federal job, not a Mob special. But they left it all as a potential threat, not a definite one, just to give the poor woman some peace of mind. Telling her about the casino boys getting interested in some land deals down in the Gulf, post Rick-the-reporter's expose, was one thing; she'd faced them with the family before and they'd all survived. However, explaining about the Jamaican tie-in would send Najira into apoplexy for sure.

Talking in code, they ate in public, preferring to play the game rather than risk hiding as a group that could be snuffed out in one easy hotel hit. All agreed that it was probably safer to walk across the street from The Ritz-Carlton to McCormick & Schmidt's for seafood. There, they could go over the travel logistics, drop a cool grand, and then get an invisible VIP escort through the Broad Street building out a delivery exit in kitchen staff gear. It was better than making one mass exodus to travel to a new hotel as a group.

They had to make it appear like they were cool, not dodging the people watching them, but then get lost so smoothly that it would seem like they'd literally melted into the buildings. But they were under no illusions—getting lost and working the system in Jamaica where they didn't know the lay of the land was definitely going to be a bitch.

James and Laura checked into the Hyatt; Steve and Najira took a room at The Doubletree; Jamal checked into the Marriott—each only a few blocks from the other, each with an Air Jamaica ticket in hand and the agreement to catch a cab to the airport with cell phones synced to call each other at the appointed hour. Anyone missing the call-in meant there was a problem.

By the time Laura followed James into their hotel room, her hands were shaking.

She numbly watched James case the room with a Glock, having seen him do it a thousand times. The moment he nodded, she put the extra bolts on the door and turned quietly to watch the adrenaline slowly ebb from James's system. She didn't say a word as he set his gun on the dresser, pulled off his leather bomber jacket, found the courtesy bar in the room, and extracted a small flight-sized Johnny Walker Red. In one uninterrupted motion he twisted open the cap and downed the amber fluid within the individual-shot bottle.

"This shit reminds me of being on the force," James muttered. "I want a cigarette so bad, you just don't know."

"They have red wine in there?" Laura asked, slowly coming deeper into the room and leaving the suitcases by the door. She'd heard him loud and clear—this shit was enough to make anyone need a light.

"Yeah, baby. I'm sorry," he said, smoothing his palm over his close-cropped hair. "They've got merlot. Want some?"

"That'll do," she murmured and set her purse on the dresser next to his gun. She didn't want to talk about what they'd discussed ad nauseum at dinner. Right now all she needed was enough mental distance to get past the panic, get clear, and to calmly work the angles. It was impossible to address the butterflies in her stomach that took flight each time she thought of her uncle over in Jamaica possibly doing something very heroic and very foolish.

Rather than focus on the myriad horrible fates that could befall her elderly uncle, whom she loved so dearly, she watched James's muscular back, the way it expanded and contracted beneath his black turtleneck sweater as he breathed deeply and reached for the wine. The shift in reality made her feel safe, even if safety was a fantasy . . . a luxury she couldn't afford.

She allowed her gaze to caress the deep sway in his back that seemed to carve out real estate at the base of his spine before the thick sinew of his symmetrically devastating ass rose to perfection beneath his charcoal-hued wool slacks. Six-foot-five and absolutely fine. She loved his stone-hewn thighs and chiseled calves—pure carved ebony.

When he turned to bring her the glass of wine, she slowly dragged her gaze up from his belt to his face, lingering along each brick of his abdominal firewall, up his massive chest and along his broad shoulders, reveling in the steel cable of his biceps and forearms. She adored his hands, the slightly rough texture of them, the way he kept his nails clean, short, trimmed, but not professionally manicured. James Carter was a working man, regardless of their wealth, and she admired that about him. Liked the little bit of rough around his edges, just the way she loved how his jaw-line was now shadowed and would rub rough against her skin.

Laura accepted the wine he offered, her gaze now held by James's intense, dark stare. They understood each other. She took a sip from her glass, watching him watch her, his gaze slowly finding her damp mouth. It was all over his face—last mission mode. He didn't have to say it; he'd told her about it a long time ago. That place where every man who carries a gun gets to when he knows tomorrow might be his day to die. His gaze drank her in as she slowly drank her wine, clearly gauging whether she could handle where he wanted to go. Sensitivity didn't have a damned thing to do with it. She understood that the man needed to turn off the battle being fought in his head. Not a problem.

She set down her glass on the dresser with determined precision. Yeah, she knew her husband—tonight he needed to be fucked and fucked well. Tender endearments, sweet, gentle caresses, soft kisses against delicate skin were not where his mind resided at the moment. If they lived though this, then she'd make love to him later. If not, then the entire concept was moot anyway.

James didn't move but stared at her with a subtle tilt of his head, as though wondering. They'd been through so much shit together; a torrid memory might be all they had to cling to while bleeding to death from a gunshot wound in the streets of Jamaica or Philly. He didn't have to ask her. Panic, now, served no purpose. The game had been set in motion by the Mob. Deadly family was in the mix, too. They had to play it to the bone.

Laura fit against James's tense body and leaned up to take his mouth hard. A granite erection stabbed her thigh. His breath filled her lungs in such a rush that it made her dizzy, but two strong arms caught her and crushed out an exhaled groan.

Her arms immediately encircled his neck as he roughly spun her away from the bureau to walk her backward toward the bed. Her tongue fought with his, her hands aggressive as she yanked his sweater up out of his pants and went for his belt, then let him strip her of her clothes hard and fast. Her hands mirrored his as he worked, urging him to take it all out on her, to give her the stress, the burden of worry with his body so that by tomorrow he'd be a marksman with a steady grip on his nine.

The heat of his touch against her back, her ass, her torso made her cry out. His face was burning up as it seared her neck and then found her cleavage, his hands covering her breasts and causing her to arch as he spilled their bodies onto the bed.

Instant weight flattened her; two hundred and twenty pounds of driving force was between her legs, an entry so hot and so good that her fists hit the duvet with a wail. A shudder claimed her, opening her wider, wanting all of him within her. Thick forearms anchored around her waist pulling her up against the next devastating thrust. Her calves locked around the dip in his spine, his breaths ragged echo-chants of a man trying to forget that he could die, killing her sweetly instead, making her body scream without words, *yeah, like that—as hard as you can.*

October chill factor be damned, the room became a sauna. Sweat-slicked stomachs a slap-glide frenzy of skin-against-skin, one flesh, one breath, her man's hands in her hair, becoming unconscious fists from pleasure jags riddling his system, purging his mind, sending spasms through his sac, her silky legs now sliding against his steel ass, melting from his pummeling heat over it to his thighs and back. Anything, *everything*, to keep him moving, make him crazy, make him split her wide and deep enough to repeatedly hit that spot that drained the color from her knuckles as she clutched the sheets.

Sweat dripping off his chin to splatter her pebble hard nipples, his grazing hers, forcing a gasp while pumping crazy . . . Minds lost to cold air rushing between them as his head dropped back—impossible to withstand without calling his name.

"Oh, *shit*, Laura," his voice broke into a million pieces caught between a gasp and a deep groan. *Only* his wife knew him like this, she was *the only one* who knew how to let her hands glide over his ass at the right moment, knew when to ride him or when to let him drive her into the mattress, when to arch, her sweet, tight wetness inspiring madness.

Satin skin consumed him, delicate hands pressed down hard against his back, scrabbling for more of what he'd gladly give her. Tight, silky legs sending a now erratic message in pulsing releases, a swell of hips slamming up to meet his pelvis, a supple spine curved in an arch so hard it practically lifted him off the bed with her throaty groan, full breasts bouncing . . . and just as swiftly, he felt her body erupt into jerking spasms that fractured her voice, fractured his scrotum, opened up everything within him in hot spewing waves until tears cascaded down his face.

When he dropped against her, she gasped as though shipwrecked and coming up for air. All he could do was roll over and drag her with him, hoping she could breathe on her own. It took him a moment to realize that she was still climaxing as she straddled him; the ecstatic agony was clear on her face as her head dropped back and she began to move against him again.

The sight of her need stole his breath. Her beauty was magnified by the sheen of dampness that covered her body, making her gorgeous caramel skin glisten beneath the room lights.

Through heavy lids he watched her grind pleasure in a slow, hard swirl down into his groin. "*Laura*, baby . . ."

His hands were drawn by both instinct and need to her pendulous breasts just to deepen her expression, make her eyes squeeze shut tighter, cause her to bite her lip as he lifted to thrust against her, waiting for that stuttering gasp, that point where she'd drop forward on a deep moan and buck hard with her mouth open, her breathing short pants.

He could feel her edging there, her thighs tightening, her lazy hip-swirl beginning to become more determined thrusts while his mouth teased a taut nipple, his thumb finding her bud. He wrapped his arms around her hips to help her forget, half sitting up for her with a hard pull that made her fingers cradle his skull.

"Uh-huh," he murmured from deep within, sending the understanding against her breasts with a rush of heat while pulling her against him hard. "I know," he said between his teeth with another hard thrust. They were so alike it was scary.

Her agonized voice was breaking him down, straining his system to bust another nut with her. He knew what she needed— they'd make love if they lived, right now she wanted a roughneck ride. Oh, shit, yeah, she could have that if she kept pumping like she was. She could smother him in her cleavage, he was beyond caring as her nails ran over his scalp and she found their mutual rhythm one more time.

"Oh, God, James!"

"I know, just get it."

His voice was a tense, muffled plea against her damp skin; hers was an open-air shriek that lifted him up off the wet bed deeper inside her. His grip around her waist suddenly tightened as his long strokes went to short jabs, her voice unraveling his sanity, her spasmodic contractions dredging his sac.

He came so hard his body was dry heaving. No sound exited him, just air until she stopped moving. Tremors passed through him, out of him, into her, and back again as though they'd both touched the same live wire.

They clung to each other, gasping, rocking, shivering, and then finally fell against the thick white duvet in slow motion, exhausted.

"Oh, my God," she whispered.

He couldn't speak, just lightly squeezed her and allowed his arms to drop away.

She kissed his chest; he couldn't even open his eyes or acknowledge the caress.

"I love you," she whispered.

He simply nodded and hoped she understood that that was the
best he could do for right now.

Chapter
7

"Whaduya mean you lost 'em!"

Tony Rapuzzio cringed as the senior Caluzo shouted into his Bluetooth earpiece and walked farther away from the casino entrance dragging hard on a cigarette. He looked up and down the nearly deserted boardwalk and hunched his body against the cold blast coming off the Atlantic Ocean.

"What happened is," he said, glimpsing his gold Rolex watch and choosing his words carefully, "the tail followed the signal up to a beauty shop where the broads musta gone to get their hair done. Maybe they even had a dye job, ya know, to change their looks so we wouldn't spot 'em. But then they split up. One went to the moolie section of Germantown, the other up in the heart of the ghetto in North Philly. But when my man got a second driver on it and they e-mailed the pics, one was some fat old broad that ain't nowhere near Laura Caldwell, and the other was some teenage chick going out to a club who I know from my own two eyes ain't her cousin.

"Well, if she slipped you—you moron—then she could be on her way to Jamaica to see her relatives and to cut a direct deal with them. If that happens, we're screwed. How in the fuck are we gonna do what's necessary without the extra resources? You think about that shit and tell Mikey to call me."

The call disconnected in Tony's ear as he took one last drag on his cigarette before pitching it over the boardwalk rail. He was not looking forward to a replay of the conversation he'd just had, but what was a man to do. At least Caluzo was in Vegas. Joey was upstairs in the suite with a bimbo, and could be a real sonofabitch when pissed off.

He hit speed dial and connected with Caluzo's nephew. "Yo, Mikey. We got us a problem. You think you can call that kid Steve you went to high school with . . . you know, get him to tip off where they're at?"

Rapuzzio waited, his nerves wound tight. "Yeah. I just got off the phone with your uncle and he's getting real nervous about the whole thing. And in a minute, I gotta go upstairs and tell Joey we lost the fuckers—and I ain't too partial to doing that, ya know?" Again he listened for Mikey's response. "Good. I'ma smoke another cigarette and take a fuckin' Tums. You get back to me and call your uncle with some good news, and I'll work on Joey. This shit has to go down right, Mikey, or I'm a dead man walking. You don't screw Scapolini and then go have a celebration like you won some fuckin' election. Don't forget me when the change goes down, what you promised. Yeah, all right. I'll wait for your call."

"How could you have lost them?" Donny shouted, his voice echoing through his spacious Pine Street brownstone. He stood and gathered his paisley silk robe tighter around himself, crossing the living room to make a martini, and leaving the two men facing each other as they sat with hunched shoulders in the overstuffed, leather wingback chairs. "That is *unacceptable.*" He whirled around, sloshing his drink. "I thought you were a professional, had worked for the feds. I thought you put the same kind of device you used to use in her travel bag? I'm not committing campaign funds in the double-digit millions to your candidate for this sloppy shit, Townsend!"

George Townsend glimpsed the ex-federal agent next to him who now did freelance work, measuring his words before he replied to Donald Haines Jr. Drawing on the most cultured, political tones within him, he kept the larger goal before him and tucked away his visceral disdain for the late, great Donald Haines Senior's spoiled, pampered son.

"Donny," George murmured in a tone designed to pacify the high-strung heir, "the beacon led to a club down on Front Street and when Mr. Bradley went in to investigate, none of them were there. But I assure you he will pick up the lead again." George Townsend's steel gray gaze slid from Donny's icy blue eyes to Bradley's unreadable dark brown gaze.

"We'll find them," the ex-agent stiffly replied. "I always find them."

"Good," Donny snapped, taking a liberal sip of his drink before pulling his fingers through his disheveled blonde hair. "My father was murdered, my mother lost her life, my lover was put behind bars—all of it happened around these people. I don't care that I became sole heir to my parents' millions. I don't care about the money, don't you people get it?"

"Donny, it's going to be all right," Townsend said quietly, trying to calm his distraught patron d'politics.

Shaking his head, Donny leaned against the mantel and looked up at the cathedral ceilings, his nervous gaze skirting the gilded crown molding. "If they'd never started digging . . . I want everything they ever owned with my father seized by eminent domain and then sold to the highest bidder."

"In due time," Townsend soothed. "But in an election year, we can't afford to openly do that. The national focus would crucify our candidate."

"I know. But I want whoever that bitch Laura cut a deal with to think it will happen immediately. I want her ass stripped of power so the underbelly of society will come looking for her, will go after her loved ones, will leave her without a family the way this travesty left me! That's what I'm writing a check for." Donny pointed at Townsend. "Anything less and you've fucking reneged and I don't drop shit in your war chests, understood?"

Tears sparkled in Donny's crystal blue eyes and his voice broke as both men simply stared at him during his impassioned outburst. He flung his martini across the room, shattering the glass. "George, they fucked you so badly you had to go into witness protection in Ohio! I'm counting on you—you're the only one who knows the game like my father did. How would Sir Donald have gotten retribution? If they had left well enough alone, Mother would be alive. Moyer wouldn't have killed her."

"Don't worry, Donny. It is my sincere pledge to you to make Laura Caldwell-Carter's life miserable. Trust me."

Townsend allowed his voice to take on a psychiatric, stabilizing drone as he watched the young Haines practically unravel before his eyes. Ever since Haines Sr., had died, the landscape had lost its old world charm. Everything was unbalanced, unpredictable, and subject to the unplanned. He wasn't about to live out the rest of his life as a non-player—some loser, suburban auto insurance broker in Ohio—not when he had been at the top of the key at the Micholi Foundation, The Redevelopment Authority, part of the who's who in East Coast political power. Never. He thought about the woman who had come up the hard way from the streets to an Ivy League institution, to Wall Street. She'd traded on the inside like the Good Ole Boys, and even beat them at their game. She was still standing. Too many had died, too many had gone to jail, and most important of all, too many had been stripped of money and power at the hands of one Laura Caldwell.

Steve glimpsed the clock as his cell phone vibrated across the nightstand. Gently extricating Najira from his hold, he flipped the unit open the second he recognized the number.

"Hold on, Mikey," he murmured and eased out of bed, hoping the reception would last as he went into the bathroom and quietly closed the door.

If Mike Caluzo was calling him at three A.M., some serious shit was about to go down. Najira had wept herself to sleep, and his eyes felt like grains of sand were scraping his eyeballs as he blinked against the harsh glare bouncing off the gleaming porcelain.

"What's up, man?"

"Need to know where you're at to be sure you're outta harm's way," Caluzo said. "I'm sure you know by now that Joey is under some pressure from the family to act decisively about the situation in the Gulf. No reason for you to get fucked in the process—since me and you go way back. Let that black bitch go, meet me for a drink in Atlantic City, and it's no skin off your nose."

Stunned silent for a moment, Steve hesitated. Rage made him want to shout at Caluzo; common sense told him to throw him off the trail. Najira was carrying his child, was his fiancée, and was soon to be his wife. Anything he and Caluzo had from the past evaporated.

"You there?" Caluzo asked, his voice strained.

"Yeah, I had to get out of bed with her and she don't need to overhear this convo," Steve whispered.

"That's a good look, Sulli. So, where you at?"

"It's that bad, man?" Steve asked, stalling so his mind could begin to work on all cylinders.

"'Fraid so, *pisano*. But you're one-a us and ain't got no cause to get nervous. Just tell me where you're at and clear out of there, and it's all good."

"At the Dock Street Sheraton," Steve lied, his blood running cold.

"What room?"

Steve paused, not wanting to put innocent people at risk. "You gonna whack her?"

There was no answer for a moment and then Caluzo chuckled tensely. "Now why would we do that? Just wanna scare her a little, send a message to her cousin, Laura. We won't bury the broad. So go wash your dick and come on down to the casinos—I'll buy you a steak and we'll get drunk together. All right?"

"Yeah. Room 907. Give me a half hour." Panic swept through Steve and made him walk in a tight circle.

"You're a good egg, Sulli."

Steve began hyperventilating when the call disconnected and immediately called Captain Bennett at home. "Cap," he wheezed when his former boss groggily answered. "Get a car down to room 907 at the Dock Street Sheraton and make sure the room is empty—don't ask, don't tell is in full effect. Just trust me when I say some shit is about to go down, and if the room is occupied, the people need to move."

He hung up and called James, pulling his fingers through his hair. Panic sweat covered him as James's sleepy voice filled the receiver.

"Yo, man, be very alert. It's worse than we thought. Caluzo is sending enforcers and they wanted me to duff on Najira. We'd better call Jamal in case he gets caught solo." Pacing in the small confines, Steve filled James in on the balance of the menacing call.

"Stay put. I got Jamal," James said in a low, angry voice. "Follow the script and don't forget to breathe, man."

"Send da motherfuckas a message," Terrence said quietly, cleaning beneath his manicured nails with a letter opener off Hakim's desk. "Dey wanna pick up de old mon, and pick up blood—den give the Italians blood."

Hakim stared at his cousins as he picked up his crystal rocks glass and took a sip of aged rum. "Daoud, who do we have in New Jersey who could make a run at a house there to send a message?"

Daoud sat back in the high-back leather chair and stared at his brother. "Someone crazy enough to spray Scapolini's house?" He smiled and trimmed the end off his Cuban cigar. "You ready to go to war?"

"Da war already start, mon. You heard dat shit me da and yours talk 'bout in da bush house." Indignant, Hector slung his bundle of dreadlocks over his shoulders.

Daoud and Hakim shared a glance at their less cultured cousins who were always ready to rumble. The disparity between them was glaring. One set of Braithwaite brothers looked like the hard-faced, street enforcers they were; the other set of Braithwaites looked like the suit-wearing, conservative Oxford University graduates they were, but no less deadly.

Hakim rubbed his palm along the side of his almond-hued jaw, his gray eyes piercing Terrence's dark, smoldering stare. "You're ready for a long siege?"

"We'll blow the motherfuckas up—been leaning on all our trade, the Caribbean casinos, too, mon. You tell me. You ready? Word has it in Vegas that his own people want him whacked for a coup."

Hakim leaned forward and made a tent with his fingers in front of his mouth before speaking. "We can finance this bullshit for a very long time with Scapolini. But you'd better pray that this bitch, Safia, has her story straight. And make it look like it could've come from one of their family lines."

"Then how will it be a message from us?" Daoud glimpsed Hector.

Hakim smiled. "Call the bastards in Jersey and tell them we sent the present to them from their people in Vegas. Let those bitches argue among themselves trying to figure out if where there's smoke there's fire." He sat back in his posh, butter soft chair, swirling his drink around. "The Vegas branch will be desperately looking for a leak, trying to figure out who aligned with us or just what the fuck went on. Scapolini won't trust a soul, which will make him crazy, vulnerable, and might make him do something stupid to cut himself off from his family lines." He took a calm sip of the amber liquid in his glass. "No trust among a family is a dangerous thing, mon."

Rattled and sleep deprived, Laura got into the cab, trying not to fidget with her short blond wig. Every instinct within her was poised and coiled to strike—but at what? In a matter of hours they'd be in the air and on their way to Sangster International Airport close to the northern coast of Jamaica.

Until she saw Najira and Steve clear the security area, followed shortly by Jamal, she'd had difficulty breathing. It was as though a stone had been lodged in her chest since James took Steve's panicked call. Somehow it spelled more than the pending doom it forebode. She knew it also meant that every single alliance they'd each ever had was suspect. No one was to be trusted. All they had was each other.

Laura kept her gaze out of the window, each couple being extra careful not to seem like they were traveling together, and Jamal kept his face partially hidden by a magazine. She only wondered what would happen once they reached Mahoe Bay Ironshore— ten miles east of Montego Bay, and just five miles from the airport. The private beach resort they'd stay in was only a couple of miles away from the Braithwaiteses establishment. Akhan had given her the name and she could only hope he and Brother B could deliver the artillery they might need without being spotted.

As it was, they were lucky to be able to get three suites at sky-high rates, and she could only pray that the underground betting would keep her vicious cousins somewhat occupied in collecting all the gambling proceeds. The only reason they got any rooms at all on such short notice was that skittish travelers preferred the sanctuary of the bigger named chain hotels, which had heavily police-patrolled beaches and solid security to scare off beach hustlers.

October was the perfect month for the Braithwaites to be raking in the cash—and they could ill afford an incident that might scare off eager, well-heeled, European tourists from the World Championship Dominoes in Montego Bay, the International Marlin Tournament in Ocho Rios, the Brown's Town Motor Race Meet, and the Jamaica Pro-Am Open Golf Tournament near Montego Bay.

She could feel James's tension like a palpable blanket tightening around her body as they waited for their flight to be called. They had no real plan. Akhan was already over there and potentially in harm's way. Scapolini's boys were getting restless, and he'd broken his promise to give her a week. Something crazy seized her. She hated not being the one in control of the game, not knowing how the ball would bounce on the roulette wheel. Laura suddenly stood and James jerked his attention up.

"I have to go to the ladies' room," she said quietly.

"All right, baby," he said, glancing around, briefly making eye contact with Steve and Najira and Jamal. "Hurry back."

She pecked his cheek and moved away from him quickly, her cell phone burning a hole in her purse. Taking the farthest stall from the door that she could, on a hunch she speed dialed Joey Scapolini on his private number and waited. The moment the call connected she spoke quickly.

"Joey?"

"Yeah, Laura—what's up, baby?"

"Something bad happened, and I know you couldn't have known."

"What, hon? Talk to Joey."

Making her voice shaky and afraid was easy—but it was also important to make him think she still trusted him. However, she had to cover for Steve to keep his communication lines cool with Caluzo.

"Joey," she hissed. "Can you hear me?"

"Yeah, and you're making me fucking nervous, Laura."

"My cousin Najira overheard something."

There was a long pause.

"Like what?" Scapolini finally said.

"You know she sleeps with James's old partner, Sullivan, right?"

"I'm aware of the soap opera, but what's that—"

"She was in bed with him and he thought she was asleep when Mike Caluzo called him. Caluzo told Sulli to get out of the Dock Street Sheraton and to leave my cousin there so she could get roughed up." Laura swallowed hard so that he would hear it, and then breathed out her next statement. "Oh, God, Joey, what's happening? She pretended to be asleep while he got his god-damned clothes, and the second she heard him get on the eleva-tor, the girl was out like a shot and she came to me in hysterics."

"Hey, hey, hey—I didn't authorize no such bullshit, Laura. You know me better than that. You sure the girl got the story right?"

"I'm not crazy, Joey, and neither is she."

There was another long pause. "Where were you last night?"

She sighed hard, thinking fast, now crystal clear about who had planted a bug in her luggage. "Trying to get some new fucking clothes and luggage," she snapped. "Fucking hotel staff robbed me on top of everything. They claimed nothing ever happened like that in their establishment, and stars even checked in there with no problem—but some asshole took my LV luggage. You know how expensive that shit is, Joey?"

"Fuck the luggage, Laura. I'll buy you a new set. The info you gave me is very important. You always come through for me, doll, and I love you for that. About what time did this call hit Sulli's cell?"

"Like three something in the morning . . . and Najira dropped an anonymous tip to the cops to pick up anyone who came to the room. She lied and said her boyfriend threatened to have her beat up because she was pissed at Sulli for leaving her like that. But, please don't go after her, Joey, okay? Promise."

"The way I see it, the girl was justified," Scapolini said slowly. "I guess I'll have to make some inquiries to see who the cops mighta bumped into, huh?"

"Thanks, Joey. I knew it wasn't you," she whispered. "I love you for not letting me down . . . but I gotta run. My husband is coming."

"All right. But where you at now?"

She paused and then threw caution to the wind. "On the way to Jamaica to do what I promised you."

"Good girl. Call me from down there."

"Done." She hung up and slumped against the stall door for a moment, perspiration making her crisp black linen suit cling to her beneath her winter coat.

She opened the stall and slipped out, hedging the biggest bet she'd gambled in a while, betting everything on black.

*   *   *

Joey Scapolini walked through his suite and buzzed his security guard center on the second floor. "Yo, anybody seen Rapuzzio this morning?"

A series of disgruntled mutters responded in the negative. He tried Rapuzzio's cell phone again, frustrated by getting only his voice mail. An uneasy feeling threaded through him and then he tried Caluzo, getting the same response.

He left his room and went to find several family henchmen gathered at the bar in the security area. "Yo Vic, Julie—where's Caluzo and Tony?"

Shrugs responded.

"What the fuck, you deaf? Find the bastards. Something's wrong. I don't like it."

Bodies began to move and his cell phone vibrated in his hand. He rolled his eyes when he saw his wife's number in the display. "Not now, baby. I'm busy, you know—"

Her hysterical shrieks made the security room go still as the men standing around drinking coffee froze to watch Scapolini.

"Where's the kids! You hurt? I'm coming."

Scapolini gripped the telephone as his wife's sobs filled his ears. "Okay, okay, listen to me. Go to the school and get the kids, take 'em to your mother's. No! Don't go back into the house for nothing, you hear me—you listening to me, honey? You back out of the driveway—fuck the plate glass and the dog; we'll buy the kids another one. That's why we got insurance and I don't want you nowhere near there when the cops show up—now move!"

"Joey, what the fuck?" Vic said, his gaze holding Joey's as the other men in the room remained paralyzed.

"Find Rapuzzio. Somebody sprayed my house with an automatic while my wife just so happened to be dropping the kids off to school. If they was home—who the fuck knows!"

Panicked, Joey snapped his attention back to the phone in his hand, trying desperately to calm his wife while dispensing orders. "Baby, listen, you gotta calm down so you don't kill yourself driving, all right? Do that for me. You at the school yet? Good. I'm on my way. I'll meet you at Mom's. Yeah, yeah, I'll stay on the line until you get there. It's gonna be all right. I ain't gonna let nothin' happen to you or the kids. On my father's grave. No, just do as I say!"

He looked at the men in the room as he bolted for the door and checked the gun in his waistband. "When I find out who did this bullshit—they're dead."

"So you still don't wanna tell me why you two barged into a room at the Sheraton with guns drawn?"

Captain Bennett watched silently with the DA from behind the two-way mirror as one of his detectives grilled Tony Rapuzzio.

"I know my rights and don't have to say shit to you without my attorney," Rapuzzio said, leaning back in his chair.

"These guys ain't gonna break and the charges will be minor at best—they'll make bail for carrying an unregistered weapon and kicking in a hotel room door . . . a good attorney will make them go with the 'I was drunk and thought it was my friend's room, and as security for the casino, I carry a weapon and thought I heard a noise in my buddy's suite' routine. They'll walk in twenty-four hours. We've been at it all night with these jokers."

Bennett rubbed his hands down his face. "Yeah, you're right. Since when has justice been just, huh, Ed?"

But both men's attention jerked toward the door as one of Bennett's officers came into the room.

"Cap," Luis said, scratching his head. "You are not gonna believe this. Either Christmas came early or it's the last days and times."

"What's up?" Bennett asked suspiciously, folding his arms above his belly.

"Joey freakin' Scapolini is on the phone wanting to know which one of his boys we picked up from the Sheraton last night—line two. And the boys in Jersey just gave our unit the heads-up that Scapolini's house was sprayed with an automatic this morning. Sounds like a power shake-up is in the works."

"Hold him on the line," Captain Bennett said anxiously. "And bring me a phone into the room with Rapuzzio. I want you in there with me, too, Ed. Let's see if a little theater might shake things up. Luis, hustle that fat asshole, Caluzo, in the room with Rapuzzio."

Bennett walked into the interrogation room with a sly smile and accepted a telephone as he watched his men put it in a jack while Rapuzzio and Caluzo glared at him and the DA.

"Excuse me, fellas, you don't mind if I take this call while you're here, do ya?" Bennett smiled and picked up the receiver when the secretary made it ring. His smile widened. "Joey Scapolini. Long time no talk to. So to what do we owe the pleasure of this call?" Bennett paused, listening to Scapolini's request for information. "I might be able to give you the names of the guys we have . . . but lemme ask you, is everything all right? Our Jersey task force heard you had a problem at your house this morning—somebody shot up your driveway, your deck, really did a job on the windows. Terrible. We'd be glad to help."

With great amusement, Bennett and the DA watched both henchmen pass disbelieving smirks between them.

"Yeah," Bennett continued. "They were at the Sheraton, kicked in a door—but our boys apprehended them before they got a shot off. Uh-huh. Clearly they were looking for somebody. Rapuzzio and Caluzo. Yeah. They're sitting right here, wanna talk to them?"

"Cut the bullshit, Bennett," Rapuzzio said with a tense chuckle. "You boys are reaching."

"Okay, Joey. Here. You talk to your man." Bennett shrugged and handed Rapuzzio the telephone and watched the color drain from Rapuzzio's face.

Caluzo looked like he was about to have a heart attack as he realized Rapuzzio was indeed talking to Joey Scapolini.

""I can explain everything, Joey," Rapuzzio said, his voice faltering. "It was just a little . . ."

Even across the table everyone could hear the garbled, profane shouts blaring through the receiver.

Caluzo leaned forward, his gaze shifting between Rapuzzio, Bennett, and the DA.

"What the fuck happened, Tony?" Caluzo said, becoming suspicious.

Rapuzzio covered the receiver with his hand.

"Talk to me, motherfucker," Caluzo said, and then turned to the DA. "What the fuck happened to Joey's house and wife, man—we didn't have shit to do with that!" He stood, toppling his chair, pure fear blazing in his eyes.

Rapuzzio was on his feet, getting tangled in the phone cord as he began to pace. Every officer in the room simply smiled as Captain Bennett extracted the telephone from Tony Rapuzzio's hand.

"Joey, I hate to cut this short, but these guys wanna cut a deal," he said, causing both mobsters to shout and lunge for the phone as officers wrestled them to the floor.

"That's bullshit, Joey!" Rapuzzio bellowed, his voice sounding like it was near a sob.

"Fuck you, lying pussy cops!" Caluzo said as Luis ground his cheek against the floor.

"Sounds like you got some organizational problems, Scapolini," Captain Bennett said calmly. "But I suspect we can process these gentlemen out within the hour, unless they decide to turn state's evidence. You know how that goes." He chuckled as the phone went dead in his ear.

"I'll fuckin' kill you!" Rapuzzio shouted.

The DA shook his head. "Attempted battery against an officer, terroristic threats—keep digging a hole. Just make my fucking day."

"Rapuzzio, you're a dead man," Caluzo shouted as three officers subdued him and handcuffed him.

"I didn't tell Joey shit!" Rapuzzio yelled back. "You threatening me, you prick—you set this shit up, huh? Call Joey—you think I'm stupid? Joey would never call a goddamned police station! This ain't over!" he hollered as the two men were restrained and separated.

Bennett and the DA left the room and went back to the two-way mirror observation room.

"Talk about fate," the DA said, rubbing his hands down his face.

"It always works like that when Sullivan and Carter bulldog something." Bennett shook his head and stared through the glass, watching Rapuzzio bang his forehead against the table. "They'll never trust each other now, and it's only a matter of time before we can divide and conquer 'em."

The phone rang. "Who the hell is this?" the elder Caluzo don said through his teeth. He stood quickly, almost toppling his chair. "Listen, you Jamaican sonofabitch. We don't need no help enforcing shit within our ranks—who the fuck gave you the right to hit Joey's house on my motherfuckin' behalf! If I find you pussies, you're dead!"

He slammed the phone down hard as one of his top men barged into his Vegas office.

"Boss, Lil' Mike is down at the precinct in Philly—The Round House, Leo said." Vince's nervous gaze held Caluzo's.

Caluzo wiped his palms down his meaty, flushed face. "For what? For chrissakes—some really bad shit just—"

"Him and Rapuzzio kicked in a door at the Sheraton looking for that black chick's cousin . . . one of the old dude's kids, but got ambushed by the cops—"

"Oh, fuck me!" Caluzo said, slapping his palms down on his desk. "This is beyond dicked." He let out a rush of breath. "The whole thing has gotten way out of hand, Vince. All that was supposed to happen was to scare the punk son in Hawaii with a little make-believe Jamaican heat—but it was never supposed to involve a real alliance with 'em."

Vince remained tense and silent as Caluzo dabbed nervous perspiration from the shining horseshoe in the middle of his scalp.

"It was supposed to be simple . . . we lean a little on the old black guy's kids, make it seem like the Jamaicans did it—some shit nobody wants to deal with . . . the owners of Xavier Mortgage sign their shit over to us to keep the heat off them because we're making them an offer they can't refuse. Then we back our Jamaican competition off because the weak link is removed from the chain. We own the land, we build the new casinos. The blue-bloods will have a canniption because one-fifth of the nation's exports go through that port city, but hey. They'll get over it. Beautiful, neat, end of story. Joey stays happy, I stay happy, the family gets richer and everyone is happy—even the moolies are happy because nobody is leaning on them, and we don't have to worry about any possible eminent domain crap. The bluebloods will yank with anybody but us, but if they get it first, those cock-suckers will sell to the highest bidder—which brings in other syndicates from around the world. We don't need that shit."

"It gets worse, Boss," Vince said, standing near the door just in case Caluzo needed to take out his frustration on the closest thing near him. "Scapolini is on line one and thinks we sent somebody to do his house while his wife and kids mighta been there. He's calling an early meeting, since Caluzo and his number one lieutenant, Tony Rapuzzio, are still down at police headquarters."

Caluzo swallowed hard. "I gotta call Cyd and Art before Joey gets to 'em. The other members of the family might not understand things so well." He looked at Vince, his gaze searching for answers Vince didn't own. "How'd Joey sound?"

Vince shifted nervously by the door as the older man sat slowly. "He didn't sound good, Boss. It won't be long before the other members of the family will be on the phone talkin' crazy and wanting to know what we're doing. Plus, I think Joey might be pissed enough to be calling for a war."

Hector looked at his brother as Terrence jumped into the Jeep and pulled out of the resort driveway.

"You tink tings gwan be cool, mon?"

Terrence kept his eyes on the road. "It was de only way to make sure we get our cut." He glimpsed Hector. "Hakim and Daoud are direct blood to de old man—we just cousins. Shit don' go down right, we ass out in de col', mon. We have to trust Hakim and Daoud to get a big 'nuff share, den break us off proper based on old debts. Eidder dat or Akhan would look after his brother-in-law, our fodder! Den it's all good."

Hector nodded, sending his gaze out the window. "No worries. Fuckin' Hakim tink he better den us, him and his brother wit dey high-yellow asses and wavy hair like a white mon. Education flauntin' bastards speak like damn British bitches—his hands dirty like mine and yours, elbow deep in de blood killin' for real estate, gamblin', or bricks and blow, what matter, 'eh? Blood is blood."

"Blood supposed to be thicker den de mud, but you and I bof know friendship turn to hen-shit when it comes to men and money. Ain't never been no real trust dere or love lost, so don't get it twisted, mon. I'm not sentimental on no cousin vibes, neither is Hakim or Daoud."

"*Irie.* The Vegas Italians need more muscle against the Colombians for the powder and against the Mexicans for da weed. We want in on the gamblin'—which Hakim is stingy wit . . . whas a man gwan do?"

"Make a pact wit de devil," Terrence said with a half smile. "Dis way, anyting go wrong, we say it come from da bullshit after the drive-by at Scapolini's house. Italians lie, Hakim know that." He pounded his brother's fist as they sailed along the narrow road, casually driving with one hand and enjoying the breeze as it whipped through the open cabin.

Both brothers laughed, and laughed hard.

Cyd Balifoni and Art Costanza sat quietly listening to Bradley's proposal. The older dons slowly sipped their espresso and cappuccino, in the South Philly private diner. Sausage with pepper and onion eggs scented the air that was in the back of the Front Street restaurant, which only opened at this hour for VIPs. An elderly man shuffled forward balancing heavily laden plates on his arms and slid them down carefully for the three men in deep conference, hearing and seeing nothing.

Balifoni brought the small porcelain cup to his lips, his gaze going through the window past the ex federal agent who'd always worked for them. He stared at the infrastructure of I-95 that ran parallel to his lucrative real estate investments along the waterfront. Costanza had the Camden, New Jersey, side of the river. Taking a chunk of New Orleans and the Mississippi riverboat business away from Caluzo was an interesting proposition.

"So let me get this right," Costanza said. "Townsend is fleecing Haines's fag son out of enough millions to position our man in office. That's where he gets his cut. Then once our man gets in, you're proposing that the D.C. boys work with the Main Line pricks to eminent domain the whole area—everything we want, to keep it out of the hands of the Jamaicans, who could do a grab based on some family will and ownership bullshit. Then we come in like great white developers in New Orleans and put in casinos to bring jobs to a blighted region."

Bradley took a careful sip of coffee as Balifoni and Costanza began eating. "Yeah. That's basically it."

"What's your cut?" Costanza asked, waving his fork as he spoke and speaking through a mouthful of eggs and peppers.

"Two mill and a house in the islands," Bradley said calmly, beginning to pick at his plate.

Balifoni glanced at Costanza as he slowly chewed a mouthful of sausage. "You can guarantee the properties we identify will get turned over to us?" He set his fork down on his plate. "I wanna talk to Townsend directly. A lot of things have changed since the Micholi Foundation bought it."

"That's why Townsend wants to do this—he wants to make amends with the family. He used to be a past director of the Foundation, and then had ties to the Redevelopment Authority. He was an old player in this game."

Balifoni leaned forward. "Joey will fuck him up the ass, first. He tried to call Scapolini at his house with a federal tap, and Joey was insulted." He sat back and began eating again, casually waving his knife and fork to punctuate his words. "That's why George did right to come to us, and not Caluzo who, word has it, got himself screwed this morning by trying to cut a side deal with the goddamned Jamaicans directly around Joey. There's gonna be a lotta fallout from that. The boys at the Round House called us, a little birdie in the precincts, ya know. Caluzo should have let us handle the real estate, and he could worry about putting the casinos on it—but the bastard got greedy, and now Joey is gonna fuck him, too."

"I don't know what's happening in the world," Costanza said with a sheepish smile, buttering his toast. "Ain't no decency, no trust."

"That's why I came to you and only you with this," Bradley said. "Donny Haines is two seconds from a nervous breakdown. He's weak but rich. Townsend has a target on his head put there by Joey, but he's useful until he gets whacked. Caluzo is a dead man walking. And if Joey doesn't watch himself, he could accidentally get popped by some Rastas, fucking around and getting soft over that Caldwell chick. No good can come of any of that. Plus, you know the chaos that's been dogging Capitol Hill. A lot of people are interested in things settling down now that Haines is gone. Stable is good for business, chaos isn't. I'm just trying to secure my future, gentlemen, and work with real businessmen."

Costanza nodded, Balifoni smiled, as only two seasoned hitmen could.

"Wise move," Costanza said flatly and then concentrated on his plate in earnest. "Logical. No bull, no emotion. Let us know when Donny and Townsend are no longer of use to you. Every transaction has to have a sacrificial lamb. Joey will demand it. Rather them than any of us."

Bradley didn't move or breathe. Just like that, the deal was done.

Balifoni motioned to the shadow of a server to refill their coffees. "As always, Bradley, it's nice doing business with ya. Just don't say nothing or trust anybody outside of the three of us sitting here, *capice?*"

Chapter
8

The vision of sugar sand beaches and jewel green hills framed by crystal clear azure blue water was a jarring contrast to the dark clouds of worry that filled every crevice of her mind. While lovers held hands on the plane and excited vacationers chatted amiably, she and her family sat silent and morose. Random, totally ridiculous thoughts would also worm their way into the black soil of her mind that was fertile with despair. Najira and Steve should be coming here to marry, not potentially be killed. Jamal should be here to learn at his family's knees about how to run real estate that could last for generations.

Laura cast down her gaze, becoming philosophical. What the hell? Landed wealth did no less—they took what wasn't theirs, fought hard to protect it, even started wars over territory, and then passed it on for their children to live in luxury. So who was to judge her? They were all pirates. By rights, Akhan and Haines had actually come by the holdings within Xavier Mortgage the honest way; hard work, solid investment, and a shrewd gamble in an undervalued area that skyrocketed. She released a slow, weary breath. Fine . . . then she would protect it the old-fashioned way.

The dip in altitude made her heart race as the plane's descent signaled their imminent arrival. Dissecting each player in the game in mental quadrants, Laura's mind sliced through the options like a razor.

One: It was no secret the Mob had many factions—they were large and had to be divided and were all sharks. This morning she just threw blood in the water. The Main Line developers also wanted this land in the worst way, and murmurs in the news had suggested that they were rallying legislation to take over major, prime segments. She made it her business to stay plugged in. Years on Wall Street and under Donald Haines' tutelage had taught her to always follow the money. Therefore, she needed to call Rick, her man inside the media, who now had a prized position on CNN thanks to her. Not only was he a long-time friend, but he also owed her a juicy favor. The only one who hadn't gone to jail in the Micholi Foundation trials was George Townsend. No doubt his political allies had distanced themselves, but someone in Washington always had an axe to grind. If Rick could find out anything, she could begin to unravel their old boys' network and cause several realignments.

Scavenging for anything to grasp as the ground below loomed larger, she clawed for Megan Montgomery's name. Two: She knew Donny Haines, was like a sister to him, and could find out what was going on with him. If anyone could get Junior to help her piece together his father's old allies, hence create a road map of who might try to push through a land grab, it would be Donny. But he'd changed his cell number, his address, and had virtually gone into hiding in Philly. Still, Megan's father, Richard Montgomery, worked for the State Department. If there was ever a man who knew some people who knew some people . . . The problem was, he still blamed her and James for involving his daughter and her cousin, Sean, in some very dangerous liaisons in order to bring down the Micholi Foundation.

Hmmm . . . Laura pressed a finger to her lips, feeling much improved. Three: Sean . . . Yeah. Insane hacker, now living in the islands where the computer systems didn't have the security levels of the U.S. Working for his uncle, who worked for the State Department, which meant security clearances that many couldn't fathom. Information always had a price. Townsend had gone into the witness protection program. Interesting.

Now all she needed to do was set the Jamaican nemeses on the Mob or themselves, a tactic already begun this morning by several well-placed phone calls. The only worry while she set the board in motion was that if they went Neanderthal and took a hostage—started delivering body parts until the papers were transferred—she'd have a problem . . . which was why Akhan's getting ammunition and her getting in touch with someone with State Department connections was vital. Oh, yeah, she had work to do.

Her head bobbed as the plane bounced to a smooth roll. People clapped and cheered; they were on vacation. James simply looked at Laura, worried; Najira seemed like she was about to cry. Laura knew she couldn't indulge either range of emotions; she had too many calls to make and people to go see. But first order of business was locating her Uncle Akhan.

Thankfully the plane soon taxied to the tarmac and came to a stop. Nervous energy made her pop up out of her seat and almost hit her head. Jamal looked so fatigued he had bags under his eyes, like Steve, and Najira just looked like she was about to upchuck at any second. However, James's no-nonsense focus sent a mild current of relief through her. The muscle in his jaw pulsed as he donned his sunglasses and looked straight ahead at the stalled line. He had a very imposing cop look about him, even after all the years off the force. It was the same vibration bouncers had: that *Terminator*, destroyer aura that was so important when negotiating with thugs. Cool. All they needed was some heat and they could play good cop, bad cop together to the bone.

The line started moving and she forced herself to be patient. This was the islands, she reminded herself, and nobody rushed for any damned thing.

Strands of calypso threaded through the cacophony of voices, accents, and vibrant colors. Humidity wilted everyone and brought out every pungent aroma human bodies could generate. Here, patience was more than a virtue; it was a necessary life skill.

"*Hotep,*" Akhan said, embracing them one by one once they'd finally cleared Customs.

Brother B gave a round of familial embraces, and the younger members of the family studied the unconcealed worry in both pairs of aged eyes.

"Let's get you out of the heat," Laura said to Akhan, monitoring his weakened condition. "Have you eaten today?"

He smiled sadly. "For reasons unknown to me, Brother B insists I have some fruit and a little toast each morning with juice."

"Good," Najira said, hugging her father. "C'mon. We'll check in and you can fill us in while sitting somewhere cool."

"They all came?" Hakim said to his inside man at airport Customs, smiling as he pressed his cell phone to his ear. "This is better than expected."

He looked up as his brother entered his suite. "Thank you. I'll send an envelope." He clicked off the call and stared at Daoud. "You're not going to believe this, mon. Our father and Uncle Edgar want to meet with the four sons and the family who came over from the States."

Daoud and Hakim looked at each other for a moment and then burst out laughing.

"Are they senile?" Hakim said, shaking his head. "The old bastard leaves here for over thirty years and now wants to do a family reunion—as though that would change things." He slapped his forehead.

"It could make it easier. Maybe he wants to just sign everything early so there'd be no inheritance taxes from the States or whatever bullshit tariffs could be applied, you know?" Although Daoud was still chuckling, his logical statement sobered them both and caused Hakim to nod.

"Good. Yes. Although I never agreed with Akhan, he was very consistent with his own brand of logic. Rather than see the white man have a dime, he'd throw it in the ocean first."

"You know our problem will be Terrence and Hector," Daoud remarked coolly.

"Of this I am aware."

Daoud leaned against the window sill. "Did you know Terrence was in Maui . . . and shot at Jamal?"

Hakim became very, very still. "How do you know this?" His voice was a menacing whisper.

"Because we are in the casino business, primarily . . . and something went extremely wrong today with a deal Caluzo from Vegas was trying to cut on the side. It seems that he wanted to know if we had any involvement in sending out pit bulls, as he called them, to spray Joey Scapolini's house." Daoud smiled. "I, of course, stood behind plausible deniability. But as he lost his cool and started talking about how Terrence was out of control on even the smallest matter in Maui, he tipped his hand."

"Terrence never said anything about a job in Maui that the Italians asked him to do."

Both brothers stared at each other.

"No. He didn't. Wonder why not?" Daoud smoothed a tapered palm across his freshly shaven jaw. "Interesting, isn't it?"

"Extremely." Hakim smoothed the lapels of his unstructured, custom-tailored suit and calmly took out a nine-millimeter from the large mahogany desk drawer.

For a moment, only the circular drone of the woven palm fan blades could be heard in the room, plus the distant pound of the surf, and a far off strand of resort calypso music.

"So, when we all meet, I wonder if Jamal will recognize TB, eh?" Daoud held his brother's gaze with his own. "Moreover, you know Akhan and Edgar are like two peas in a pod. Although Edgar had no real assets, if those two old men think there will be death over the property, they may just opt to split it fairly down the middle giving each child an even slice of pie. Terrence and Hector could have been playing this outcome all along, using the Italians to scare everybody."

Daoud began to pace and gestured wildly with his hands as Hakim's expression clouded with rage. "Our father was always

into fair, the collective—you remember his idealistic, tribal insan-
ity—but fuck fair, Hakim. *We* are his firstborn, legitimate heirs.
Terrence and Hector could have played us. Let them take that dilapidated barracks house in the bush when Edgar Braithwaite,
the great Brother B, croaks! They can turn it into the only thing
it's good for, a manufacturing plant. They did some shit behind
our backs, and I want to know what the old men were told, what
happened. That's important to know going forward because we
might have to take internal action at a time when we just poked a
stick in the Italian hornet's nest."

"I think until we further understand who has set up the dominoes and what game they're playing," Hakim said, "we might
want to protect Akhan and his second family. Roll out the red car-
pet and let's watch a bit, eh?"

Getting from the airport to the hotel was always an interesting
experience in the Caribbean, but once Brother B's station wagon
pulled up behind the resort bus, Laura could really see the strain
that both the travel and the stress had placed on Akhan.

Apparently the others in their group saw it, too, and James
made quick work of ushering Akhan inside to turn him over to
Najira and Steve in the lobby so he could sit as he checked their
group in.

"Okay, I put Jamal in with you and Brother B," James said,
handing a stack of keys to Jamal. He stooped down and leaned
next to Akhan's ear. "In case anything goes down, all you warriors
will be together. Cool?"

Akhan nodded, slightly short of breath, his eyes holding a
silent thank you, and knowing James did that for the protection
of both elderly men while also preserving their dignity. "We have
canned goods in the back of Brother B's station wagon that only
family should bring to the room."

James nodded and stood up, handing Steve and Najira their
keys, and handing Laura hers. "We can either wait for the bellman to come up, or everybody hauls their own bags and gives the
brother a tip anyway."

They all looked around at the lobby filled with tourists and without a word, collected their own bags—James and Jamal getting the sparse items Akhan and Brother B packed as well as the box in the station wagon.

"Five minutes, Jamal's room," Laura said quietly, glancing around their group.

There was nothing more that needed to be said as they advanced toward the room elevators through the pristine aqua and white lobby that was loaded with lush elephant grasses potted in huge vases, along with broad-leafed palms, ferns, and bright-hued hibiscus. Birds took a shortcut though the open space, stopping at the edge of the patio-like structure to beg for breakfast muffins or to steal abandoned sugar left by the coffee cart. Gleaming tile floors bounced the sun's rays against wicker furniture padded with overstuffed floral print cushions, and the sound and smell of the surf beckoned one to not worry, be happy—impossible under the circumstances.

Laura watched her husband drop his bag by their door and continue down the hall to Jamal's room balancing a ragged brown box of ammunition topped by old food cans, and the backpacks of the two old men. Najira and Steve glimpsed her for a moment as they opened their room door. Laura inserted the key and entered her room, further saddened by the gorgeous mahogany appointments and four-postered bed. Paradise was not supposed to involve shoot-outs, kidnappings, and whatever else their enemies had planned for them.

However, getting sentimental was not an option. She dragged both suitcases over the threshold, double-checked for safety, and left the room, headed for Jamal's. Without consulting Akhan, the moment James opened the suite, she headed for the phone and placed a room service order. The old man needed to eat, needed some liquids. As it was, he'd become diabetic with advancing years and had to eat on a consistent basis.

Laura gripped the phone trying to efficiently rattle off the best choices for him. When Najira came into the room, her eyes glassy, it finally hit her. Akhan was not immortal. Her uncle's time was imminent. She didn't mean to but snapped at the woman taking her order when the lady requested that she repeat herself a third time.

"I'll be fine," Akhan said calmly, slightly reclining on the couch. "I'm not even hungry, my young queen."

His voice was ragged and weary and it made everyone gather around closer and sit leaning forward, perched on the edge of their seats to hear the dying words of their tribal king.

"I have figured out how to resolve this problem," Akhan said slowly with a sad smile. He closed his eyes and spoke through slow, breathy sentences. "I took my wisdom from Solomon . . . so I am going to cut the baby in half."

Najira was on the floor sitting closest to her father and she leaned her head on his knee. "Daddy, our nerves can't take a riddle. Just tell us what you want us to do."

There was a quiet finality and resignation in Najira's voice that seemed to make the room go still.

"Brother B and I are going to show how close our brotherhood has always been—the way it should be. We will tell them we are going to merge assets and split things right down the middle. Of course you, Steve, Jamal, Laura, and James are already well off and are afraid of the Mob—you all have relinquished any and all interest in Xavier Mortgage. The four Braithwaite sons will have an even share in the Gulf assets, and we will say that Brother B and I only asked you all to come so you could meet them, they could meet you, and they could see from your own eyes that you don't want these assets. I will also tell them that part of the condition is that nothing is to ever happen to any of you, and that I intend to try to walk my daughter down the aisle while here. So I wanted you all here and safe while the Italians get the shock of their life. They can't bully civilians; they'll have to come up against the Braithwaite clan."

Akhan adjusted himself on the sofa for more comfort. "Then we will sit back and watch the feathers fly."

"But, Daddy, you always said you wanted the people to . . . Are you telling us that these people who have been doing all this mess are *family?*" Najira's voice trailed off in horrified awe as eyes admonished her.

"It's a brilliant plan," Laura murmured, ignoring Najira's obvious question. It was what it was. Terrible.

Brother B nodded and looked out the open sliding glass doors. "Four fighting cocks in de yard, and me and my good friend will never haf to bear arms . . . dey will do demselves."

"The universe is always efficient and beneficent," Akhan murmured. "This will buy you some time, sweetheart." He touched Najira's hair. "Get a dress and you and Laura work on a wedding. Leave the ugly business to us old men. Once we all have dinner together and your half-brothers and cousins understand that I will give them all they desire, there will be no reason for any struggle . . . with us, at least."

Laura nodded and helped Najira adjust pillows behind her uncle so he could fully recline. It was a truly brilliant plan. One set of brothers thought they'd been given three quarters of it all, only to have it snatched back to a fifty percent share because their dying father wanted peace. Doing a wedding here really would drive home the point that Akhan meant business, while also subtly giving her and James faces to place with names so she could also set plays in motion behind the scenes. They'd blow each other away, just like the Mob boys were imploding over the divisive issue. Greed was a powerful motivator. The old man was a master, and if it wasn't his own flesh and blood, he probably wouldn't be laid out on the sofa because of it. Akhan had to make what was probably the worse decision any parent would ever be forced to make. He had to choose between two gangster sons that had gone hardcore, or his second set of children—Jamal and Najira and her unborn baby, his grandchild. Clearly Akhan had chosen, but it was breaking his heart. That was the part that pained her so deeply to witness. This last game, more than the cancer, was what was killing her uncle Akhan.

*   *   *

Laura ripped open her suitcase and James just stared at her. "Don't look at me like that. We've got five hours until dinner with the Braithwaites and I've got to set the table."

"I'm going with you," James said calmly, "so you might as well just run down your itinerary."

Laura sighed hard and laid out a burnt orange sundress, grabbed a large tube of shower gel, and then headed toward the shower. "The Montgomerys need a call. I can't get to them all the way in Kingston fast enough, but I can start the ball rolling. Megan's up here in Montego Bay with her own tourist shop. That's visit number one. I gotta call Rick—he owes me a favor. You gotta call Captain Bennett to see what's up in Philly. You can stand there looking evil or get in the water with me."

Her outrageous offer made him smile. "You're joking, right?"

"No, I'm serious." Laura stopped walking and offered him a sexy pout. "Akhan bought us some time, the Mob is in disarray, and anybody else possibly after us will get backed off by this very weird family until they know what's up with the paperwork." She placed one hand on her hip. "You want a quickie—which really does help me think better—and want me to fill you in while we get dressed, then you gotta make a decision, man." With that she spun on her heels and strode out of the room.

Although by now he should have been used to his wife's sudden, seductive ways, she never failed to catch him off guard. James ditched his shoes and hurriedly undressed, getting a rise as soon as he heard the shower go on. It annoyed him a little to think his woman knew him so well and had him so damned conditioned that the sound of running water could give him wood.

But he forgot all about his mental complaints as he opened the glass door, entered the spray behind her water-slicked body, and fit against her like a glove. She leaned back against him, squeezing the aromatic gel into his palms with her eyes closed and her chin tipped up toward the ceiling, resting her head back against his shoulder. Slick lather built in his hands as he swirled them slowly over her breasts and belly and hips, returning to her erect peaks that dug into his palms while he paid homage to her shoulder and neck with gentle kisses.

She rewarded him with a soft moan, drizzling more gel down her chest, and then pulled away a bit to let it run over her shoulder and down her back, emulsifying under the now slippery friction between then. Gel suds foamed in the crack of her firm, wet ass, stealing his breath as she abandoned the tube to a small shower shelf and stroked his hips with well-lathered hands.

Breaking contact, she turned to take his mouth and take him into her hands. Runnels from the shower cascaded down her breasts, down her sleek torso, pooling eddies in her navel, rushing over the dark, silky hair at the v between her thighs. It was truly a sight to behold; his wife was absolutely amazing. His palms ached to touch her everywhere at once. Her long legs glistened and shimmered as the water ran over the curvy swell of her hips down the length of her all the way to her pretty French-manicured toes.

The dual sensation of her deep, sensuous kiss and soft slick hands working up and down his engorged shaft almost caused him to lose his equilibrium as she tore her kiss away and sucked water rivulets from his nipples. Water droplets clung to sections of her hair like frozen crystals while still more rushed through it, turning it to black silk as she slid down his body and forced him to hold onto the glass door and tile wall with flat palms.

The blast of cooling water, then the furnace of her mouth and the spiral of her tongue forced a groan up and out into the echo-rich enclosure. Watching her do him under the spray like a sun-bronzed mermaid was almost too much to bear—the sensations and the vision of her toffee-hued skin wet and glistening, her dark, tight nipples at the ends of her heavy breasts . . . her mouth drawing him in as her graceful hands choreographed rhythmic pleasure with her flickering, delicate pink tongue . . . he was losing his mind.

One thought, one purpose—the quickie she'd promised. All soap had vanished from her squatting form; he had to get inside her and had to do it now.

Caressing her cheek, he got her attention, and thank God she could read the look that he knew had to be on his face. She glanced up with her large, smoky eyes and drew him out of her mouth in such slow, agonizing increments that it made his stomach clench. Then she smiled as she stood, kissed him deeply, releasing his lower lip last, and turned around.

The hot glimpse she gave him over her shoulder at the same moment her sweet ass slid against him did it. An arm instantly wrapped around her waist of its own volition and he almost heaved her off her feet to get inside her. Feminine hands slapped the tiles; he held the overhead plumbing to keep from falling, praying with every stroke that he didn't accidentally yank the showerhead out of the wall.

But, oh *god*damn, it felt so good. How this woman always took him there was anyone's guess but his. The water was getting chilly, but her body was so hot he didn't care. Gooseflesh pebbled her arms as she snap-jerked her spine to capture more of him harder and faster and with resolute authority. This time when she started falling over the edge of a hard climax, his sudden release rushed her into a second one that dragged him with her hollering, voices bouncing off the tiles.

Breathing hard, he heard only the sound of the spray and their ragged, unified exhales filling the room. He leaned his burning face against her shoulder and gathered her in his arms. She laid her arms above his and hugged as much of him as she could grasp.

"Here's the downside of a quickie," he murmured against her ear, smiling with his eyes closed. "Now I need two hours to crash, and then I'll want something to eat and you with me in bed all day . . . and it's just not that type of situation."

She nodded, winded. "I know. That's why I was trying to compromise . . . seemed such a shame to waste paradise."

He nodded, reaching around her to turn off the water. "Good looking out." He brushed her earlobe with a kiss. "But you are gonna have to feed a brother after this . . . a burger, anything. However, don't think that I'm not eternally grateful." He deepened a kiss against the sensitive part of her neck, wishing they had more time. He wanted to taste her so badly, to make her arch and weep with pleasure all afternoon, but they had business to address that was of a potentially deadly nature. He hugged her more tightly and had to allow words to be a temporary place-holder for any future actions he dreamed of. "Laura, I swear you turn me on so much sometimes that it's incredible."

"I try," she whispered with a sated chuckle, reaching back to run her fingertips across his close-cropped wet hair. "Honest, I really do."

Chapter
9

A quiet, satisfied smile coated her insides as she sat across from James. Watching him scarf down a huge burger and fries just made her want him all over again. Try as she might, the thought wouldn't leave her while she tried to focus on, and enjoy, a shrimp Caesar salad and cool iced tea with mint and lime.

The problem was, right now, the only thing she really wanted to consume was him although she'd been ravenous for shellfish when they'd sat down to order. A moment could change everything.

Somewhere between handing back the server the leather-bound menus and enjoying James's peaceful, silent company as they waited for their entrées to arrive, she'd fallen in love with him all over again.

That part was no surprise, though. It happened all the time; the renewal of what they shared. That was the very thing that now drove her to begin forming a final exit strategy. No more. She was sick of the game, the high finance three-card monte, the political shell games and maneuvers, and most certainly she was done with revenge. Her soul was finally settled. *This* was what she wanted: tranquility.

Laura chewed her salad, deep in thought. She refused to become like the political widows and matrons she'd seen on the campaign trails from Philadelphia to Washington, D.C.—bitter, angry, aggressive, striving, grasping bitches. For what? Money? She already had enough; so did the family. Enough to last generations. Maybe if Elizabeth Haines had realized that, she'd still be alive today.

But the men in Liz's circle had been no better, in fact they were worse. She wondered, too, if Joey Scapolini ever figured that part out—that there was a threshold one could cross where life would never again be carefree—and losing that freedom had a severe price. The man had kids; was the game worth it? She wondered if that was the main reason Akhan had walked away from his sons. Had they gone somewhere so far, so deep that even their own father had to step off? Akhan and Brother B might have been revolutionaries, but were righteous. There were never drugs and gang murders involved.

The concept gave Laura the willies and she shook off the uncomfortable thoughts. She knew what they had to do; dwelling on it would not make it go away, nor would it provide immediate solutions. All worrying would accomplish was to put an acid hole in the lining of her stomach. Nah . . . why go there when Hershey chocolate perfection and the most sacred space in the universe, the Caribbean, worked at a leisurely pace to make all that feel irrelevant. With everything the two of them had been through, the one thing she and James had learned was to live in the moment. Now she hoped if she could string enough moments together maybe they'd survive.

The shower was a moment. This was a moment. Laura sought mental moments now to preserve her sanity. The interlude at the Hyatt was a moment. James had always been her alternate reality, even back when she was quietly, insanely, on a mission bent on revenge. He had been that moment to change her destiny. Their moments strung together in frenetic lovemaking that was never supposed to happen between a cop and an uncharged felon. He had also changed their destinies the moment he'd dumped all the evidence that would have jailed her for life in international waters over the bow of a cruise ship. There were places a man or woman could go from which they could never come back.

Moments changed lives. It was imperative to focus on the right ones and choose wisely.

Her hand in his, she and James had watched the water, saying nothing, lost in their own thoughts until their server had returned with aromatic dishes garnished with passion fruit and mango slices. James had calmly sipped his Red Stripe beer with a smile and had cast her a devastating glance before she'd lost to the competition of golden French fries. All she could do was silently chuckle and shake her head as she stabbed a huge, succulent shrimp with her fork.

Brilliant blue sky and glaring white sand with jewel blue water licking it framed him as they ate on the wide restaurant patio. The intense sunlight seemed to add polish to his dark chocolate skin, and the stark white Polo shirt he wore acted almost like an additional reflector so that she could observe every delectable, exposed inch of it.

Too bad the white wrought iron table hid all that his khaki shorts would have revealed. Fabulous thighs and a great butt. The way the cotton shirt spilled over his stone-cut chest and abs was to die for. And he did everything so casually. . . . Didn't he realize that the mere act of bringing his burger to his fantastic mouth caused every muscle in his arms and shoulders to move in a way that stole her breath?

"What?" he said after a moment, looking up from his food.

She had to laugh at herself. The fork was in her hand and suspended midair between her plate and her mouth. "I love you," was all she said and all that she'd admit to right now.

He smiled and wiped his mouth, finishing off the last of the burger. "I love you, too—now that you fed me—but stop."

She tilted her head to the side, smiling wider. "Stop what?"

"Stop," he said, chuckling, and hailed a waiter for the check.

"You're rushing me, man," she said, taking a few quick bites of her salad and laughing harder as she chewed.

"The last I heard we were *supposed* to be picking up the new cell phones with local service for everybody from the concierge, since the ones we have get spotty connections down here, and then we're *supposed* to be taking a cab to Megan's."

"The plan is *still* the same," she said, teasing him through mouthfuls. "We all have to be able to stay in touch—communication is critical."

"Uh-huh. Then stop making me wanna change the plan by looking at me like that."

He smiled wider and paid the check when it came. She chuckled, shook her head, and quickly finished her salad, trying to ignore the shiver he'd sent down her spine when his gaze raked her.

"You're twisted, you know that," he said in her ear as he helped her out of her chair.

"Yeah, a little, maybe."

He chuckled near her neck and kissed the place where her sundress exposed her shoulder. "Why is it that you give me the best sex when we're in a jam?"

"Just making the most of the moment," she said with a wink, and then breezed away from him toward the lobby where they could catch a taxi.

Steve kept his voice low so as not to wake Najira while he stood out on the room balcony and talked to Captain Bennett. The voice mails had loaded his phone but he couldn't see it—nothing was registering on the display; everything lagged. He hated that shit; technology was his link to the world. Not trusting the room phones, it wasn't until James dropped off the new cells with local service that he felt comfortable dialing in and got the series of cryptic, crazy messages from their old precinct.

Every now and again he glanced at Najira's prone form, glad that the poor woman could finally rest. Whether it was sheer fatigue that laid her out, or finally getting to a calm place of acceptance about her father and feeling that his plan would keep them all safe, he wasn't sure. But what he did know for a fact was that the insane shit Cap was telling him was raising the hair on the back of his neck.

"From what we could tell, Rapuzzio, the dumb bastard, refused to take our offer to turn State's evidence and go into the witness protection program. He headed right from the Round House to the airport to get a ticket to Vegas. They must have known that's where he was headed, and whoever he called and asked to get him an e-ticket had to give the tip-off, because he never got the ticket. Our boys were following him and monitoring his destination, but he went into Philly International and never came out."

"Oh, shit," Steve said, rubbing his palms down his face as he crushed the phone to his ear with his shoulder. "He could be in a food service bag, a cargo container, or compacted garbage by now. You know with all the contracts the South Philly boys have at the airport, anybody coulda done him. Homeland Security, my ass."

"Yeah, well, we found his body in Tinicum in the wildlife preserve marshes by the airport. Anonymous tip. They wanted us to find him."

"Damn . . ." Steve murmured, rubbing the tension away from his sweaty neck. He wanted to get out of the sun and heat and simply sit in the air-conditioning, but the last thing he wanted to do was to alert Najira that bodies were beginning to drop.

"Screwed, ain't it," Bennett pressed on. "We owe you for the Sheraton tip, because otherwise we would have never collared him and Caluzo. But you know at some point, you, me, and James are gonna have to have an off-the-record conversation about how you knew to send us there."

"I hear you," Steve said, not committing. Guilt consumed him as he thought about his old time friend, Mike Caluzo. Even though he could be a real bastard, they went way back and had helped each other over the years. He just hoped Mikey would make some good choices. "Cap . . . you give Caluzo a protection plan offer?"

Steve waited and held his breath.

"Yeah, yeah, we gave 'em both a shot at amnesty. But that crazy bastard started yelling about how our agents were dirty, like Bradley, and he wasn't getting set up in some bullshit house in the sub- urbs—he'd take his chances on his own. Go figure. So we let him go, just like we did Rapuzzio, and put a tail on him."

"Okay, do me a favor," Steve said, knowing Cap would never commit but might do it. "I know Bradley is out of our jurisdic- tion, is federal, and—"

"No, no, no, no, no! Don't even start that shit, Sullivan."

"Hey, you want me and James to have a long conversation with you over a beer, then all I'm saying is, in your spare time just ask a few questions."

"Kiss my ass, Sullivan. You know how many feds are watching this South Philly crew?"

"There were a lot of agents involved in that whole Micholi thing, I'd start there—especially since the federal boys are always trying to yank with our jurisdiction in Philly. All guts and glory and then we get blamed for letting murderers slip through the cracks."

"Last I heard you and James were retired for years, so what's with the *we* shit, huh?"

Steve smiled, hearing the smile in Captain Bennett's voice. "I am, *we* are, but once a civil servant, always one. Besides, I figure if Caluzo threw out a name while panicking, you might wanna fol- low it up." Steve paused, his voice and mood growing instantly sober. "Cap, you and I both know that a dirty man on the inside could get good cops killed, especially one with federal clearance or contacts."

Intense silence filled the line for a moment.

"You and James were always good men, Sullivan. Clean. The department misses you—a lot."

"Thanks, Cap," Steve said, knowing that Captain Bennett under- stood he was thanking him for much more than the compliment.

"If Caluzo turns up, I'll call you."

"Appreciate it."

The call disconnected as abruptly as it had begun. Steve closed his eyes for a minute and then leaned on the balcony rail staring at the gorgeous white beach, crystal blue water, and happy vacationers below. Mentally weary, he let out a fatigued breath and opened his cell phone again to call James.

When James's cell phone vibrated, Laura just looked at him. She sat very still as their taxi meandered down the congested streets away from the resort area. She could tell by James's expression that the news was dire. Whatever moments of respite she'd claimed, mental or otherwise, were over.

The moment he closed his phone he shook his head and sent his gaze out the window, his voice low and ominous. "The bullshit is starting."

"Since when is it a fucking crime to call the police station to find out if one of my security personnel might have gotten involved in a little fracas?" Joey said, glaring at the police captain through his mother-in-law's screen door. "And how is it that you have the right to come to my wife's mother's house here in South Philly with some bullshit allegations, upsetting my family that's already upset when yous sonsabitches oughta be going after the fuckers who bullet sprayed my house!"

"What happened in Jersey ain't in our jurisdiction," Captain Bennett said with a smug tone. "Is it, Luis?"

"Nah, Cap. Can't cross the state lines, only the federal boys can do that," Luis said, eyeing Scapolini with a smirk.

"Then fuck you! Go tell your Jersey boys that they can kiss my ass, too, until I cross the bridge to go home." Scapolini's voice rang out on the narrow street causing window curtains to flutter in neighboring houses. "You can get off my steps, too, asshole, unless you've got a warrant—and since I ain't do nothing, fat chance a judge will give you one."

Captain Bennett nodded thoughtfully, smoothing his palm over his jaw. "See, that's just the thing. We were hoping you might be able to help us understand a tragedy that did cross over into our jurisdiction . . . and we figured, who better to ask but the man who'd spoken to the victim last."

Bennett paused for theatrical effect; Luis popped a toothpick in his mouth to take the place of the cigarette he wanted and allowed it to roll around on his tongue.

Scapolini's gaze narrowed, but he didn't slam the door, obviously curious about what the officers were referring to. "Stop jerking me off, all right."

"We found Rapuzzio in the marsh by the airport. Weren't you guys friends for a long time? Almost family, or something?" Ignoring the minute flash of shock that Scapolini quickly concealed, Bennett turned to the detective by his side. "Thing that's bothering me, and the only reason I came out of the office and didn't just turn this over to my boys is the fact that Joey's call came to me—ain't that right, Luis? Then I was sitting there as a material witness to Joey cursing the man out. We got that on tape, right?"

"Yeah, but Cap, there's no real crime, per se, in shouting and yelling at somebody . . . unless they happen to die from suspicious causes. But I'm sure our friend Joey has an alibi. He always does." Luis made the toothpick tumble over his tongue.

"Yeah. Joey is good that way," Captain Bennett said, now turning back to stare at Scapolini without a smile. "Always has a concrete alibi. I'd just like to ask him to humor me down at the station and tell me a great bedtime story."

Scapolini turned his head and began yelling to his wife over his shoulder through the narrow row house. "Call my lawyer, babe! Get Archie on the fucking phone and down here now!"

"Relax, Scapolini," Captain Bennett said calmly. "I know your foul ass is capable of anything and everything—and one day, I'll bust your balls. However, a strong hunch on this one tells me even you ain't that stupid. . . . But I *am* interested in knowing who might be—so, shall we dance?"

"We've got to play this easy," Laura said as she and James got out of the cab two blocks away from Megan Montgomery's shop and began walking with other tourists. "The last time and only time she met us, we caused her to flee her home, get chased

through the streets of Baltimore in the dead of night, and have to
get out of the States on a phony passport. Her father never wants
to hear from us again, either, I'm sure. So, this is going to be a
very delicate reunion, James."

He stopped at a window falsely admiring some athletic gear so
they could talk. "True, but that wasn't our fault. Bottom line is,
we actually saved her life because she was on Moyer's hit list for
being too close to Donny and knowing too much."

"People have a way of forgetting the basics when under stress,
James," Laura replied, threading her arm around his waist and
guiding him a few more stores down the row before street ped-
dlers could become aggressive.

He chuckled as she stopped him in front of a designer dress
boutique. "So, you trying to say I'm not subtle?"

She smiled. "As subtle as a baseball bat when you want something, brother. Just your presence is intimidating."

"Aw, baby, I'm hurt."

"Let me be the bad cop this time," she said, her voice pleading.
"Be nice, be accommodating, and go with my flow, okay?"

"Yeah, yeah, yeah, but what's the angle?"

Laura let out her breath hard. "The only thing that got her to
open up to us before was her solid friendship with Donny. This
time, I'm going for a heavy hand of truth in the equation, all
right?"

"You're the master strategist—me, I'm just your enforcer . . . so
I'll go look at postcards if you want," he said with a wide grin.
"I'm easy."

She just sucked her teeth and rolled her eyes with a half smile,
and tugged him to begin walking.

Mike Caluzo sat in the cramped airport chair with his right leg
crossed over his left at the ankle, his knee nervously bouncing.
Perspiration made his face, back, and armpits damp. He kept his
eyes glued to the window, intermittently glancing at the depar-
tures board while saying silent Hail Marys that there'd be no
delay from Newark International to Vegas.

Everything had gotten all fucked up. None of it was supposed to happen like this. When his cell phone rang, he nearly jumped out of his skin. The number was blocked. It could be anyone he knew. Could be his uncle calling to help him out.

Unable to resist he picked up the call and uncrossed his legs so he could lean forward as though talking to the floor.

"Yo."

"Mikey?"

"Yeah. Who's dis?"

"Bradley. Your uncle told me to make sure you got to Vegas safely, given all the shit going down."

Mike Caluzo closed his eyes, tears wetting his lashes. "Tell Big C I said God bless 'im."

"Family is family, will do. Now tell me where you're at."

Laura and James entered the cheerful tourist trap that specialized in a selection of cameras and other electronic equipment. Casing the establishment with their eyes peeled for Megan, they split up. James headed for the electronics, Laura toward the sarongs and beach wear as they scoped out the small shop.

The eclectic mix of merchandise made sense. Megan had been a computer whiz on a university payroll in Philly before her life was interrupted. But judging from the well-stocked inventory, the nice hubbub of activity, and the gorgeous location, she could have done much worse for herself with the severance pay her Dad probably finagled from Penn and whatever else he did to help Megan reestablish her life.

Laura kept walking, taking note. It was important to understand what a person had to lose or gain in any transaction. After a short while of browsing and diplomatically declining assistance from eager employees, she spotted Megan coming out of the manager's area to greet her female cashier in a very personal way.

By instinct, James turned away so his face was hidden, as did Laura, preferring to watch the dynamic for a moment to get a sense of who was who. Megan caressed the young blond's cheek, asking if she'd like anything for lunch when she made a bank run. The two shared a look. Okay, it was established—lovers in the house. Megan had clearly rebuilt her life. This was going to be a delicate information extraction. Laura looked up and walked to the register with a lime green sarong in her hand and smiled cautiously.

Megan immediately blanched and her lover tensed.

"Hi, Megan," Laura said as gently as possible. "You look well. I'm glad." There was no fraud in her tone; she'd meant what she said. Megan had helped her and James, and the converse was also true.

"What brings you back to Jamaica, Laura?"

Megan's expression closed down to a tight, horrified expression that pinched her otherwise beautiful brown face. She tossed her rust-toned dreadlocks over her shoulders and folded her athletic arms over her breasts. Laura patiently watched as the blond got the wrong impression and took a possessive step closer to Megan.

"My cousin's wedding," Laura said and then let out her breath. "My uncle isn't doing so well—prostate cancer, time is marching on, and we have family business interests here. My husband and I are just down here to try to kill several birds with one stone." With a slight nod that was actually designed to relax Megan's partner, Laura indicated James. "You remember my husband, right?"

James offered a brief wave and a smile, but didn't come over, pretending to be enamored of the camera cases. "Hey, ladies."

Megan relaxed, her friend relaxed. "Oh, well . . . that's good—about the wedding, but I'm sorry to hear about your uncle."

"He's lived a good life," Laura said, again meaning it. "Thanks, Megan. I told James I thought you had a shop here and wanted to patronize it . . . since you'd been so good to us in the past." She let the reference drop and dangle, and then gave it time to sink in. With her most ebullient smile, Laura extended her hand to the woman nervously standing near Megan. "Hi, I'm Laura Caldwell-Carter. I'll introduce my husband James once the rapture fades from his technology dazzled eyes."

The three women laughed, and Megan looked over at her partner, her eyes brimming with a combination of pride and quiet joy. "I'm so sorry. This is Kaitland," Megan said quickly as Kaitland extended her hand.

Laura smiled warmly. "It's a pleasure. Megan is quite a lady," she added, meaning every word she said. "Honest, dear, true."

"Yes, she is," Kaitland said with open affection, glancing at Megan with a shy smile. "I'm glad to have met you. Megan is lucky to have friends like you in the States. We hope you guys will visit us while you're down here?"

It was the perfect opening and Laura took her time threading the needle for the delicate social surgery that needed to occur. From the brief, tense expression that flitted across Megan's face, it was obvious to Laura that Kaitland didn't have a clue about their former relationship dodging hit men and that Megan wanted it to stay that way. A passing, chance meeting in their shop was one thing, but Megan clearly didn't want to encourage anything beyond that, which could imperil her new, ordered life.

Accommodating the unspoken request, Laura dug in her purse and found a small piece of paper and a pen. "That would be lovely, but with the coming nuptials that my cousin sprang on us—and I'm sure your schedule keeps you busy—it may be hectic. But here's my cell phone number while in Jamaica, as well as the resort we're at." Remaining politically correct, Laura pressed the information into Kaitland's hand. "Oh, speaking of friends, have you all heard from Donny lately? I'm so worried about him. He's not returning calls and just seems . . . I don't know . . . distant."

Megan relaxed and let out a sad rush of breath. "Laura, I am so worried about him, too. He's gone recluse on all of us and the last time I spoke to him, he just seemed so angry at the world. He's not the loving soul I once knew. It's terrible."

Laura covered her heart with her hand. "Oh, how awful. I am

so very, very sorry to hear that." While it was the truth, it was a bit over the top, yet necessary.

Leaning in to draw both women into her confidence, Laura glanced over her shoulder at James and spoke in a conspiratorial tone.

"My husband used to be a cop and is still so paranoid about everything. I'm glad he's off the force, but some old habits die hard. He got worried that some of the people who we'd heard about in the news might try to contact Donny and begin pressuring him for donations, campaign contributions, even old favors that his father and mother took to their graves with them, unfulfilled. Now that I'm hearing this from you, Megan, I may actually have to apologize to James—much as I hate to admit being wrong. Plus, Donny has been through *so much*, and no matter what all transpired, his father and I were fast friends. I hate to hear this."

Laura shook her head as though deeply disgusted and stepped back with a dramatic sigh. She'd effectively kept Megan's cover by speaking of only knowledge made public by the media and by leaving the unspoken lines wide open for Megan to interpret without making Kaitland suspicious.

Appearing mollified that Laura would abide by her parameters and respect her new relationship, Megan glanced over her shoulder at James, who still seemed to be out of earshot. She closed the small circle again and dropped her voice to a private murmur. "The last time I spoke to him, like I said, he was so angry." Megan paused, her gaze boring into Laura as she skirted the depth of their past affiliation, but obviously wanted to convey whatever she could to Laura.

It was all in Megan's eyes, the yearning to get information across without divulging too much in front of an innocent, that Laura picked up on.

"Losing loved ones is so hard, can do so much, especially with someone who has delicate sensibilities, like Donny." She released a sad sigh. "Finding out that his lover, Alan, betrayed him . . . so horrible. Then his father's death—even though they were at odds, that was still his parent. And, oh, God, when Liz was killed . . . that was probably it for him." Again, Laura just shook her head and sent her gaze to the floor, raking her short curls. "It may have all been too much for him, really."

Kaitland hugged herself. "That is so, so sad." Her furtive gaze went between Laura and Megan. "I never met him, but if he's a dear friend and so vulnerable, it would be just a travesty if users went after his inheritance."

Laura nodded and took up Kaitland's hand. "This is why I was so worried. His father and I were in business together *for years* in Philadelphia, and *I know* how cruel people can be. They don't care what he's been through, or that he's alone and confused . . . even possibly lashing out." She glanced at Megan, their eyes meeting in understanding. "He may be angry at anyone from the past who was close to his parents," she added to give Megan an in. "Regardless of his mental state at the moment, I don't want to see him further abused by all the hangers on . . . predators, sharks, scam artists."

Kaitland squeezed Laura's hand. "I so agree. No one needs that."

Megan sighed. "I know you mean well," she admitted. "But he's blaming everyone for how alone he is . . . like I said," she added quietly, giving Laura a direct look. "He's very angry and flinging illogical blame around onto everyone."

Laura caught the look and the reference. Donny blamed her and James for his plight—not realizing that Alan, his lover, was a vicious, usury bastard, his mother a murderous bitch who'd been instrumental in having his own father murdered by his mother's lover—all of which she and James saved his narrow ass from . . . but if he wanted to lob twisted anger at her, so be it.

"I'm so sorry about all this," Megan said quietly.

"Yes, so am I," Laura replied, not surprised that things took this turn. She knew the apology was about more than what they'd directly spoken of; it was about all that went unsaid regarding Donny and his warped sense of who did him wrong. Still, she needed information that now she was sure only Megan could provide.

"Here's the thing that really just . . ." Laura let her arms fall to her sides in mock defeat. "I guess I'll just never know."

Megan and Kaitland both leaned in, moving away from the register so that another sales clerk could wait on a customer. That's when Laura knew she had them.

Glancing over her shoulder, Laura nervously glimpsed James again. "Before we came here," Laura whispered, "my husband got word that an ex-federal agent that had been involved in all that Micholi trial business on the news was possibly dirty . . . and you know one of the key players in all that, George Townsend, once a very good friend of Donald Haines Sr., never did a day of time. In fact, he got relocated to some witness protection program. Now, call me suspicious, but who knows who could be in Donny's ear coaching him, trying to fleece him in an election year, Megan?" she said, glancing around.

"Oh, shit," Megan said, closing her eyes.

Even though she'd added hunch and yeast to the story to draw Megan in, not a flicker of guilt ran through her. If Donny was pissed off and crazy, his dumb ass was vulnerable—and there was too much temptation down in the Gulf for the Main Line developers and Washington hacks to ignore. They'd go after Donny, trying to ride on his dead father's coattails. If anything, one day he'd thank her for keeping him from going from wealthy to homeless once the bloodsuckers got through with him.

Giving Megan time to digest what she'd told her, Laura pressed on, using a slice of guilt trip as her final parting shot. "If you're his friend, you might want to just . . . I don't know . . . check, if you can—given some of your father's resources, to be sure no one is taking advantage of your dear friend."

Laura looked for James again as though nervous he'd be angry that a marital confidence had been broken. "Maybe even Sean could find out so your dad wouldn't know . . . but if you care about Donny, you'd advise him of any foul activities around his philanthropic efforts—you understand? A lot of people were aware of what Donald and Elizabeth had monetarily. Donny is their only heir, which makes him a prime target, especially in an election year."

"Say no more," Megan murmured, her voice low, tense, and angry. "I hear you."

Laura hugged her and Megan hugged her back. "Well, I'd better hurry up and pick out a wedding present for Najira and Steve before my husband buys so much camera equipment we'll never clear Customs."

"I'll go introduce myself to him," Kaitland said with a smile. "I'll be sure he leaves with something reasonable while you and Megan figure out a nice wedding gift." She hugged Laura and brushed Megan's cheek with the tips of her fingers. "It was good to meet you. There's still so much about Megan that I'm learning."

Laura just smiled and watched the pretty young woman in a white sundress walk away. She followed Megan's eyes, which followed Kaitland's ass, and decided to finish off the game as though she were talking with one of the boys downtown. "Real nice," Laura said with unabashed appreciation. "I'm glad for you."

Megan shoved her hands in her olive cargo pants pockets. "Thanks. Means a lot that you're cool with it . . . and that James is, too."

Laura smiled. "He just looks like a caveman, but he's really evolved." She was glad that made Megan finally relax enough to laugh, and Laura almost chuckled thinking about James and Steve's initial reaction to learning that Donald Haines Jr. was gay and screwing his father's former legal partner's son. She nearly had to bite her tongue to keep further commentary about it at bay. But one thing all of them agreed on, having dealt with the slimy underbelly of politics and the Mob—good people were good people, bad people were bad people, and if one fell into the former category, who they slept with was their business. Those in the latter category could get you killed.

"We have your number down here, right?" Megan said, glancing at Kaitland as she and Laura headed toward the section of the store loaded with silver gift wares.

"Yeah," Laura said, forcing the butterflies of anxiety and elation to be still in her stomach. She wanted to praise dance; Megan was going to help. But she couldn't seem too elated. After all, this was a somber occasion. "Just let me know if we can help in any way. That's the least we can do."

Chapter
10

"Very strange thing that's been happening here," Captain Bennett said, making a tent with his fingers before his mouth as he and the DA stared at Scapolini across the interrogation room desk. "See, my detective goes to get a cup of coffee while we wait for your lawyer to get down here so we can clear all this up and have a conversation, and oddly, our guys in Jersey say that another guy you had a recent argument with just bought it."

Scapolini turned his head and sent his gaze out the window. "I don't know shit and ain't got jack shit to say until my lawyer gets here."

"No problem," Captain Bennett said. "We've got time. All day, all night, this year, next year, whatever. Makes no difference to me. So, we'll wait. I'm just curious though, Joey. What'd these guys do to piss you off so badly, huh?"

Scapolini just raised his middle finger and folded his arms.

"Oh, get the hell out of here," Steve murmured. "In the fucking men's room?"

"You heard it, Sulli. Slit his throat clean through and sat him on the john with his pants pulled down so it looked like the man was taking a crap and a sweatshirt wrapped around his neck to absorb all the blood. Was a few hours before the blood soaked into his clothes enough to finally drip on the floor, and that's when maintenance freaked out and called the cops. So, I need some insight for all this divulging I'm doing, which breaks every policy on the force and could cost me my well-earned pension. Talk to me."

Steve sighed and stepped away from the bar, half wishing he'd never answered the phone. He began walking until he got to a secluded spot, but dropped his voice nonetheless. "Listen, Cap. Killing Rapuzzio wouldn't start a war for Scapolini. That would be like an internal house-cleaning scenario—putting his house in order if one of his own did something out of line. But the Caluzo thing is iffy. That would cross family jurisdictions. Just like us, they can't cross lines without severe bullshit repercussions. Okay, you follow?"

"Yeah. I got you. And it was clear when they left here that the family battle lines were drawn. Even though Scapolini was hollering at them both for being dumb fucks—he never said about what or why, just how could they be so goddamned stupid. The drama happened between the two we'd thrown in the same interrogation room together." Captain Bennett chuckled. "We sorta let them think that one of them was responsible for Scapolini calling, which broke down any trust they had. They went at each other like it was WWE *SmackDown*, and it took half the department to restrain 'em. What can I say, we used the opportunity."

Steve raked his sun-kissed hair, wistfully considering the huge pool. "Tell ya what, Cap . . . and this is just a hunch, not even a good one, just my gut."

"We'll take it, at this point. This crap has been blowing up in our yard, and I'm sick to death of the federal boys coming in and pulling rank, taking all the credit for all our hard police work."

"I feel you," Steve said, nodding in reflex, even though Bennett couldn't see him do so. "Ya know, those two together is really pretty odd. Rapuzzio was Scapolini's top man, and Caluzo was always sorta distant—did basic enforcer jobs in Philly and kept a presence there for his uncle from Vegas. Why those two would be a matched pair to go after my lady is really curious. Caluzo I could see, because he warned me . . . but Rapuzzio—without Joey's knowledge. Judging from the weird call you got, doesn't ring right. Plus this fed name that Caluzo flung out there. Cap, I'm serious, you'd better run a check on this Bradley dude."

"Yeah, well, we're on it—discreetly. Follow?"

"Ain't that the only way?" Steve began walking again as tourists passed.

"But what's the whole thing about, Sullivan? Seriously."

Steve let out his breath hard and began walking parallel to the edge of the surf. "You've got the Jersey casino family and the Vegas casino family trying to muscle in on some prime real estate in the Gulf that could be made available if the owners cave—and they've gotta make the land grab before the Jamaicans figure out a way to pressure the owners for it, too. Don't forget, you've got the boys in Washington who ain't above going for it, either, but they have to wait until the election year is sealed up. They'll try to jack it through legislation—then if that fails, might have the owners made real uncomfortable from every agency at their disposal; you know how they do things."

A long whistle filled the receiver and it made Steve stop and begin to angrily pitch shells into the rolling waves.

"Damn," Cap said, "and here we thought it was just drug territory."

"It is," Steve said, feeling fury rise with the bile in his throat. "Layers of money. First you make money off the waste removal, then leveling the joint, followed by the construction contracts for real estate development. Then layer on the casinos—straight bling. Then add in the restaurants, rental income from major stores, concessions, hotels, prostitutes to service the high rollers, and all the powder, pills, and weed that the newly renovated area can stand. All worth millions in the country's port that is the gateway for one fifth of the nation's imports and exports, once it's all said and done, if not worth billions." Steve closed his eyes for a moment, allowing the impact to truly sink into his own brain. "*Now* you get it?"

"So when you and James decide to piss somebody off, Sulli, you really know how, huh? This is a tiger by the tail, if ever I heard." Bennett tried to make light of the situation, but the strain was evident in his voice when he chuckled.

"Yeah, it's been a barrel of monkeys, Cap. A complete three-ring circus."

"Sulli . . . why don't you guys come home and let us try to cover you? We can't do shit for you internationally—even though Philly is probably hot for you guys at the moment. But you hear where I'm going . . . you said Jamaicans were involved, so it would seem like that might not be the place to be." Captain Bennett waited, his silence laden with worry.

"Appreciate it, Cap—but you know once me and James get onto something this big, there's no running from it. Just like old times, we either drag it down or have it on our asses until it eats us." Steve just stared at the ocean, his voice detached and philosophical.

"I kinda figured you'd say that," Bennett replied, and then let out a frustrated sigh. "One last question, then, so we can do whatever we can to keep the pressure on these assholes on this side of the water."

"Shoot," Steve said, heading back to the hotel.

"All right—how the hell does your girlfriend factor in? Like, no offense, but she didn't strike me as a Paris Hilton–type heiress. So what sent the odd couple, Caluzo and Rapuzzio, through her hotel room door at the Sheraton in a way that got 'em in enough trouble with Scapolini to get themselves whacked?"

Steve chuckled, the sound coming out hard and brittle. "Get this, Cap—her dad is one of the landowners . . ."

James exited the store behind Laura loaded down with brightly colored shopping bags. A digital video camera, webcam connectors, a laptop, a small micro recorder, and Laura's wedding gift choices as she walked beside him still window-shopping, authenticating his role as a dutiful husband for anyone who might have been following them.

Remaining casual, Laura opened her phone and dialed Najira, waking her cousin with a series of crisp instructions.

"I know you're tired, boo, but you have to get up, go down to the concierge with Steve and start planning your wedding."

"What!" Najira protested groggily.

"It's our cover, it's your father's ruse. You have got to do the bride thing—hell, you were gonna get married anyway and wanted him there, and we need a way to make sure James can get pics to download and e-mail to the right people, so just—"

"Laura, you're insane, you know that? I don't want my wedding day tied up with an operation you've—"

"You wanna live? You want everybody to be safe? Then stop playing! If that's all I had to do, dammit, you know—"

"Yeah, I know you would, but—"

"You can get married for real, romantically and the whole nine later. Okay? Just start having the meetings, get moving as though that's the only reason you're here. *Later* we can get sentimental and technical." Laura clicked off the cell phone feeling her blood pressure spiking in her ears.

"I take it she doesn't get the severity of the problem," James said in a dry tone.

"Not at all." Laura kept a false smile plastered on her face sure that they were being watched in the small tourist area. She could feel eyes from some remote place crawling over her like mosquitoes.

"Najira doesn't have to get it," James said calmly, pecking Laura's cheek as though they were out for a casual lover's stroll. "As long as Steve gets it—and he does. Trust me."

Laura relaxed. "Good," she murmured, kissing him back so she could talk into his ear. "Because the ball is in motion, especially if bodies are dropping."

James's cell rang and she pressed her face to a window to allow James time to seem to casually talk. Although his body was rigid, his expression remained unreadable. When he got off the phone he slung an arm over her shoulder and kept her moving, explaining the most horrifying information without missing a beat.

"He'll break it to 'Jira, and then you won't have any more bull-shit out of her," James said calmly. "He knows what they've gotta do and why."

It was completely outrageous, but they couldn't refuse. Hakim Braithwaite was sending a limo to collect them all to bring the family to his resort, where they'd be his dinner guests in a private room, and then could partake in the club and gambling at his closed door operation for VIPs and dignitaries only. Under normal circumstances, honoring Akhan would have been a beautiful gesture. But after spending nearly an hour going through the room to check it for surveillance equipment, the gesture was any-thing but nice; it was ominous.

Laura stood with her back to James as he pulled the zipper up on the little black linen dress she'd selected. Resentment coiled within her like a serpent; she knew this had to be the very thing sending Akhan to his grave: his sons rich on illicit drug money. Opulent, decadent displays of wealth, with a hidden threat of deadly power if their father refused to comply. The people who Akhan had dedicated his life to helping in the grassroots com-munity would be screwed over by his own flesh and blood—no different from, and possibly worse than, if *the man* had taken it all and done no less.

She was so angry that she could barely put her diamond stud earrings in. She almost couldn't get black, strappy stiletto sandals on without wobbling all over the place with fury.

"Very nice," James murmured, trying to compliment her. She looked like a million bucks, even though practically shaking with rage. "Is the dress for them or for me?" He smiled, hoping he'd put her at ease by teasing her a little.

"Both," Laura snapped.

"How's that?" he said, raising an eyebrow when she walked away from him to powder her nose.

"*This*," she said angrily, smoothing down the dress, which stopped mid-thigh, "is *always* for you. However, it also distracts very chauvinistic men who think I'm a bimbo based on packaging. In situations like this, the element of surprise is always best."

While she'd given him a straight answer, he hadn't expected the hard delivery. "Baby, you're gonna have to calm down before we do this dinner thing. Your claws are showing."

"I am so gonna deal with this mother—"

"Laura," James said calmly. "Breathe. If you could deal with Paxton and his Philly crew of black elitists robbing the city and the people blind through insider contract manipulations, then you can deal with this."

"This is much worse, James," she said in a quiet hiss between her teeth. "They're blood."

True, she had a point, but if she was going to pull this thing off, she had to lighten up. He watched her close her eyes and mentally count to ten.

"Your plan is working; the Mob is unraveling—already imploding on itself. Megan is getting you data, right? So . . ."

She held up her hand. "I know, I know. Okay. I'm just so . . . I can't tell you." She spun away from the mirror to face him, a compact in her hand. "He's dying," she said quietly and swallowing hard. "And they don't even give a rat's ass. They don't know what this man has done for untold communities and families over eighty some years. He was a grassroots organizer, loaned people money who couldn't get a fair deal anywhere else, lobbied, marched, gave his all for the common man and woman. They don't fucking know, James!"

Her voice was a tight, anguished whisper that broke off into a near sob. He'd known she was torn up, but until this moment, just how much he hadn't fully understood. Laura was always one to deeply bury the most painful emotions within her, just to drive through the ugly business at hand that had to be dealt with. But as he crossed the room to hold her he remembered just how soft her heart truly was, which was why there was such a hard, protective layer around it.

"Hey, we're gonna get through this," he said, gathering her into his arms. To his complete surprise she stiffened.

"I know," she said, extricating herself from his hold to apply some powder. "And if we don't, my plan is to put a bullet in their heads."

James leaned on the dresser and stared at her, becoming slightly disturbed. Even though he was pretty sure that Laura had never actually taken a life, tonight there wasn't a doubt in his mind that she could.

"That's my line, baby." He watched her meticulously apply a little more makeup but knew for her it was go-to-war paint. He also figured out why she had stiffened as she tilted her chin up to the ceiling and refused to cry, forcing back tears so she could apply mascara. One hug and she would have dissolved. Right now she couldn't afford that. "How're we playing this, then?"

She sighed hard. "I'm rich, spoiled, and cannot be bothered with the fucking community," she said, briefly pressing her lips together to even out her lipstick. "You're an ex dirty cop that couldn't give a shit. Scapolini leaned on me and I want out. You're not feeling it either. Najira and Steve have enough and just wanna get married . . . and we throw in the wild card—Jamal. He was roughed up in Maui via some circumstances we don't have the full details on, but shooting was involved. He's done. For him, it's not worth it. We're middle-class Americans who can't relate to the travesty that happened in the Gulf, which is now someone else's problem. The only thing we agree on is that the government doesn't know what it's doing . . . and then I drop the tidbit about potential eminent domain being forced by politicos in the hip pocket of the Italians—which isn't a stretch."

James nodded and found his khaki-hued linen suit jacket that had been lying across the chair and slung it over his shoulder, making sure his new camera was in his pocket. "Cool."

The family collected in the lobby with faces so somber it looked as though they were going to get into a limo to attend a funeral, not a so-called family reunion dinner. Steve and James glanced around the group and leaned into the huddle.

"Everybody looks nice, except the expressions, which are a dead giveaway." That's all James said and then stepped back.

Akhan nodded and adjusted his embroidered, royal blue African robe and matching cap, which was now so big on him that he was practically swimming in it. Even his pantaloons ballooned out and sagged, yet he still had the regal carriage of a proud, ancient king. Laura took note of the significant weight loss the elderly man had experienced, which until now was harder to tell. She neared him and slipped her hand into his as they waited for their ride.

"You lead the dance, Uncle," Laura murmured touching his face and pecking his cheek.

Brother B forced a smile, fidgeting with his brightly hued floral shirt that needed ironing. He looked totally uncomfortable in his white linen dress slacks and thick leather sandals, but appeared as though he'd made a supreme effort to get dressed up.

"I guess we're just a little bit antsy . . . thirty plus years gwan by, now what to say?"

"For both of you?" Jamal said, incredulous. "Damn. What happened?"

"You look good, brother," James said, deflecting the comment and rounding Jamal. As a distraction, he lifted the lapels on Jamal's white casual Armani and nodded his approval of his black silk T-shirt weighed down by the heavy platinum and diamond disk with his name emblazoned on it around his neck—something that was far from his taste.

But he kept ribbing the younger men, turning his focus to Steve once Jamal smiled.

"You know, you know," Jamal said. "This is how we do it in Philly."

"Steve, man, you're slacking," James teased, opening his arms. "Where's your suit jacket, man? You can't represent in a collared T-shirt that's almost screaming Eagles' football jersey, and a pair of pants, brother."

"I tried to tell him," Najira fussed, "but he said it was too hot."

"I was going for boardwalk casual," Steve complained. "In and out of the air-conditioning to the heat is taking a toll, all right. If I gotta put on a jacket, forgedabout it. And, besides, Brother B has on just a shirt."

"He's an elder," James said flatly. "Brother B can wear what he wants."

"Steve, can't you just go get a jacket to put over your arm?" Najira said, rolling her eyes.

"That's all right, because you, my dear, look lovely," James said, kissing the back of her hand to make her smile. He turned her around a bit so that her light cotton, African mud-cloth print sarong skirt breezed out a bit. She truly looked elegant in her flat patent strap sandals and tastefully low-key black silk shell—such a far cry from the wilder Najira they'd all known.

Although Laura and Akhan were eerily silent, James kept up the meaningless banter. It was imperative that they loosen up, and any discussion with the old men in their group about what happened to make them step away from their sons would keep them all tight. He continued to mess with Jamal, and playing the dozens and commenting on his costly rags, so he wouldn't go there.

"How much you got on, bro, seriously?" James said, laughing. "A house note, a car note—right here, this mess around your neck is an Escalade."

"Can I help it if I know how to style, boss? If Laura would let me, I'd school an old brother on the newest trends, but I'm not trying to come between man and wife."

They carried on until the lines of strain seemed to ease on Laura and Akhan's faces. Even Brother B had to laugh at some of the ridiculous commentary. James just prayed that the revelry would continue in the limo, as word was sure to travel fast about their mood.

"We're gonna invite them to the wedding and just seem like as women we're caught up in that," Laura said in Najira's ear as they were helped into the stretch first.

This time Najira nodded and clasped Laura's hand. "Steve explained . . . I'm sorry, girl," she whispered. "I didn't know how bad it had gotten."

Laura squeezed her hand back and gave her the eye to chill. Once the driver stepped away to assist Akhan and Brother B, Laura whispered quickly and quietly in Najira's ear as the others entered the vehicle.

"No more conversations, not even in the rooms until all of them are swept for listening devices . . . which are going to be impossible to find each time. It's better to speak in code and get disciplined until this is all over. If you just gotta say something, write it and then flush it down the toilet. I know your dad and Brother B will school Jamal, and Steve already understands the drill from his days rolling with James. All right—don't answer, just nod."

Najira nodded and then scooted over to be close to her fiancé so that Laura could sit next to James.

Chapter
11

Despite the fact that it was a relatively short ride, only a few miles from one resort to the next, Laura felt she would jump out of her skin by the time they pulled up to the elaborate facility. Smaller by comparison than a mega hotel chain, what the structure lacked in size it made up for in ornate amenities.

A grand, hand-laid flagstone semicircular drive welcomed their white stretch limousine to a palatial front entrance littered with expensive foreign vehicles being valet-serviced. Eager valets jockeyed huge Mercedes sedans, BMWs, Jaguars, Escalades, and Bentleys to more remote parking, while tuxedo-wearing greeters spoke to VIP guests in cultured, dignified tones as they entered the impressive, polished mahogany and marble ensconced lobby.

Laura kept her gaze sweeping but not gawking. Her mind was clicking like it was a calculator, and she was admittedly impressed by the tact the Braithwaite brothers took . . . they'd gone for old world charm and plantation refinement to hide their illegal earnings behind the facade of dignified elegance.

Yet as they left the expertly landscaped exterior that boasted a profusion of fragrant, color-rich blossoms and entered the lobby past the lush interior gardens, she fought not to scream as she glimpsed Akhan slowly, and ever so briefly, close his eyes, clearly dying a thousand deaths where he stood, she knew. How could he not as he watched his sons take the lessons he'd probably taught them about hiding in plain sight, how *the man* did things at the upper echelons of society . . . only to see his sons bastardize his teachings with a sick hybrid of revolutionary, *Spook Who Sat By the Door* tactics, and something as insidious as drugs.

Akhan turned away as though to step outside and leave, but his and Laura's eyes met, and then he slowly looked at Najira and then Jamal and lifted his chin. Brother B landed a hand on his shoulder, and both old men put on the faces of veterans of war and became stone. If nothing else shattered her heart, seeing that transformation surely did. James obviously caught it, too, and she watched him shake his head so very subtly while staring at her that one had to really focus to even see his head move.

Surrounded by glass-like marble floors, gold-gilded cathedral ceilings were held open on each side by white antebellum columns to allow in the flow of tradewind breezes. Ornately upholstered Queen Anne chairs were positioned by large fireplace hearths, and sumptuous leather recliners. Delicate settees and chaise lounges were grouped before plantation sugar chests, Chippendale coffee tables, and English tapestries. They waited, trapped, but didn't sit amid the splendor.

Finally after fifteen agonizing minutes, two men strolled toward their party as casual as could be. They made no apology in their gait or expression, but simply approached and looked the group over with a slight air of disdain.

Laura felt her blood run cold as she stared at a male version of herself that she knew by age and description had to be Hakim. His gray eyes locked with hers instantly, a challenge in them as well as something else that troubled her to her core, but she refused to look away.

"Akhan, long time," the eldest brother said, extending a business-like handshake to his father.

Akhan looked at the extended hand with deep sadness in his eyes and accepted the gesture with a weary sigh. "Yes . . . a long time," he said as he shook his son's hand like a stranger.

A younger version of the first stepped in and only offered a nod. "Way too long," he said, his voice curt. "But, then, that is history."

Both cultured Braithwaites turned to Brother B, as they eyed James and Steve and gave Laura and Najira a cursory glance.

"T and Hector said they were on their way and will meet us in the dining room," the eldest son announced.

Akhan and Brother B shifted nervously where they stood.

"This is Najira and Jamal Hewitt," Akhan said, his eyes never leaving the eldest son's face. "This is Hakim and Daoud Braithwaite," he added. "You are siblings."

An awkward silence fell over the group as Akhan took a labored breath. In the decades that separated his children, his double life in the states and the islands had never come face to face until now. They hadn't even known of each other; at least Jamal and Najira had been unaware. Everyone stood tensely in the small circle, not sure what to say.

"Steve is your sister's fiancé—Steve Sullivan."

Steve leaned in and shook both Braithwaites' hands. "Pleased to meet you," he said stiffly.

They simply nodded and released his hand, unimpressed.

His gaze unblinking as he stared at Hakim, Akhan introduced Laura and then James. "Laura Caldwell-Carter, your cousin, and her husband, James Carter."

Laura watched them each shake James's hand and could tell by the biceps flexes beneath suit jackets that each man was trying to crush the bones in the other's hand. A wry smile appeared on Hakim Braithwaite's face as he released James's hand with a nod of respect. Then he turned to her.

"Cousin, is it? A shame that such a lovely woman is a blood relative—but a pleasure to finally place a face with a name." He took her hand and gently caressed it within his and released it.

Laura saw James and Akhan bristle from the corner of her eye but had to ignore them. "It's nice to meet you. I'm so glad that we're here," she lied, looking around and turning on every political acting skill she owned from years of working the circuit.

"This is absolutely *fabulous*, Hakim. You've clearly developed one of the finest establishments in the Caribbean."

"We like to think so," he said, clearly pleased that she seemed impressed. "After dinner we should take a little tour so you can see the rooms. We spared no expense."

The blatant suggestion and reference to rooms was so inappropriate, but she decided to max out the situation to see just how far she could run with it. Taking his arm, she began talking and walking with Braithwaite.

"Yes," Laura said brightly. "You must show us your rooms. Najira and Steve were planning their wedding at the other resort—because we didn't want to impose . . . but after seeing this . . ." Laura turned around and stared at Najira hard, and then gave James a look to be cool.

"I'm just stunned, it's so gorgeous," Najira said, catching on. "But I couldn't even imagine having a wedding here, plus this place must be booked up years in advance." She gave Laura a look that contained a plea in her eyes and then turned her gaze on Steve for help.

"Yeah, wow," Steve said, "this is awesome. "We probably couldn't—"

"I always keep a few rooms held back for VIP events that may occur on a moment's notice," Hakim said with arrogant pride lacing his voice. "As owner, we can make certain things happen."

"That would be more than this old man could hope for," Akhan said in a low, defeated tone. "Thank you."

"Not a problem," Daoud said. "Why don't we take this discussion down to the dining room?"

Laura glanced at her husband, and there was such an extreme mixture of emotions within his expression that she couldn't process them all. Part of it seemed like he was sulking to help falsely hype Hakim's self-importance, and yet there was also something very primal and deadly going on behind his intense gaze. Brother B seemed mortified but held his peace. His elderly eyes radiated disapproval, but he kept his lips pursed in a narrow line as they headed to the elegant, mahogany appointed restaurant a floor below the lobby via a massive white double staircase that emptied out to the beach level,

Not sure what she'd expected, Laura felt every mental stereotype come crashing down. The Braithwaite brothers' crisp British accents, their ultra-conservative, clean-shaven style, their understated business casual suits—all of it was disorienting, considering what financed it all. Then again, as Akhan had always told her—so she was sure he had to tell his firstborn sons—the founding fathers made their money on illegal trades . . . everything from slavery, gun running, rum running, slave ship insuring, flesh peddling, opium, you name it, all while keeping up the Puritanical trappings of civility. Okay, fine. Then let the good times roll.

The maître d' practically genuflected as their party entered through the leaded, beveled glass French doors and hurriedly escorted them to a private room with eighteen foot windows that cranked open facing the beach. Hibiscus and honeysuckle grew in huge, fragrant blossoms beyond the screened-in windows, and thorny bushes guarded them like silent sentries along the cobblestone path that tapered off into pure white sugar sand.

A large round table set for twelve and skirted in the finest white linen fit perfectly into the circular, castle-like window nook. All stood around, not sure of the protocol of who should sit where, but stepped aside so that Laura was on one side of Hakim to his left, James was on her other side to her left, and Akhan was next to his son, taking a position on Hakim's right, followed by Daoud on Akhan's right, then Brother B. Jamal instinctively moved down three seats from Brother B to allow room for his two missing sons and whomever else the table was set for, should they decide to show up, choosing to take a position next to his sister, Najira. Najira held Steve's hand, with James on Steve's flank.

Still, no one moved until Hakim shrugged and smiled. The moment he did, servers who'd seemingly come out of nowhere rushed to pull out high-backed, heavy gold brocade chairs for Laura and Najira. Crystal stemware glittered in the low dimmer lights and soft candle lights, which bounced off gold charger plates, gleaming gold flatware and gold-rimmed, fine bone china.

Beautiful oil paintings and tapestries graced the walls and long-stemmed solitary lilies stood proudly at the table's center.

Helping each guest get settled, ebullient servers made a grand show of placing linen napkins on laps, and producing a thick, leather-bound wine list for the boss. Laura fought a scowl—all the pomp and circumstance be damned, the Braithwaites would put a bullet in a person's skull as quick as look at them, and she knew it. However, the disorienting irony was intriguing. Under different circumstances, she might admire their brass balls. She could relate, since she had a pair herself.

After much ado about wines and such, all of which she participated in through a very remote part of her mind, she had to admit that Braithwaite was so reminiscent of her Wall Street days that it was eerie. Akhan had always said that the universe was efficient. Just watching things come full circle made her know that was true.

"Well, shall we order some appetizers until the rest of our party arrives?" Hakim said, his attention constantly drifting to Laura.

She smiled and sipped the Chardonnay that had been produced with great flourish. "That would be nice," she murmured, holding his gaze. "Your father is diabetic and should eat." With a wry smile she watched him accept the jab like a true gentleman and he simply nodded.

"Sir," he said, glancing at Laura with a sarcastic smirk, "what can we bring you?"

"My appetite isn't what it once was," Akhan said, looking suddenly very old.

When Najira sat forward, her expression alarmed, Laura covered her hand.

"How about some fruit and some cool, unsweetened tea?" Laura said, looking at her uncle.

Akhan nodded. "I think I can keep that down."

For the first time since they'd met, a flicker of concern flitted behind Hakim's distant gray eyes. Ready for battle, Laura leaned forward pursing her lips with her fingers and ignoring all protocol. "His prostate," she said, not caring that she'd thrown a grenade on the table. "He must eat; it is prudent to do the wedding this week, and he needs medical attention. Fruit would do him good."

She sat back, glanced at her uncle, and took up her wine.

Hakim hailed the waiter. "Do you always speak your mind so directly and so elegantly?"

"Always," Laura murmured and never lost eye contact with Hakim. "Especially when time is what it is."

"Again, I will say, then . . . I am very glad we had this family reunion so that we could meet."

She couldn't even begin to glimpse James who was seated at her left, and smoldering by now she was sure. But it was about a command performance. If the twisted bastard had interest in a blood cousin, and if that would buy time, so be it. He needed to think that she was equally ruthless and down for whatever. Although Akhan was quietly cringing, he understood the game. The topic had to be dragged kicking and screaming out into the open so there was no room for an ambush.

Faces sought leather-bound menus for cover as the tension mounted, and then something so totally bizarre happened that Laura nearly broke her mask and laughed.

The complete, diametrically opposite Braithwaites rolled into the restaurant like they were on their way to a rap concert. The contrast between the more sedate but seemingly deadly ones that were seated and the pair that came in with a chick bordering on hoochie made Laura sit back in her chair and stare.

Seated, Hakim and Daoud wore lightweight beige and taupe linen suits, respectively, and expensive, Italian leather slip-ons without socks. Their only jewelry was a classic Rolex each, and their hair was trimmed down low in close-cropped, silky waves. They shared the light almond hue and hazel-gray eyes with Akhan.

But their walnut-hued cousins rolled in like one would imagine Shaba Ranks—dreadlocks swinging, one wearing an electric blue sharkskin suit, the other doing cobalt-gray in shiny, pressed leather, sporting so much bling that even in the low lights one had to squint. Fingers, necks, wrists, and mouth jewelry set off their look. Air Force 1's were the shoes of choice. The woman with them had on a skin-tight white halter dress that stopped at the bottom of her butt cheeks and practically lost her double D cups from behind thin strips of white silk that showed her dark areolas and pouting nipples.

For Laura, it was an interesting study in family genetics and family dynamics. However, the thing that stole her complete attention was Jamal's reaction when the eldest of the dreadlocked brothers skidded to a halt, and laughed.

"Oh, shit, we share the same taste in women. I'll just be fucked." Terrence shook his head and reached over everyone to pound Hakim and Daoud's fists. "Pops," he said with a sneer and then found an open seat and plopped down before his lady. "Safia, go ahead and sit next to the motherfucker," he instructed the woman in the halter. "I don't care," he added and then made room for his brother to take a seat between him and Brother B.

"Yo, long time," the other brother said, looking at Brother B like he was inspecting a bug under a microscope, and then gave Akhan a nod. "It's all good, though."

Laura watched the dynamic unfold very, very carefully, monitoring all reactions. The two more conservative brothers were cool but she could tell they were absolutely undone by the wild entrance. Good. A schism in the ranks. She could work with that, and this had obviously been what both Akhan and Brother B were counting on. The two off-the-hook brothers were high. Loose cannons like that were unpredictable, but good for getting their asses killed when pure strategists like Hakim required absolute control. However, Jamal wasn't breathing and James was poised in his chair for a lunge for some reason. Najira seemed confused, and Steve was on red alert like James, while both old men seemed very, very sad.

"Hi, I'm Laura," she said, ignoring all protocol and ready to get the show on the road. "Nice to meet you."

"T and H," the eldest of the two dreads said, getting up before a server could help him to take the dripping bottle of wine from the silver stand. He gave Laura a leering up and down and poured himself a full water glass of chardonnay. "Tell me you ain't blood, girl—no cousin."

She chuckled. "Blood cousin with Hakim and Daoud, but not with you. However, let me introduce my husband, James."

Terrence walked around the table. "My bad. You cool, though."

James was on his feet eye to eye with him. "Terrence, right?"

Terrence smiled as they pounded each other's fists like about to begin a heavy-weight bout. "Yeah, mon."

"That's Jamal and Najira, her fiancé Steve," Brother B said cautiously. "Terrence, Hector," he added, motioning with his hand before lowering his eyes as though ashamed.

Terrence smiled. "Na-jira . . . pretty name." He totally ignored Steve and looked at Jamal. "We met, but it's cool. You know my girl, right?"

Jamal didn't move or blink, nor did Safia.

Hector reached around his brother and pounded Jamal's fist. "It's cool, mon. No worries. Drink your wine and later I'll give you a blunt. You'll forget all about the bullshit."

Laura sent her gaze to Hakim whose eyes smoldered a very quiet and lethal warning as Akhan's fruit appetizer came.

"Let's order and get that done, then we can talk without interruption."

Never in her life had she experienced a level of drama like that at the table surrounding such a seemingly simple task as ordering food, but once the servers returned to place entrée selections of lamb, veal, quail, broiled Chilean sea bass, salmon, tuna, filet mignon, and five orders of lobster, the room fell silent. Yet the drama had served a vital purpose and she was thankful for it—because it illuminated where the fissures were in Braithwaite philosophy and power structure.

Diametrically opposed in the methodology and approach to getting rich and staying that way, but with similar goals and ambitions of wealth building, Akhan's offspring clearly wanted to follow the route of the quiet, entrenched power structures of old world money. Their clientele at the resort mirrored that desire, as wealthy Saudis, Europeans, and Africans flooded the lobby. To her way of thinking, Hakim and Daoud stood a better chance of cutting a side deal with the Main Line than the Italian Mafia, whereas the muscle that Brother B's sons, Terrence and Hector, openly flexed would help those Mob factions that were battling South Americans and Mexican drug lords.

Even more interesting was the fact that mild shock flickered in Hakim's eyes when Terrence acknowledged having met Jamal and stated in his inimitable way that the woman, Safia, also knew him. While a detailed conversation, later, would reveal more, just like James's grisly expression could be dissected in the inner circle family meeting, she was about to lob another grenade across the table now that the servers were gone.

"I'm glad that we have all come together, no matter how long it's been—*Ashe*," Akhan said slowly, reading Laura's eye signal cue to begin. "As Laura mentioned earlier, it's no secret that I'm not well and at my age, I've been blessed. My days are numbered." He took a slow sip of tea, parceling out his words and making the four Braithwaite sons listen intently, then leaned forward with a glass of water in his hand and held it above the lily. "I ask the ancestors for permission to begin and for guidance . . . and pour libations so that I may speak wisely. *Ashe.*"

An inner smile warmed Laura's soul. She knew Akhan believed but was also playing it to the bone. Yet, a very remote part of her wondered if the ancestors really could hear. If so, and if there was any spiritual correlation to all the times she'd gotten out of a jam by the hair on her chin, then she was glad Akhan had not wavered in his approach. It also seemed to quietly freak out the big bad Braithwaites, who seemed to hold their collective breath until the old man was finished.

Brother B assisted, making sure Akhan could reach the flower, and all haughty conversation had stopped as the elderly men worked in tandem. Despite the glaring disrespect and anger coming from their wayward sons, some things even they didn't seem ready to mess with.

"It is done," Akhan said, sitting back in his chair, seeming winded. "Now, let me speak plainly." With no emotion or judgment in his tone, his gaze roved the table and settled on Hakim. "I had two families, this is clear. I loved my first wife dearly, and her death changed much—that is history. I left, for reasons those here understand. Perhaps that was not the thing to do. I make no excuses or apologies. It is what it is."

Akhan lifted his chin and spoke calmly with determination. "I made alliances, just as you probably have. Mine matured and bore fruit. Some may say it is strange fruit, but it produced what I could have never dreamed of and do not have time left on this planet to spend. So, rather than see *the man* eat half of it in inheritance taxes and other tricks and schemes, I'd rather dispense it now."

"Wise move, mon," Terrence said. Hector pounded his fist.

Hakim sat back in his chair and clasped his hands in front of his mouth, staring at Akhan.

"Laura has always been my executrix because she was educated at fine universities and spent time on Wall Street. She was my honest eyes and ears in the States. Now, my daughter, your younger half sister and cousin, is ready to marry, and I want her to have a chance to live in peace," Akhan said with strained emphasis, his unfaltering gaze sweeping the table. "I do not know my grandchildren, assuming there are some—which is my fault. They don't know their cousins. Philosophical differences have torn this family apart. I cast no blame; I am simply stating sad facts."

Akhan drew a shuddering, weary breath and then briefly looked at Jamal. "I almost lost this son to the system and violence on the streets, and I want him to have a chance, like you, for self determination. No favors, just the freedom to walk through this life unmolested if his choice differs from that of his brothers, of the family." He looked at Brother B. "The blood was always thicker than the mud, even though this was my brother-in-law," Akhan said with a smile, pounding Brother B's fist. "If he had a dime, I had a nickel, and so forth—this is how we made it."

Terrence and Hector were bobbing their heads. Hakim and Daoud seemed extremely distant but attentive.

"Laura had shared her bounty gleaned on Wall Street with your siblings, Najira and Jamal, as well as her sisters. She doesn't care about the Gulf, nor do they. We'll sign it over."

"Good choice, mon. Why be burdened?" Terrence said with a wide grin.

Akhan sat back, eyes smoldering. Brother B's expression was so tight it seemed like every wrinkle in his face had smoothed. Hakim's gray eyes became a dark, intense, silent storm, just as Daoud's hazel tempest raged behind his silence. Laura sat forward.

"Gentlemen, here's the deal," she said abruptly, going for shock value and playing many aces at once. "I've made sure that the Stateside family won't go broke. But who gives a damn about money if you're looking over your shoulder and scared?" She held Hakim's gaze and then looked at Terrence dead on. "That's no quality of life. Personally, I want to go to the beach without looking over my shoulder."

"*Irie,*" Terrence said with a dangerous chuckle. "The woman makes too much sense, and overstands the situation."

"I need a lawyer, though—one who can draw up iron-clad papers," Laura bluffed.

Hakim sat back, his gaze now locking with the Braithwaite clan. "While I agree, would you care to elaborate on your thinking?" he asked, carefully choosing his words.

She leaned forward using elements from the table setting to draw a picture. "Let's stop all the bullshit. We've got white boys from the political arena about to eminent domain the area to keep you out. I got pulled into a very uncomfortable meeting with some Italiano SOBs at their casino in Jersey—and found out they'd put surveillance equipment in my travel bags." She looked at both senior Braithwaite brothers. "I do not need that shit at this point in my life over some land I am so not interested in developing."

Laura sat back and dramatically dragged her fingers through her hair. "Then, poor Jamal had some asshole shooting at him for the Italians to send a message to us, I guess? Who knows what that was about, but the timing was awfully suspicious to me," she said, seeming oblivious and watching Hakim almost imperceptibly glance at Daoud as Terrence and Hector eased back in their chairs. She noted that Safia hadn't spoken and was frozen like a deer that had wandered in front of an eighteen wheeler.

On a roll now, she threw up her hands. "You're obviously millionaires. I've got money—not as long and strong as yours, but enough so that we're okay. We're here so you can know that whatever went down thirty years ago with you and your fathers, we didn't have shit to do with it and really don't wanna know. These old men are ready to bury the hatchet and as such will turn over that entire portfolio of assets—splitting it right down the middle for you guys so there's no drama. Okay?" She looked to each Braithwaite seeing how very okay it was for some and how very not okay for others.

Smiling as though she'd reached some kind of unilateral agreement, she motioned to Najira. "All we've gotta do is sign everything over to you all—and we can let this poor girl and her fiancé—God bless Steve to have stuck around through all of this—get married. We can throw a nice shindig here."

Her gaze went to Akhan and became soft, which was no act. "Her father can see his only surviving daughter walk down the aisle. We can hang out here until the people with interests in the region in question are told that we no longer control it and they need to step to you if they want it. That changes the power paradigm completely. Obviously, an old man and some chick who digs the beach, me, and my ex-cop husband alone—no offense—are no match for the people who'd want to pry this out of our hands."

"You making so much sense you giving me wood, cousin," Terrence said, laughing, and hailed the waiter. "Bring some Cristal—a bottle for each person."

"I think this requires some thought, however," Hakim said in a controlled tone. "While generous, there are issues—"

"What the fuck issues?" Terrence said, raising his voice and leaning across the table. He pointed at Laura. "De sister says dere divesting. Period. They got leaned on and wan no parts of de shit, good choice."

"Now that's the gospel," Laura said, baiting the two Braithwaites into a sure power struggle. "Let me tell you this," she said, causing them to give her their undivided attention. "Joey Scapolini— and I *know* you know who he is—gave me one week to come down here, make you back off, and return with the paper redone in his favor." She folded her arms over her chest. "This coming Sunday, the casino families meet and I'm supposed to be back on a plane."

"Screw that," Najira said, entering the game gingerly. "I'm not trying to go back—I'd rather stay down here with family, get married, and chill. It ain't worth it."

"Word," Jamal said. He looked at Terrence and held up both hands before his chest. "Dude, I ain't know about the relationship you had with certain people and wasn't trying to play you. I told Laura, take my shit and put it in the family pot. I ain't dealing with the Italians and can stay down here on the beach smoking a spliff, if you really wanna know."

"Look, me and James did our time working behind the lines— if you catch my drift," Steve said, adding in his two cents. "We know these families real well, and ain't trying to go there."

James nodded and sipped his wine. "Especially now that bodies have started dropping in Philly."

The table went quiet for a moment.

"What bodies, mon?" Terrence said carefully, his gaze steady on James before it slid to Hakim and Daoud, then to Hector and back.

"Rapuzzio and Mike Caluzo—while they were trying to make a run to Vegas. Nobody is sure because it happened while we were down here, but somebody screwed Scapolini some kinda way and he's cleaning house. So, like Laura said, it ain't worth it." James went for the bread and began casually munching.

"Then if you all feel comfortable," Akhan said, "I guess it's agreed." He shook with Brother B and then pulled him into an embrace.

"Like Akhan said," Brother B replied, his gaze furtive. "We were idealistic old men even back then. We made mistakes. We thought the revolution and the cause of the common man was worthy. We stood on principle, and we perhaps lost our way. But you all became strong anyway. Good." He sighed and dabbed his eyes, and the emotion that welled up in him was no act. "I hope one day you can forgive us for doing what we had to do." He swallowed hard and looked at his sons. "Four ways, clean cut, no one of you has more than the others, all my assets are yours, all Akhan's assets are yours . . . and Laura can work the paperwork before the Italians and politicians try to get to it first. We just need your lawyers to draw up everything to be sure it's the way you all want it written. We're at your mercy."

Terrence nodded. "All is forgiven with dat, mon."

Brother B blinked back tears as Hector and Terrence pounded each other's fists.

"I'll have my lawyer—"

"Our lawyer," Terrence said, cutting Hakim off.

Daoud and Hakim shared a look as Hector glanced at his brother. Violent tension crackled in the air. Laura smiled as their entrees came.

"Well, that's a complete load off my mind!" She flopped back in the chair and waited while the wine server opened champagne, clearing away the wineglasses and replacing them with flutes while entrées were presented. "I don't care who does it, which lawyer or both attorneys as long as we get this done and one of you all calls the Jersey and Vegas guys to tell them there's been a change—oh," she added, placing her finger against her mouth, "plus, those old Haines affiliates have to get a notice to not even try to jack it from you with that eminent domain mess."

"We'll handle it, Cousin," Terrence said with a wide smile. "I like you a lot, a woman after me own heart."

"Trust me, Laura," Hakim said in a low, threatening tone not directed at her. "We'll handle it."

"Fantastic," Laura cooed, sweeping up Najira's hand as she leaned past James. "Now we can do the wedding without worrying about anything. I'm so glad we all met and just did this—and we wish you all the best." She looked around. "You guys are the ones who know development and real estate, not us. Just look at what you've built here—simply gorgeous."

"It is so pretty down here, I'm so ready to plan a small, private gathering," Najira mewed for theatrical effect, gazing lovingly at Steve.

"Whatever you want, babe, I'm down." Steve finished his wine quickly before a server removed his glass and handed him a flute.

"Then I guess it's settled," Laura said brightly.

"Cool," Jamal muttered and closed his eyes. "Damn, it didn't have to be all this."

"They cool, I'm cool," James said, and pounded Hakim's fist and then leaned in to get Terrence, Daoud, and Hector. "Good looking out. Y'all got that."

Laura smiled wider. "You can tell Scapolini that you held us hostage in your resort until we signed—please do that so he won't come looking for us. But if he ever comes down here, we'll have some explaining to do because it is absolutely breathtaking, whether a hostage or not," she said with a light chuckle, slathering on praise to ensure dissension in the Braithwaite ranks. "I bet the four of you custom designed each room with rice beds and Jacuzzis and everything . . . oh, I love the décor here—a wedding in your gardens will be beautiful."

With no small measure of satisfaction Laura watched Hakim and Daoud bristle at the mere concept that she could have been confused enough to believe that Terrence and his brother, Hector, might have had anything to do with building their resort. They seemed positively outraged, too, that their cousins made no attempt to correct her—and the fact that they didn't was also quite intriguing.

She nearly laughed aloud just watching the silent feathers fly at the female blunder. The affront was the final icing on the cake that she knew would begin the fall-out. Yet, watching Akhan and

Brother B's eyes stole any satisfaction that might have been gleaned from the minor triumph. The two old men were heart-broken, clearly knowing that their blood was about to go to war over land that was due to anyone but them.

"Good," Akhan murmured, raising his unsweetened iced tea. "Then let me propose a toast, since we have unity and complete cooperative economics."

Seizing the opportunity, James removed the camera from his jacket pocket. "I was saving this for the wedding, as best man, but since we're all one big happy family . . ."

Chapter
12

A bundle of sticks had just been scattered. The tension between the Braithwaites was palpable all through dinner, although they remained quite amiable toward everyone else. As the haute cuisine meal was completed, the groupings became extremely interesting for the tour.

Ever so discreetly, Hakim had maneuvered himself to fit between Akhan and Laura, leaving Terrence to lag behind with his brother, Hector, and their father, Brother B. Daoud, Jamal, Steve, and Najira were oddly dismissed into a group with Safia, who seemed to remain mute and terror-stricken as the family moved in a loose collective through the hotel with Hakim leading the way.

The establishment spared no luxury from its Scandinavian-inspired spa to Euro-chic clubs, with plantation-motif bedrooms that boasted huge antique armoires and high, overstuffed four-poster beds that seemed to have been transported from an era gone by. Details as minute as linens and towels had been carefully selected to present only the best. Everything had the mark of a craftsman upon it. Multiple pools and bars littered the property, as well as state-of-the-art exercise rooms, full tennis courts, saunas, and a pristine, private beach.

As Laura walked and openly complimented the eldest Braithwaite on his achievement, she secretly begged the question: with a mind like this, what could he have accomplished with resources that weren't dirty? She already knew the answer. Her admiration wasn't false, it was simply conflicted. She understood the economics of the game very well. Some groups of people had been kept out of legitimate enterprise, and thus muscled their way in. Scapolini was no different; none of organized crime was. The genesis of it all was the same—if you marginalize a group, it will find a way to first survive and then thrive, and the methodology might not be to the majority group's liking.

How many philosophical debates had happened with these business mavericks and her uncle Akhan? Laura couldn't even venture a guess. She could envision her uncle and Brother B on one side of the porch in the bush, arms waving with impassioned statements about the greater good of the people, while Terrence and Hector sat back smoking a spliff and Hakim and Daoud lobbied their case like expert attorneys.

Who might they have become if they'd had access to wealth and the resources of, say, someone of Donald Haines Jr.'s, ilk? Did seeing that access blithely taken for granted and squandered by rich kids at Oxford and Yale do something to Akhan's sons? Did having their noses pressed up against the glass, knowing they were smarter, take them to a dark place in their souls that eclipsed the last of the light their father tried to instill in them for their communities? Or did something else much less altruistic occur?

It was a question that nagged her, as much as what was the final straw that broke the camel's back. Her uncle Akhan and Brother B were clearly impressed with the monument of achievement that Hakim and Daoud had built, just as assuredly as they were conflicted to the depths of their souls.

Finally Hakim brought them around to the members-only club— a private casino that could circumvent the cumbersome gaming laws of the country because it was not open to the general public.

In the quiet recesses of Laura's mind as she watched Hakim Braithwaite tout his accomplishments, she wondered how many kilos and dead bodies it had taken to build a palace like this.

* * *

Donny clutched the telephone receiver and listened intently. He couldn't believe what was being said. The caller drew an agonized breath that brought tears to his eyes.

"Just stop," he whispered. "Please stop."

"I can't, Donny," Megan wailed. "I'm more than worried about you—I'm scared. This isn't you; this is the way your father rolled! These people are dangerous, and as your best friend who loves you I have a right to have you at least hear me out. We go back too far for you to close me out. It's not fair . . . it's not even you, Donny. I don't know who this person is."

"I don't know who this person is anymore, either," he said quietly.

"Then come visit me," Megan pleaded. "You're my family. Ever since college—you and I were the only ones who understood each other."

"That's the thing," he said with a sad chuckle. "You still have family; I don't."

"Yes, you do—me," she argued.

"You know what I mean . . . at least your parents finally accepted your lifestyle, mine never did. They never saw me."

"That's where you're wrong." Megan released a long sigh. "My father, no less than yours would have and did, protect me because I was his kid. But the reason he's in Kingston, five hours away, and I have a shop in Montego Bay is because he doesn't want my choices in his face. That's not acceptance, that's . . . tolerance. What I had to come to terms with was the fact that that's the best they could do. Sean is only in Kingston working for him because he's not been honest with the man. But I will say this, at least my father stood up for my life when it counted most, even if he turns a blind eye to my lifestyle. We have to accept some things too, Donny. They're human and flawed."

"Well at least yours stood up for you, mine—"

"Saved your fucking life." Megan's voice was strident as she pressed on. "Stop this depression spiral, Donny. Haines put

Laura in your path; put the best barracuda on the case to protect you and your interests—so how you can turn on her now—"

"That bitch is responsible for—"

"Making you see that your love, Alan, was poisoning you slowly through your mother's lover, Sutherland!"

Donny's sobs made Megan press harder to force the mental breakthrough, even if it might cause a nervous breakdown.

"What if she hadn't outed him, Donny? You would have died thinking you had the dread disease! You can't blame her for your mother's karma catching up to her. Your father tried to warn you. He might not have agreed with you, he might have been a real bastard, but he protected you as his son. And for all his totally screwed up ways and double-dealing and political intrigue, the one thing he tried to do was leave a mark somewhere on the planet where justice was served—now you want to undermine that legacy by forcing an eminent domain land grab? Are you insane! I won't stand by and allow it, Donny! Not as your friend! How many times had we sat in the dorms, or martini bars, espousing lofty rhetoric about idealism and the people, huh? You do this, and I am done with you, because you know better."

Donny closed his eyes and sat down on the sofa slowly. "Oh, Megan—I'm so lost. I remember. But it's too late . . . wheels are in motion."

"Please come here, before something tragic happens. I would die if anything happened to you. I want you on a flight tomorrow. "

Bradley sat in the Center City Holiday Inn Express hotel room with Townsend and turned off the recording.

"Houston, we have a problem," Bradley said without emotion. "Should I eliminate it?"

Townsend smoothed his hands down his face. "No. At least not the one you're thinking of." He stood and paced to the window.

"I think you know how important it is to protect our interests at all costs." Bradley fixed a hard gaze on Townsend.

"Donny is high-strung and unstable, but has an inexhaustible checkbook, courtesy old Hainsey. If you eliminate his longtime friend, Megan—the only link he has to stability—he'll know he's been watched and will freak."

"We can easily make it look like a boating accident, salmonella poisoning, E. coli . . ." Bradley smiled. "You know my specialty is coincidental demise."

"No, even if it doesn't appear suspicious, he'll go into a funk, Megan will become his martyr, and her opinions will be what he follows like some sort of death-bed promise. Megan isn't the danger, it's that Laura Caldwell bitch. If he gets down there and *she* gets her claws into him, then we've got a nightmare on our hands."

Bradley nodded. "Then it seems to me that I should get my beach wear together to make sure that doesn't happen."

When he got voice mail, Captain Bennett spoke rapidly in code into his cell phone receiver.

"Listen, it's next to impossible to find out info on guys behind the federal barrier, unless you're one of them. He retired with a clean record and commendations out the ass. But the word in the hallways is that he was always suspect. That's the best I can do right now."

"Whatduya mean they *found* Mikey?" The senior Caluzo sat back in his chair within his Vegas office and listened hard, completely disbelieving the information that was pouring through the telephone line. Quiet rage filled him as his nephew's death was described in grotesque detail. "He was trying to get back here, back home to Vegas where it was safe, when they did him, then?"

Syd Balifoni and Art Costanza shared a glance and silently waited until Caluzo hung up. Syd's thick, squat frame flanked Art's lean, gaunt build in plush leather chairs that faced Caluzo's desk as they studied his expression.

"What happened?" Balifoni asked, his eyes boring into Caluzo's.

"My nephew," Caluzo said in a garbled croak and then crossed himself. "That fucking Scapolini musta got to him."

"I don't understand how Scapolini could've known that we did his man, Rapuzzio—not this fast," Costanza said, his gaze ricocheting between Balifoni and Caluzo as he used his hands to punctuate his sentences.

Syd shook his head and kept his voice low and ominous. "This is all fucked up now. It was supposed to be simple. Mikey was to lure Rapuzzio into thinking we'd actually do business with the Jamaicans and cut him in. Then, we'd whack him and make it look like they did it. There'd be enough of a trail between Rapuzzio and the Jamaicans so that the family couldn't deny that's what happened. Mikey even got one of 'em stupid enough to break ranks with his own, thinking we'd work with him—greedy bastard. Then, with all the problems caused by the so-called Jamaicans, it would only be a matter of time before Scap went after them— being a hothead and all. Between the Jamaicans hitting Scapolini and Scap hitting them back, that branch would be so weak that they couldn't do shit when we cut our deal with the Washington boys."

"That's why I don't understand what happened," Caluzo said, scratching his scalp. "Something either screwed up with the Jamaicans and Joey, because word on the street is, they sprayed his house. So, when we hit Rapuzzio, why the hell did Joey come after one of us if he had every reason to believe it wasn't us? When they found Rapuzzio, the first thing Joey shoulda done was call the rest of the family and put out a call for war against the Jamaicans. I shouldn't be finding out about my nephew being dead in a fuckin' airport."

The threesome fell quiet for a moment and finally Syd sat forward.

"Joey is a pretty sharp ace. You think he got wind of our little meeting with key players in Philly and D.C.?"

Art glanced at Syd and then sent his gaze toward Caluzo again. "Nah . . . I think something happened at the police station. Like, what was Mikey doing getting picked up with Rapuzzio? Maybe Joey freaked and thought they said something to the cops and just decided to whack both of them—one for betrayal, one as a precaution he wouldn't squeal."

"But without informing the family, though?" Caluzo shook his head. "Where's the fucking trust—the old way of doing things? You think you have a problem, then you bring it to that branch of the family." He stood, hoisting his rotund form up from his chair. "I'ma tell you something—I've never felt comfortable about Lil' Joey taking over from Big Scap when he died. He moved up too fast and isn't patient enough, he's pissing people off."

"Yeah, and now we've got an even bigger problem," Syd said, looking from one don to the other. "We've got loose ends in Jamaica that sprayed Scapolini's house, and truthfully, for all we know, coulda had something to do with the argument that happened between Mikey and Rapuzzio. I don't like not knowing."

"We should send somebody down there to whack the big Rasta and cut off that dangling string." Caluzo walked over to the bar. "We need to make all of this shit go away . . . and at the family meeting, I'm gonna have some real hard questions for Joey."

"Are you shittin' me?" Scapolini said as he paced, pressing his cell phone to his ear. "The Hawaiian chick Tony was doing was some huge Rasta's woman?" He closed his eyes and leaned against the private bar in his Atlantic City suite. "So how does that translate into my house getting bullet sprayed, huh?"

Pure outrage throttled him as he listed to his henchman's report.

"Oh, get the fuck outta here! So, now, because Tony was my top guy, they send him a message by doing a drive-by on *my* property?" Joey pushed off the bar and began to pace. "No, I'll tell you what I think—Tony got greedy and tried to cut a deal with them, and the chick you're telling me about was supposed to keep tabs on him . . . obviously she did. So find the chick and lean on her until she explains everything she knows. Then I want every single one of those fuckers that had anything to do with this wiped out! But you don't touch Laura or her people until the meeting . . . she's gotta sign those papers with the old man. She didn't have anything to do with this part of it. Yeah, I'm sure."

He listened some more, growing more frustrated by the second.

"Well then send a cleanup team over there to Jamaica, if that's where the broad is!" Joey bellowed.

Sean picked up the telephone and hit speed dial, his eyes glued to the State Department computer screen. "Yo, Megan, your hunch played out. These are some very, very bad dudes."

"Talk to me, Sean. I've gotta know how deep Donny is into this."

"Okay," Sean said quickly. "Turn on your fax. I'm gonna send you a pic of Agent Bradley. You should show it to Donny, maybe see if Laura or her husband, James, know who he is. But according to his file, he won a bunch of citations, was clean as a whistle . . . then retired. That's where it gets real murky."

"How?" Megan hissed into the receiver, her nerves wire taut.

"It seems he became some sort of lobbyist, or something—job description totally murky. Donny has been sending him mega checks—"

"You pulled up Donny's banking info?"

"My kung fu is strong, girl," Sean said, laughing. "You want to do identity theft, you come to a hacker. You want top security clearance info and a hack down to the transaction level, you come to a maestro—me."

"Okay, okay, but get back to Donny's expenditures. Please, dear God, tell me he's not letting people just suck him dry."

"You've gotta talk to him, Megan," Sean said gently to his cousin. "Suck him dry? Maaan, they're gonna turn him into a husk, that's how bad they've been in his pocket."

"Oh, God, Sean, how bad?"

"Try seven figures bad and still climbing."

A gasp cut through the receiver.

"What's this ex-federal agent Bradley doing with the money? What service is he rendering?"

"I can't tell all that from the screens I have access to, there's no detail on the transfers, just who they go to. But it's to some other guy, John McHenry, who's cleaning Donny's clock."

"Who the hell is John McHenry?" Megan's voice snapped through the line.

"Are you sitting down?" Sean said sarcastically, "For two million, your final answer is—"

"Sean, c'mon, stop playing!" Megan groaned.

"George Townsend—ex-Micholi Foundation executive, old political hack, ex-Redevelopment Authority boy, who turned State's evidence in the trial against Alan Moyer in exchange for a walk and full lifestyle makeover as insurance baron John McHenry of Ohio."

"Oh . . . my . . . God."

"Yep. Taking campaign contributions and doing political fundraising, so to speak, because from his accounts I noticed some fairly substantial campaign checks going out—but, of course, nowhere close to what Donny had given him." Sean paused for a moment and then released his breath in a nervous rush. "Listen, Meg, call me crazy but the last time shit like this went down, a lot of bodies started showing up—you understand what I mean."

"Yeah, I do," she replied in a tense whisper.

"For this kinda cash, going to support who knows what, the stakes tend to be pretty high."

"I know," she said, her voice becoming small and tight. "That's why I wanted him to come down here."

"Well, my two cents says that you ought to call Laura, be sure she has the names and pics, so she can keep her eyes open when she gets back to the States—who knows what kind of old axe they have to grind? I mean, even if it's just to confirm her hunch, she's good people, Megan, and has a right to know that she wasn't off base."

"I'll call her, text message her, e-mail her, and might even stop by her hotel if I don't get her. But rest assured, I'll make sure that she knows."

Behind two highly polished mahogany and gleaming brass doors, Hakim showed them his penthouse pride and joy—the members-only club.

Taking up the entire footprint of the top floor of the building, with access to roof-top gardens replete with hot tubs, carp pools, and lush garden seating with two staffed bars, one could lay wagers on any sporting event in the world, or simply enjoy the basics of cards, roulette, or craps. The only thing Hakim had disallowed as a matter of personal choice was slot machines.

"I find the slots create an air of transient desperation," Hakim said, lifting his chin a little as he described his disdain for the machines. "The noise, the lack of skill . . . no. Not here. They can do that in Atlantic City or Vegas. My goal was to create a different and much more discriminating environment."

Laura watched Akhan purse his lips and she allowed her gaze to sweep the small but exclusive casino. Inarguable elegance permeated every aspect of the establishment, and it was impossible not to become momentarily mesmerized by the domino championships being heatedly played on large, flat screen HD-TV units strategically hung throughout the gaming floor.

As she watched the experts go at it, the notion that everything was a game took root in her. Everyone was playing it, and like dominoes that had been set to launch, one false move and they'd all fall one against the other. Laura smiled. She had set them all up, now the key was to hit the right one at the right time to make them begin to collide against each other. At the right angle, there would be no gaps or stops in the quickly moving lay-down.

"Fascinating, isn't it?" Hakim murmured, looking up at one of the screens with Laura.

"Absolutely amazing," she said quietly, not seeing the methodical championship game but rather the entertaining image of standing dominoes that was staged to fall.

"Not like the way we've seen it played growing up, though."

Hakim smiled at her and she offered him a chuckle in response, noting that their group had begun to disperse to peer at gambling options now that the full tour was over.

"Definitely not," she said, glimpsing Akhan from the corner of her eye. "Smack talking, and the way a player slammed the domino down on the table with attitude—it was an art form."

Hakim laughed warmly now and nodded. "It was that, indeed." In an odd turn of events, he glanced at Akhan across the room watching the elderly man sit and rest a while on a small velvet sofa. "You may never believe this, but I do miss those days sometimes. He was quite amazing, you know."

"He still is," Laura said quietly. "Don't speak as if he's gone yet."

"I'm sorry." Hakim's gaze searched her face. "It's force of habit. Something that made things easier to accept, thinking of him as dead to me. But now he's back like an honorable old spirit. . . . What am I to do with that, Laura?"

She sighed. "Enjoy the rest of the time left and get to know him."

"He doesn't know what he just did by giving away half of everything to Terrence and Hector."

Laura didn't flinch or blink. This was the conversation that she'd wanted to have and the sole reason she'd left the rest of the group, knowing Hakim would try to quietly lobby her on the side.

"I know," she finally said and sighed. "I know."

"You can fix it, you know," Hakim said quietly. "With patience."

She stared at him, trying to catch his meaning.

"His time is nigh. Things take a long time here in Jamaica. It could take us months to have the attorneys finalize the paperwork and by then, who knows, after much observance, as sole owner and executrix of my father's will, you might have had a change of heart."

Laura hesitated, not willing to commit but processing Hakim's strategy. If she didn't have to change the paperwork, at the same time could get them to back off, the only problem would be when she returned home to face Joey Scapolini.

"I could definitely have a change of heart," she said. "But I would need serious protection. Like I said at dinner, I'm going for quality of life, not quantity."

"That could most assuredly be arranged."

She nodded and accepted a glass of white wine from a serving tray that passed. "Do you have children and a wife, a family?"

He smiled. "My wife is from Belgium. Yes. I have two boys, ages four and six."

"Good. Then be nice to your father in his last days," Laura said, still smiling but her eyes not. "Show him pictures of his grandchildren, tell him the legitimate parts of your life, and I will make sure Terrence and Hector don't get a dime."

She sipped her wine calmly. It wasn't a lie what she'd said. True, it was leverage, blackmail . . . maybe even extortion, but he'd done no less and Akhan deserved so much more. The one thing for Hakim didn't understand was that he wouldn't get a dime, either. After seeing all that she'd just witnessed on the tour, there was no way in hell she was going to allow him to wipe out hardworking people's homesteads to put up a bastion of decadence for the rich and famous.

"I can do that, so can Daoud," Hakim said.

"Good," Laura said coolly as she sipped her wine. "That's all I want—for that old man to die at peace."

"Enjoy the casino. Maybe tomorrow you'll accept my offer to stay the rest of your time here on the house, wedding included. Once you've awakened and had breakfast, I'll have someone come to transfer you to our resort."

"Thank you . . . that's very hospitable of you," Laura said in her most even tone, knowing that not only would she and her family be under a pretty version of house arrest, but surveillance was a sure bet, too. However, without much choice they both knew she had to comply.

Hakim nodded at her and walked away to begin his task of acknowledging his father. Laura was galled. That was a first, bribed with a sweet land deal to treat your elderly parent right. When she saw Terrence break away from his conversational group to approach her, she already knew the deal. Even still, she wanted to hear what his offer was all about. More important, since he was the loose cannon, she needed to get inside his head.

"So, lovely cousin Laura," Terrence said with a half smile, "I see

Hakim has been hard at work pressin' you to change his father's final wishes, eh?"

She laughed, already liking his style. "Yeah."

He wagged a finger at her clucking his tongue, his smile wide and his eyes hard. "But you know it is baaad luck to go against the wishes of a dying man."

She heard the threat loud and clear and yet her smile didn't waver. "I'm very superstitious, rest assured. I know."

He nodded. "Good. Because you're too beautiful and have too much to enjoy in dis life yet to find yourself at odds with de ancestors."

She nodded. "That's why I'm always prepared for any eventuality, and try to always respect my elders," she said in her most eloquent tone.

"Den it's all good." He seemed to relax and gave her a quizzical look. "I don' suppose you smoke . . . or want anyting for de head?"

"With all this mess going on," she said chuckling. "Not a chance."

"All de more reason to relax . . . chill."

"Thank you, but no, thank you," she said, tipping her glass against his in a salute. She knew Hakim had seen it, and that was just what she wanted, each to wonder. So, to hold him, she went for something that might deepen the conversation and his very fleeting trust. "Can I ask you something though?" she said, moving in closer.

"You can always ask, but I don' promise to tell." He stepped in even closer, encroaching upon what she was used to as personal distance and appropriate space.

"What happened?"

He blinked and looked at her seeming puzzled.

"I mean, I don't understand," she pressed on, gazing up into his eyes. "Thirty years seems so long . . .Uncle is a realist, he knows what goes on in the world—so why not work with his sons and nephews-in-law? I don't get it."

Terrence's face held an odd mixture of awe, relief, and an emotion that bordered on being unsure. She'd cast out the sensitive question, positioned in such a way as to make him think she was all right with their illegal business operations, and simply couldn't comprehend why Akhan and Brother B were not. Terrence rubbed his chin and chuckled, hedging, obviously deciding how much detail to go into, if any at all. Laura waited, her gaze steady and probing, also knowing that Terrence, more than anything, wanted to win her allegiance against Hakim. Giving her a satisfactory answer could, in his mind, deepen the trust.

"Ever'ting 'appened a long time ago—old family business, you know?" he said, glancing over her shoulder to where Hakim stood with Daoud and Brother B.

Laura followed his line of vision knowing that the closer Hakim appeared to be getting to his father, the more the possibility loomed that he could convince the old man to reverse his emotional display at dinner and to keep the inheritance structured the way it had been. Of all the people here, Terrence and Hector had the most to lose if she or Akhan met untimely demises.

"I know all this goes way back, and is probably not so important," she said, withdrawing to make him think he'd offended her by taking too long to tell her something. "Besides, it's really none of my business. I just thought it was a shame and wanted to . . . overstand." She offered him a slight smile that he returned as she watched him struggle with the decision on what to say.

True, he could apply violence and pressure her with threats, but a lawyer still had to do the paperwork cleanly, or everything could be contested. He knew it; she knew it. Better still, Hakim knew it. The only thing none of them knew was that they weren't listed in any of the papers to receive jack shit. However, a phony set would be produced, seals and all, courtesy of Akhan's fast thinking and ID creation contacts in the hood—something the old man had put in place long before he'd gotten on a plane.

"It began as philosophical differences," Terrence finally said, going behind a wall of code, but giving her an explanation, nonetheless. "What can I say? And, as long as no one got hurt," he added with an indifferent shrug, "it was all so much rhetoric."

"Uhmmm," Laura said, taking a sip of wine. "I gather someone got hurt?"

"Not just someone—Hakim and Daoud's younger sister . . . dat old man's princess. Allegra, I tink, was 'bout twenty-two. Had muled many packages in latex—you catch my drift?" He paused and waited until Laura nodded. "Those were the early days, mon. But dis one time a balloon busted inside her. De old men turned dey backs from dat point on. Had said if anyting ever 'appened like dat, dey would." He sighed and gave another philosophical shrug. "De one ting I have always admired, but always hated about Akhan and me fadder—dey are undoubtedly men of dere word."

Laura's gaze slid from Terrence's to the small family gathering by the roulette wheel. She nodded thoughtfully, knowing all that she did about her uncle . . . knowing what little she did about Brother B, his best friend. Akhan's daughter caught in some bull, even being put at risk by her brothers and cousins for money—probably Hakim's plan, Terrence's powder. No wonder the old men walked away and wiped their hands once their male code of honor had been so thoroughly violated. Now it all made so much sense. This was more than Akhan's political ethics and beliefs in what was fundamentally just for the people. This was personal.

"Well, hey," Laura said, touching his arm to engender more trust. "That was a long time ago, God rest her soul. They paid, you paid, I see no reason why things can't be cool now, do you?"

"I like how you tink, cousin. Let me buy you some chips . . . play the house for a while—you and your man."

"Thank you. Maybe I will try a little roulette. I don't know anything about cards or craps beyond standing there as good luck and blowing on the dice."

"Don't even come near me to tell me shit," Jamal said between his teeth as he watched a craps game, sipping a Hennessey.

He moved away from Safia, whose eyes shone with a desperate quality as her gaze darted between him and the otherwise occupied Braithwaite brothers, keeping special focus on Terrence as he spoke to Laura with his back toward them.

"I had to," she whispered quickly as she came in closer to him but kept her eyes on the table.

"All I know is you almost got a brother killed, so I ain't trying to hear shit."

"I got played," she said quietly, glancing around quickly. "I don't wanna die." She looked at him, her eyes wide and filling with tears. "I didn't realize how deep things were until it got insane. I only had part of the story, Jamal . . . you gotta believe me. For an endless supply of coke and some cash, I figured I was just a female to all of them, so it didn't matter. Then, as I overheard more and more, I realized how deep the shit was that I was standing in."

He glanced around quickly. "First of all, fuck you. I'm not trying to die, either. Second of all, I can't make any promises beyond telling you, I'll see what I can do."

"Both your partners are ex-cops, right?" she said, her voice low and desperate. "Don't they have some amnesty programs, some relocation thing they could do?"

"Like I said, I'll see what I can do—but you need to drop some science in my ear and know that from this point on it's a one way conversation with you talking, me listening, and you stepping away from me if the big man even glances this way."

Chapter
13

Akhan's progressively weakening condition made it easy for everyone to beg off and call it an early night. Mission accomplished, the Braithwaites didn't seem to mind. The discussions during and after dinner, at least, ensured them one night of amnesty until they had to move in the morning.

Still, James and Steve insisted on checking everyone's room. There had been no breeched entry—the little pieces of paper, threads, buttons, tiny elements put into the door jambs as the room doors had been closed and do not disturb signs hung showed the rooms had not been tampered with.

Although Laura was so mentally fatigued she was ready to pass out, James held up his hand, made the sign of a zipper over his mouth to denote that the room could still be bugged, and pulled out his cell phone the moment they'd crossed the threshold. He pointed to the slightly ajar sliding glass doors. She nodded and whipped her cell phone out of her purse, noting that she had several waiting voice mails and text messages.

Sending a text message from across the room, James stared at her: *Make it seem like we've been so quiet because you were kissing me, so I can check the room.*

She nodded and text messaged him back: *Done.* But she smiled and walked over to give him a long, languid kiss and then sent him another message: *Make it authentic—talk to me in code while we hunt the room for bugs.*

He gave her a thumbs-up signal. "I've been waiting to do that all night, girl."

She smiled and sent a text message to both Steve and Jamal, telling them to be sure to check their balcony entrances. "Good, because I'm so relieved now that all that family drama is settled."

"Uh-huh," James said, going along the frames of furniture and behind all mirrors and artwork on the walls. "You think you can relax now and start enjoying this like it's a real vacation?"

"Aw . . ." she said, forcing herself to laugh as she saw Steve and Jamal's responses that their balconies were sealed tight. "It has been a while, hasn't it?" She sent a quick text to James: *We were the only ones breeched.*

He nodded. "Yeah, it's been too long." James got down on the floor and looked under the bed, growing frustrated.

"There was just so much on my mind," Laura said, her hands sweeping the dresser's interiors as she quietly opened and closed them. "I'm just glad that Akhan came to his senses and is going to split everything fairly. I don't want this problem, James. I was serious about what I said at dinner."

"I know," he replied, not looking at her, but searching the closet. "But I don't think Hakim and Daoud liked having their share cut down from ninety-five percent with five going to you as executrix to fifty in order to share with his cousins."

Laura and James shared a look and she nodded her approval.

"I know, but again, what can I do? Hakim came to me on the side to ask me to wait on the papers . . . you know, until his father passes . . . which could simplify things. But then Terrence came over while you and Steve were playing blackjack, and he wants me to rush it through, of course. Here's the thing, frankly," she added. "Terrence frightens me a little, even though he's cool people. But we're caught in the middle again, baby. What's gonna happen if they find out they've been double-crossing each other?"

"I'm not sure what you mean," James said, still searching. "Like, just asking the co-owner of Xavier to hook a brother up isn't exactly a double cross."

She stopped moving around the room; James looked at her hard knowing that she was about to lob a verbal grenade.

"It was something Joey Scapolini said to me that gave me pause . . . like, I think one of the Braithwaites might have cut a side deal with the Italian Mob—not that I give a damn, and not that it's my business, but that's why he was leaning on me so hard to sell to him. I'm not going there, James. Family first and always. But I don't want to make the wrong decision and find out Akhan and Brother B got played because one of the sons is in bed with the Italians."

James wiped his forehead and mouthed the word "Whew!" to denote that she'd really dropped a bomb. Laura covered her mouth and stifled a chuckle.

"Well, listen, baby," James said, sending her a text message as he spoke. "Like you said, it isn't your business, you don't have to decide tonight, and you need to relax."

She read his message that said: *Nice.* She typed back: *Thank you.*

"You're right," she finally said, and then released a little groan, walking away to rub her neck and begin searching in the nightstands. "That feels soooo good."

He smiled widely and sent her a quick text: *No fair.*

She mouthed the words, "Hurry up, then." He mouthed back, "Okay, I'm trying."

"I love making you feel good," he said, now searching harder for the device he was sure had to be in their room.

"Well, let me get my dress off, first. You ruined the last one."

He made a face at her and she quietly laughed and stuck out her tongue at him.

"Then take it off for me, baby," he said, but stopped for a moment to look at her.

She winked at him; he mouthed back, "For real."

"All right," she murmured sexily, and complied.

He turned over the lamp carefully and noticed that the base was a little loose. "Damn . . ." he said in a low, sensual tone. "With that get-up, you're gonna have to ride." He smirked and showed her the device.

She got it. To keep their cover it would have to seem that the lamp fell during wild sex.

"Take off your pants," she demanded, but then sent him a text: *"Both brothers are at odds. More than one could have planted a device. Keep looking."*

James closed his eyes and silently cursed.

"Oh, yeah, like that . . ." she said, getting up on the bed so the mattress would sound and she let her smaller arm fit behind the headboard and gently pulled the wire. She gave James the thumbs-up. "Oh, baby . . . shit, just put it in!"

He kicked over the lamp as she began jumping up and down on the bed, and stomped the device. "Oh, God, woman . . . get it—hold onto the headboard so you can work it."

Laura ripped the wireless device off but kept making the bed sound until he smashed it under his foot. They both stopped moving. He grabbed the small electronic cells and went into the bathroom to flush them down the toilet. When he returned he had a sheepish grin on his face.

"That shit is giving me a bad rep," he murmured in her ear. "No damned foreplay, caveman style, and two minutes before I crashed and burned."

She laughed hard and brushed his mouth with a kiss. "Aw, but I know the truth."

"It's a man thing, you wouldn't understand," James said, chuckling. "Check your voice mail, mine has blown up."

"Well, if either of the Braithwaite brothers gives you a smug expression tomorrow, you'll have a good idea of which one was listening." Laura looked at her text messages first. "Megan said to turn on the laptop you just purchased. She's sending a pic to my old e-mail address she had."

She watched James get out the equipment while the telephone was pressed to his ear and she also listened to Megan's long messages that went on in three segments.

"Donny is coming to Jamaica tomorrow," Laura said, and then

quickly pressed her cell phone to James's ear, replaying the messages for him.

James handed her his phone and did the same. "Listen to the conversation Jamal just had with that chick from Maui—who really comes by way of Vegas . . . used to roll with Rapuzzio and then tried to get cute and now is scared."

"What?" Laura whispered. "Oh, shit . . ."

"Yeah, so you'd better tell Megan to not contact us anymore— no sense in putting her, Kaitland, Sean, or even Donny in the line of fire."

"Definitely not."

Practically speechless, they both listened as the new information invaded their ears before stabbing into their brains. Multitasking, James opened up a laptop connection to the Internet and Laura immediately found Megan's file.

Soon the image of a tall, athletically lanky officer with dark hair and moody, intense eyes filled the screen. James and Laura both stared at the computer screen and then each other.

"He was in our house in Philly, Laura. He was one of the feds crawling around your place on Pennsylvania Avenue when Rick broke the story."

"I know," Laura said, returning her gaze to the screen. "What's Captain Bennett's e-mail address?" Her fingers raced across the keys as she prepared the download Sean had sent. "I'm also sending a copy of this pic to my media man, Rick, at the network, for him to sit on, like old times, until something definitive breaks. You call Cap, I'll call Rick, give Steve the low-down by phone so he can bounce it to Jamal for Akhan and Brother B. If they're watching our rooms, they don't need to see us running into each other's rooms conferencing."

James pulled out the camera and handed it to her. "While you're at it, might as well give Megan, Cap, and your man at the network these Kodak moments, too, just to be on the safe side."

Laura beamed at him. "That was such a *smooth* move—did I tell you I love you today?"

* * *

Rick sat up in bed, groggy, and listened to the information Laura forced into his ear. He stroked his wife's hair as she lightly stirred and then left her side to go turn on his computer.

"Well, hello to you, too," he said with a yawn. "I don't hear from you in months, but when I do, it's always a doozy! God bless you, hon, for making this man's career over the years."

Captain Bennett hung up his phone and got out of bed. The call from James made his already disquieted mind spin with more possibilities. Bradley, and then all the crazy shit the chick Safia from Vegas had told Jamal Hewitt. Everything had to be substantiated, of course. Donny Haines in Jamaica? Why? This was definitely out of his jurisdiction, and much as he hated to admit it, he'd have to kick this up a notch to a branch that could do international. Scapolini had made bail within hours and had walked. It would take a multi-state, coordinated effort to monitor all those wiseguys' travel movements, and with the limited resources he had departmentally, there was no way he could tip off James and Steve that trouble might be headed their way.

Intense frustration made him grind his teeth as he stood in the bathroom in his striped pajamas taking a leak. All he needed was a little break, one small favor that could be called in from somewhere. *Anywhere.* Didn't God ever hear the prayers of an honest man? For his entire career he'd been busting bad guys for lesser offenses than they'd deserved to do time for—and it grated him no end to know that they were dirty as sin, but he couldn't drop the full weight of the law on them. They knew it; he knew it; the DAs cried in their beer about it, but there was nothing he could do.

When the phone rang a second time, he hurried with the task of finishing and quick-rinsing his hands, bellowing at the inanimate object as though it had the choice of whether or not to ring. "I'm coming, I'm coming! Gimme a break, will ya!" he yelled, reaching the cordless unit before it went into voice mail. "Yeah. Bennett here."

"Detective Bennett, this is Richard Montgomery from the U.S.

State Department, stationed in Jamaica, West Indies. A while back, your men helped save my daughter's life. I'd like to help your cause, in any way possible. Please go turn on your computer."

"Are we done wreaking havoc for the night?" James murmured, watching Laura boot down the laptop in her black lace strapless bra and thong panties, thoroughly appreciating the view.

"Yeah, I guess," she said, shoving the unit onto the nightstand beside the huge king-size bed.

He traced her cheek with his finger. "You know it's gonna get real intense tomorrow. The move over to Hakim's gilded cage will mean eyes everywhere, not to mention, when Donny's flight comes in, the entire landscape could change again."

She sank against his chest and closed her eyes. "I know," she murmured, listening to his heartbeat. "I'm also worried about Akhan. He refuses to go see a doctor until he plays out this hand and Najira walks down the aisle, but all of this is taking a toll on him. I can see it in his eyes."

"I know," James said quietly, stroking her silky curls. He kissed the crown of her head and allowed his palm to slide from her hair over her shoulder and arm to revel in the feel of her satiny skin as he caressed her back. "Just rest, baby," he said, leaning his head against the wall with his back propped up on pillows against the headboard. "Let your mind be still for a little while. We set a *lot* of balls in motion tonight, and sometimes you just have to do nothing for a moment to see where they're gonna land."

"You're right," she murmured, losing herself in the hypnotic feel of his warm hand painting liquid heat up and down her spine as he stroked her back in a lazy, repetitive pattern. "We have this moment between drills, and I have to just let it go until tomorrow."

"Yep," he whispered, brushing the crown of her head with another gentle kiss.

"I love you," she murmured, and kissed his broad chest through his shirt. "You're the only one who ever made me feel safe . . . or understood me when I was crazy."

He chuckled slowly and the sound reverberated through his chest and around his heartbeat to coat her ear. "I love you, too, and who knows, maybe because I'm crazy about you, that's why I understand your brand of crazy when I see it."

His comment made her smile, the sound of his voice traveled through her as a sensual vibration.

"Mmmm . . . and who knows when the next time will be that we can do this," she whispered, running her hand over his nipples through his shirt and flipping open a button slowly with one hand.

"Then maybe I'll get a chance to redeem myself, since what they caught on tape was so lame."

She laughed low and deep and slowly as she continued to open his shirt and then pressed her mouth to the smooth skin beneath it that covered what felt like pure granite. "I think that can be arranged."

"Good," he murmured, pulling her up to him and lowering his mouth to hers. "The last time was a quickie . . . and I would really like to set the record straight with my wife."

"Good," she whispered into their kiss.

The heat of his hands melted her as they slid down her back to work on her bra hooks. There was something about him that just blotted out everything else when he got like this . . . determined, patient, driven, yet controlled. Each kiss planted with expert precision along her earlobe and neck, that right spot in the bend of her neck, lightly dusting her shoulder and collarbone with damp heat until her nipples stung for his mouth's attention.

James Carter was a man who knew what he was doing, knew her every nuance, and knew how to transport her from a mental prison of worry to sheer ecstasy. With the tip of his tongue that had just found one tight areola to circle, he left wet heat without touch at the straining peak. Hands designed by a generous God to hold her just right, a slightly rough thumb rubbing back and forth over distended skin, a lazy, crazy-making pattern that drew a gasp.

"You've redeemed yourself," she said on a light pant as he gently pressed her breasts together and laved both nipples at once.

"No, I haven't," he murmured against her fevered skin and then slid down further to kiss her belly. "Lemme get out of this suit."

The loss of his body heat almost made her cry out, but the sight of him slowly stripping away his clothes definitely helped. He looked like a marble statue that had been dipped in bittersweet chocolate, and as her gaze traveled from his heavy-lidded eyes down the length of him, in reflex she licked her lips. When she did that, she literally saw his groin contract hard, so much so that his erection jerked as though giving her a slight nod.

Acute need for him burned the saliva away from her mouth, parching her throat until it seemed as though all the fluid within her converged to spill from the swollen nexus between her thighs. Yet, he took his time, just as he'd promised he would, slowly returning to the bed in a way that made her simply close her eyes.

Somehow he'd found a way to take the moments she cherished and create an altered state of agonized eternity with them, stretching out time and her consciousness with his full lips sweeping her skin, his tongue laving distended flesh, his teeth softly nibbling sensitive zones while his heavy, blanketing warmth covered her.

She spread her legs wide for him as he found the edge of her thong at her hip, rolling it away from her in maddening increments between deep kisses that followed the smile line of her pelvis. What had just been heavy expulsions of breath soon had voice as he unlocked a low moan that had been trapped inside her chest. His slow rolling tongue transformed that sound yet again into a high-pitched gasp. But there would be no rushing him as his wide-spread fingers caressed and opened the clenched halves of her ass while his tongue carefully opened her fever-drenched slit.

Head tilted back, spine arched, she could feel her eyes roll toward the back of her skull. His attention sent radiating desire through her, making her breasts ache for his caress as he gave all his attention to her bud. Unable to bear it, her hands covered her breasts as she rhythmically lifted her hips against his tongue. Teasing her, he would remove it, denying her the soft, flickering friction, to give it to her burning inner thighs, or to unexpectedly French kiss her opening long and deep until she groaned.

Writhing under his hold, she felt the pad of his thumb in her exact tempo while he continued the languid French kiss between her legs. Nearly out of her mind, she let her thumbs mirror his rhythm against her erect nipples, causing her to thrash, but when she did, he slowed down.

She was so close, yet he was drawing it out so long that tears wet her lashes, and she couldn't catch her breath. Her stomach was contracting; so was everything else below it. She needed him to suck it, lick it, stroke it faster, yet he was still bent on messing with her mind. Yeah, he knew what he was doing and it was so not fair . . . but so damned good.

His name escaped her lips on a quick expulsion of air, and she arched hard with a moan when that made him do what she needed. More aggressive now, he captured her bud with his mouth delivering the attention she'd craved. Close to the brink, every muscle tight as a wire, finding anywhere on him that she could touch, she begged him not to play with her mind. "Don't stop."

It was a tense command spoken through her teeth—one that he heeded not a moment too late. The convulsion hit her in spasmodic waves like dominoes falling in a fast running pattern of multiple hits. Duration and the strength of the sensations made her cry out, which only made him blanket her, enter her hard and ride her slowly to start the spiral all over again.

Sure hands gripped her ass, spread fever up her spine, and flatpalmed the sway in her back. His mouth covered hers, tongue searching for its mate, returning her own sweet lacquer, sending shudders through her as he moved so slowly it almost hurt. His moan chased hers back down her throat, his thick thighs spreading hers even wider until her legs anchored around his waist. Her caresses became feral as she tried to pull him into her faster, returning his long, deep strokes in punishing, quick thrusts.

She couldn't keep her mouth on his; the spiral of pleasure was out of control. Climaxes built, crested, and tumbled her down into a shuddering mass while he moved like a steady piston—rock-solid, unwavering, refusing to be rushed.

Reduced to babbling his name between entreaties he ignored, she held him tightly and sought his ear, trying to bargain, trying to negotiate, trying to get him to hear her plea. "Oh, God, James . . . I can't take it."

When she felt him shudder, his breath hitch, and then increase the force of each thrust as though he'd shifted gears, she knew he'd heard her. His entire body was slick with sweat and she ran her hands down his hot back, coaxing his hurried return. Beyond words, he redoubled his grip on her, repositioned his hands and weight to gain better leverage, and she shut her eyes tightly preparing for the ride.

They'd found that moment in between moments, that surreal place where love transcends lust and lust illuminates love, where muscles cramp with fatigue but one still can't stop moving or get enough. His voice pushed air from his lungs in time with driving thrusts, becoming a low, sensual chant of heat. Droplets of sweat dripped from his chin when his head fell back, and she was almost sure that they sizzled and burned away the moment they made contact with her skin. An expression etched in agony covered his face, then he suddenly gathered the duvet in one fist as though trying to keep from falling. She reached for his ass and pulled him to her hard and fast, and it buckled him, making him crash.

Two seconds behind him, the convulsion that stole up his back and twisted his face slammed him so completely that she thought she might need to put a spoon in his mouth. The seizure was relentless, trapping him in a silent scream. It was several seconds before his voice returned post-mortem, triggering her wails that dissolved into husky moans. The dominoes were falling, were slipping, sliding, thundering one against the other until she rose up off the bed. Every shuddering gasp only seemed to make him heave against her more to chase the very last tremble like a junkie.

His head dropped and she caught his face in her hands and kissed him hard, then let him collapse. He was breathing like he needed to be on a ventilator; so was she. After-shock tremors made their bodies twitch in unison; after several minutes he rolled over and pulled her on top of him, yet remained lodged deep inside her.

"Damn," he murmured with his eyes closed. "Redeemed?"

"Uh-huh," she gasped in two parts. "Reputation salvaged."

Hakim steepled his fingers before his mouth as he sat behind his gleaming, mahogany desk and Daoud leaned forward, both listening to the recording again.

"You heard what she said about Scapolini and the possibility that someone may have cut a side deal," Hakim said, his gaze cold.

Daoud nodded. "But she's leaning with us—she told her husband that Terrence frightened her."

"He frightens most people, which is his objective, after all."

"Too bad the lamp fell," Daoud said with a sly smile. "I would have liked to hear the rest of the conversation."

"I think they were done talking by that point," Hakim said with a half smile. "Lucky bastard."

Daoud chuckled. "That's our *cousin*, you know."

Hakim's smile widened. "Oh, yes. I will have to keep that in mind."

"You gwan hafta ease up on de threats, mon," Hector said, his voice tight as he rolled a spliff in their resort villa. "De woman is gwan get spooked, but she seems cool. Let her jus' follow de ole man's wishes wit no more drama, and we'll be phat. Might have liked to have known her and de rest before dis."

Terrence turned off the recording. "Yeah, mon. Dat's one lucky motherfucker."

Hector handed him the thick joint. "Don't go dere 'bout Laura, even if she does give you wood. Dat's our cousin, mon."

"Twice removed," Terrence argued and fired up the jay. "It's not like we grew up wit her; now that would be perverted. But since we just met, I'm jus' admiring de beauty." He pulled a deep toke in between words and fought to hold in the pungent smoke while still trying to talk. "Knocked the damned backboard out so hard we lost the signal." With a big smile, he saluted the air by raising the reefer that was pinched between his thumb and fore-finger. "James Carter got my utmost respect. I would have done no less."

Hector laughed and lit his jay. "Next time have our boy put the bug somewhere it ain't gwan get crushed—like the damned closet or behind a painting."

"*Irie*," Terrence said, chuckling through a thick plume of smoke. "My bad."

Chapter
14

Morning lit the sky way before she was ready to cope with it, but there was no turning it back. It had made a grand pronouncement parting the sky curtain of dusty rose-orange clouds over the pounding surf, and then streamed in golden sunshine until sleep was impossible. Her husband's warmth circled around her in a delicious spoon, his heartbeat thudding against her spine, a morning erection nudging her to waking consciousness.

"Good morning to you, too," she murmured with a little laugh. "Want some coffee?"

He chuckled and kissed her shoulder. "Hmmm . . . in a little while."

"Man, you need to stop . . . we have to move hotels and deal with the whole next level of the game today."

"Shusssh," he murmured, kissing her shoulder and filling his hands with her breasts. "I'm not fully awake . . . can't hear what you're saying until I've had my coffee."

Megan rushed up to Donny, leaving Kaitland and Sean where they stood. She threw her arms around his neck and hugged him until he laughed.

"First we get you some sunblock, dude, and then some shorts and a T-shirt—out of those winter clothes, and we find us a good spot on the beach." Megan held Donny away from her and smiled brightly. "And an umbrella drink."

"How about in reverse order?" Donny said with the first genuine smile he'd owned in over a year.

Sean accepted the pass-off from Megan, giving Donny a handshake-hug. "Reverse order, for sure, dude. Umbrella drink is first priority."

"Meet my partner," Megan gushed. "This is Kaitland. Donny is like my brother."

Donny smiled at her and then simply gave her a hug. "Oh, I like the way you make Megan smile. I know we'll be fast friends."

"I've heard so much about you—stay with us, please. Why go back?" Kaitland said.

Donny nodded and looked around at what had become his makeshift family. "I should have done this years ago."

"Donny, believe me, so should I." Megan simply touched his cheek and then slung her arm over his shoulder as they began to trudge through the airport to collect his luggage.

They didn't see the tall gaunt man with dark hair and hard eyes hidden behind his sunglasses.

Akhan sat across from Brother B on the balcony overlooking the surf. He sipped a small glass of papaya juice and stared at the horizon as he spoke. "You know it has begun in earnest now, my friend. Their being nice to us last night only made it more difficult . . . made it easier to remember what time allowed us to forget."

Brother B nodded. "I'm prepared. I lost dem long ago and I am old, so if I die, what of it?"

Akhan nodded. "My worry is that we won't for a long while after this and the mind and memories create hell."

Safia rolled over and stretched, and then untangled herself from Terrence's loose hold. Her body ached and her head was throbbing. His king-size waterbed now felt like a prison, and his dead weight on her was making her legs go numb. Too much liquor and weed from the night before caused a weird combination of nausea and hunger. Coffee was calling her name for the hangover, and chocolate chip cookies, cake, maybe Danish; anything sweet right now was a must.

Naked and somewhat disoriented, she trudged into the wide, ivory-hued kitchen to start the coffeemaker and then suddenly realized that she needed to pee. Quickly setting up the Braun, she did a little dance to keep from wetting herself when she ran the water to fill the unit. But she wanted to make the aroma float through the palatial villa while she went to the bathroom and got in the shower.

Dashing across the tiles and polished blond hardwood floors, she entered a guest powder room, not chancing she'd make it all the way back to the master bath.

The open sliding glass doors off the kitchen deck had allowed the morning breeze to blow in a fragrant hibiscus scent with sea salt air throughout the luxurious home. This was how she wanted to live. True, she felt bad about Tony, but in all fairness, he'd played himself. At least Terrence was his own boss, not a flunky who had to do the bidding of someone above him. Although there was something about Jamal . . . something that drew her, even though he wouldn't commit. He'd be perfect, in fact, if he could figure out how to extricate her from mobsters and dealers, so that she could live like this without the dangers.

Safia closed her eyes as she quickly sat down on the commode and began to tinkle. She sighed heavily, wishing all the deals she'd cut and the men she'd slept with would just simply go away. She didn't open her eyes as the bathroom door opened. Annoyance swept through her—Terrence was such a pig. She couldn't even pee without the kinky bastard wanting to watch, and this morning it seemed like too much of an effort to start an argument through a hangover that could get her beaten.

"What?" she finally said, opening her eyes to acknowledge him since he wouldn't go away.

It took a second for her mind to catch up to the image before her—two seconds past too late.

"We oughta get moving I guess, because they'll be sending a car for us soon," Steve said quietly, bringing Najira a cup of tea to settle her stomach. "How're you feeling?"

"Okay," she murmured, her complexion looking ashen. "It passes after a while."

He set the tea down on the small balcony table and came up behind her, wrapping his arms around her from behind. His fingers gently splayed over her small belly bump and he closed his eyes as he laid his head on her shoulder.

"I'm going to make sure nothing happens to you, Jira. I swear I'll die trying."

She hugged his arms tighter to her. "Please don't say that. I don't want anybody to die."

Both Laura and James started and ran in from the balcony when the pounding began on their room door. They'd dressed and ordered room service, but it sounded like a raid not a food delivery. James quickly stashed a nine in the back of his cargo shorts waistband and pulled his T-shirt over it.

Flipping the security bolt, he opened the door only as far as it would allow, and saw Jamal's stricken face—then slammed the door shut to fully unlatch it so Jamal could barrel through the door.

"They did 'em both," Jamal said, eyes wide, his voice low and tense. He was sweating, eyes darting back and forth. "It was too fucked up."

"Slow down, man," James said quietly. "Did who?"

Laura stepped forward.

"Shot Safia on the toilet—right in her head. Hector never even saw it coming. He was asleep in bed. The only reason Terrence made it was because he got up to take a whiz and called her—she didn't answer and he heard movement, got suspicious, and got his nine and headed toward his brother's room . . . then started hollering when he saw Hector."

"Oh, my God . . ." Laura looked at James. "Hakim, you think he would?"

"Anything's possible," James muttered. "But Hakim doesn't strike me as a guy to go for glaringly obvious—not right after a meeting like that."

"No, I'm with James. That's who Terrence called, anyway. That's how I know. He called Hakim, and Hakim let Brother B know one of his sons took three to the chest and one to the head. I was in the room with him and my pop when he got the news. Terrence is rolling to the hillside up in the bush with a whole buncha motherfuckers who be up there. The only reason they were rolling solo and light was because they were down here meeting with us, and according to Brother B, normally they don't roll like that. So, Terrence is off da hook blaming everybody for what happened, feel me? Now Hakim is all paranoid, thinks Terrence could do anything. He says he wants us moved ASAP. A gorgeous woman is dead even tho' she was a gold diggah. Damn. This shit is getting crazy, y'all."

"He's got more than three hundred soldiers in the mountains with everything from automatics to rocket propelled grenade launchers, and the area is booby trapped and mined. There's no way we can go up there after him to force a conversation. The crazy SOB believes what he believes, and until we can prove other- wise—"

"I do not have to prove shit!" Hakim yelled, rounding his desk to point at Daoud. "We had no motive to go after Hector and the woman—even with all the bullshit going on with Xavier's proper- ties. If we wanted him dead, the timing would be suspicious and would give the old man pause . . . might freak out Cousin Laura, and she's softening. So this bull doesn't make good business sense, something that Terrence, in all his hotheaded, undisci- plined responses to situations, could never grasp."

Hakim strode across his expansive office with his hands behind his back. "Why would we do something that could jeopardize a peaceful conclusion? We can wait the old man out, have the lawyers delay—since *dis is de islands, mon*," he added with a thick Jamaican lilt. "Or, if we were to be brutal and impatient, it would be so easy to have a sick old man fall gravely ill and perish. What would that cost? A few thousand to a coroner? A switch of his insulin. Easy. But we were trying to handle this in a civilized fashion, so as not to have any street violence spill over into the tourists' areas that we're heavily invested in during all the major tournaments and events that rake in millions."

"I know this," Daoud argued. "You know this. But if Terrence doesn't believe it, then what good is the logic? A war is imminent."

"A war has always been imminent. Fuck him. Call in our security forces and brief them."

"And if he decides to take hostages to push through the paperwork quickly?"

The two brothers' gazes met in an intense deadlock.

Hakim's gaze narrowed to a withering glare. "Just go get the family and bring them here to protect our goddamned investment."

"Cops will be looking for me—fucking Jamaican authorities, mon. Like I shot my own brother and his woman, and they'll make it some bullshit setup like a fight over a female. You know dis!" Terrence shouted in the phone to one of his most trusted lieutenants as he drove like a maniac toward the mountains.

He listened to advice about which direction to come into the safe house, which roads were clear, and who would bring him in, as well as a personal opinion about Hakim and Daoud's involvement.

"I hear you," Terrence said, fury and grief stinging his mind. "Yeah, yeah, I can't say for sure—but what's fucked up is dat I can't say for sure about me own blood. But I do know dis. One— we have to bring Akhan and Laura up here to sign de fucking papers. End of story. You get our lawyer up here and I want a team to rush Hakim's resort and bring dem here. Dey sign, it's all good. Dey can go back 'ome. But I'm not sitting up in de mountains in hiding, me fadder in grief over Hector, de old men wondering and beginning to change their minds because history is repeating itself, and once again, Hakim, that foul pussy, comes out smelling like a rose. No!"

Fury had him in a chokehold as his Jeep steadily climbed up the narrow roads sans guardrails at perilous speeds.

"And for two," Terrence shouted. "I want to send a serious message to those fucking Italians who are leaning on us that, if dey come looking for trouble then they 'ave banged on de wrong door. Call Philly, our people in New York to come down to Jersey— yeah. Den get on the phone to Da Big Easy, Houston, and send 'em into Vegas. I want dem hit so hard it's World War Three, mon. Retaliation will come swift from dem—which is a good ting, and the easiest one of us to find is Hakim. So he can decide if he wants to split the Gulf fifty-fifty among family, or stand alone against invaders."

Terrence paused as his lieutenant's voice filled the receiver. "Yeah, mon. Nothing like an outside threat to make family draw together."

Lieutenants drew together in the Front Street restaurant by the I-95 overpass deciding what to do. Lil' Joey had called for immediate retaliation. No one disagreed. It was just a matter of where and when. Getting into the areas the Jamaicans controlled would draw notice, so it had to be handled a certain way. A large party of 15 discussed the merits of drive-bys, individual hits, C-4 under fuel lines. Their methods were many; all were veterans of Mob wars.

The problem was that they were used to the old way. That's why they never thought anyone would be brazen enough to stop on the emergency lane of I-95 above the restaurant, get out of a car with mud covered tags, and point a bazooka at the building.

* * *

"What!" Scapolini walked in a slow circle of disbelief in his suite, listening to fire engines and chaos on the streets of South Philadelphia. No one had made it out of the building.

Fifteen families in his network would be grieving. A neighborhood icon was destroyed. Old men and women who had served their time and had kept the secrets for generations were slaughtered as innocent bystanders simply because they'd come to work that day to serve the best pastas and gravy outside of a grandmother's kitchen. Young bus boys and dishwashers were charred remains. The media was told by the cops to claim it was a gas main so that the community wouldn't panic. But Joey knew that aside from all the grieving, the feds would move in now to lean on him hard as an additional pain in his ass.

Mike Caluzo's house was a veritable fortress. Through a pair of binoculars, henchmen crawled like ants all over the sprawling Nevada estate within the gated community. Big C came out of the house to get into the waiting Mercedes sedan, which had been thoroughly checked over by his loyal drivers. A dread stood up in the open air Jeep a quarter mile away, hoisted a bazooka, and fired.

Syd Balifoni had ordered a gin and tonic to go with his massage at the casino's spa. He lay there beneath the sheet in the warm room, trying to relax while waiting for the masseuse to prepare the oils and begin working the knots out of his back.

An unidentifiable server brought him his drink on a silver platter . . . along with a machete.

His health deteriorating for multiple reasons, Art Costanza left his doctor's office with his security forces in tow. High blood pressure, gallstones, enlarged prostate, all seemed to be converging to foreshadow his demise.

But a carload of angry young men the hue of midnight sped

the process along with Uzis and Berettas in broad daylight—no tags and V-8 engines smoking.

"My house?" Joey Scapolini said in a quiet, lethal tone, standing on his mother-in-law's steps in South Philly. *"Now they've firebombed my house?"* He leaned against the door with a thud and rubbed both palms down his face; the Bluetooth unit in his ear was splitting his skull with the information that he was hearing. He closed his eyes and spoke through his teeth. "Raze their casinos to the ground. Every last one of them."

They stood around looking at Brother B with empathy as the older man lifted his chin, tears in his eyes, and drew a shuddering breath. Akhan's familial hug just made him shake his head and release a grief-stricken sigh.

"Well, at least I got to see him before this," Brother B said quietly. "We knew it might come to this, but I didn't think it would so soon."

"I know, old friend. Nor did I, but we always knew the possibility," Akhan murmured, but shot Laura a gaze not to elaborate.

She subtly nodded her assent. There was no way that she would out Akhan's full plan, especially not to Najira and Jamal. How could that old man go to his grave knowing that his children were aware that he'd turn blood against blood to save their lives, and that this whole thing he and Brother B had cooked up was banking on the Braithwaite clan to go to war? Now that this seemed to be in full effect, she knew there was no need in belaboring the point with details.

"But that woman . . . her, too?" Najira whispered in disgust. "I'm so sorry about what happened to Hector. But they were that ruthless that they'd just kill a woman like that?"

"It was jacked up, Sis," Jamal quietly told Najira. Conflict was evident on his face. "But she was straight gangsta, told me so out of her own mouth. She got in way too deep, playing games, gold diggin', trying to get paid." He sighed hard and shook his head.

"First she worked Rapuzzio to get her a job in Vegas so she could do her thing there versus Jersey, thinking there'd be more opportunity in Sin City, and there was. She got a chance to repay Rapuzzio by going with Terrence to string him along and keep an eye on him while he was casing the Vegas joint as a high-roller."

Jamal looked at Akhan and Brother B, and then the rest of the group. "Last night, while trying to beg for amnesty, she also told me out her own mouth that Rapuzzio told her to hang with Terrence because the casino families knew he was only in Vegas, just like he'd been in Jersey, to see if there was any way to siphon profits off the old lady of the West—Big C's joint." He raked his elaborate network of cornrow designs down the glistening parts in his scalp. "The really crazy thing is, the chick actually believed she could play these boys and not get caught . . . that she was just too pretty and too barracuda to lose. But by the time she asked me for help last night, there was nothing I could do for her."

"It wasn't your fault, J," Laura said, gaining murmurs of agreement from Akhan and Brother B.

"From what you told us, man," James said, "this chick then turned on you—she and Terrence, actually. The whole thing was a setup." James looked at Akhan. "Terrence didn't know how deep the thing went with Safia and Rapuzzio, but he was there trying to cut a side deal, too."

"Yeah," Jamal said, agreeing with James. "He was down for whatever, ready to play the angry boyfriend to scare the shit out of me, so we'd think we needed to get out of the Gulf. The bull nearly worked, too—and that's why he thought we were serious."

"Wait, I don't get it," Steve said, glancing around. "She's with Tony Rapuzzio, who tells her to baby-sit Terrence . . . then at Tony's request, they spook Jamal?"

"Correct," Laura said. "There's only one reason that Rapuzzio would send his woman to baby-sit Terrence, and that Terrence—who didn't know about the affiliation Tony had with Safia—would allow her to set up Jamal for a scare job. Terrence had to

think that doing the Mafia's little job would show loyalty and ensure he had an in."

"She said that Big C was doing some stuff behind Joey Scapolini's
back . . . and she wasn't sure what it was. But Mike Caluzo knew
what that was, and because he wanted more than his uncle would
give him, just like Tony Rapuzzio wanted more than Scapolini
was willing to break him off, the two of them were gonna go into
negotiations with Terrence—thinking Terrence was the top
man." Jamal's gaze held Najira's with its intensity.

"Problem was, Terrence had lied, and the Mob boys didn't realize that Hakim was running shit, Jamaican politics inside the
organization being what it is. But Rapuzzio was gaming just as
hard as Terrence, trying to make Terrence think that Scapolini
was leaning on Laura. So he thought he'd better act fast to secure
another strong ally in him and Mike Caluzo before Scapolini
made Laura cave. And Scapolini was playing games, too. Scap was
trying to make Laura think the Jamaicans were on him and then
would be on her so much that she needed him—the great
Scapolini—as an ally." Jamal raised his fist. "May Safia rest in
peace. Wouldn't have known all this unless she'd finally wanted
out and told a brother . . . for old time's sake."

"Yeah, that one-night stand might have punched your ticket
dude," Steve muttered, "the way she was rolling. But it is great
info."

"Since you're still here, I can live with that," James said, pounding Jamal's fist.

Jamal let his breath out in a rush. "I felt sorry for the girl, actually, because she got caught up in the game. She knew too much
for her own damned good, things like the fact that Terrence was
a front man for the drugs and whatever, but as far as high-stakes
strategy, it was all Hakim's yard. Terrence wanted Hakim to think
the Mob was his problem, that's how he kept Hakim in the dark
and from having inconvenient conversations. He was always giving Hakim lying-ass reports about what Scapolini and the rest of
them were doing. Since Safia was sleeping with both sides and

the middle, and they'd be on the phones or bitching about the situation in earshot of her, she knew all this shit."

Jamal's gaze swept the group. "That *beautiful* woman would lie as quick as look at you, and was bringing Terrence info on the Mob, and taking Rapuzzio info on the Jamaicans, ready to side with whichever guy won, and getting cash and trinkets like a mercenary double agent, running info to the highest bidder."

"Well, I'll just be damned, Jamal," Najira said, holding his gaze. "That hoochie would've gotten you killed . . . not to mention, I mean, God rest her soul and all, but better her than you. How you gonna play with both the Mafia and the Jamaicans and not get screwed?"

"Some people will do anything for money," Akhan said in a sad voice.

"You got that right," Steve said, dragging his fingers through his hair. "But my question is, how do you sleep at night?"

"That's why she came to me," Jamal said with a sheepish half smile. "She was scared, wanted out, and once she saw our whole family at dinner, wanted us to work some family mojo to get her untangled from the weave and web, ya know." His smile became sad as his gaze became distant. "Yah, she was a real diggah . . . but, still, she didn't deserve a bullet in her head. I wish maybe we could've hooked a sistah up. The science she dropped on me was all that, and I'm not talking about in bed, but this mad-crazy info she just told me while running scared."

"Admirable, but not possible," Steve said. "We'd better get our own house in order, first."

"Playing those kinds of games, she'd set the ball in motion. Don't blame yourself," James said calmly. "You would have helped her, if you could've—but who knew everything was about to blow in less than twenty-four hours?"

"God rest her soul *and* Hector's," Laura said.

Akhan nodded. *"Ashe."*

A loud knock on the door that sounded like the police made everyone pause. Then a card key in the door made people draw weapons.

"Hold up, hold up," a young male voice said as he entered the room. "Hakim sent me to get you all relocated wit da quickness." Hakim's soldier held up his hands before his chest and looked around nervously as everyone in the room pointed their barrels at him. "Hey, mon. I'm just the messenger."

Chapter
15

D amage control was imperative. Making it clear to all parties that they were simply chattel moving at the behest of whomever physically had them held hostage, and nothing more, was the only assurance that they wouldn't be targeted by armed combatants. But dying simply as collateral damage was still an extremely significant possibility.

James's cell phone vibrated on his hip at nearly the same time Steve's did. James picked up as the family hustled down the hallway—someone was already going through their room and quickly throwing their bags on a cart.

He and Steve's eyes met for a second as they both recognized Captain Bennett's number frozen in the displays.

"Yeah," James said fast in unison with Steve.

Captain Bennett didn't hesitate as he barked out an urgent command on the three-way call. "Get out of there! It looks like Baghdad here in Philly. Head for the American Consulate—per Montgomery. Mob bosses got waxed, damned houses and restaurants are blowing up, drive-bys, you name it. The retaliation is serious—a Jamaican club got firebombed, four houses, every corner they controlled sprayed, convenience stores have been trashed. Like I said, get your asses out of there."

Both James and Steve closed their cell phone units at the same time, gave each other the eye, and helped Akhan onto the elevator. Each member of the family passed a nervous glance knowing something additional had just gone down. The security henchmen sent by Hakim gave Steve and James suspicious glares, but said nothing as the whole group spilled out of the elevators into the lobby.

A white Toyota minibus was already waiting in the driveway. A muscular driver was yanking bags off the cart that had come down via the service elevators ahead of them, and he was loading the back of the minibus in a quiet frenzy. The man who'd come to their hotel rooms motioned with his chin for them to enter the van. Happy tourists walked by unaware. James gave the nod and the family filed into the vehicle, helping Akhan and Brother B get settled.

Strained silence filled the vehicle as the driver and the man riding shotgun with him jumped into the front seats, slammed the doors, and the minibus careened out of the driveway. Nervous glances searched familiar eyes as well as the unfamiliar landscape. The only thing keeping Laura somewhat calm was the fact that Hakim's henchmen didn't attempt to disarm James, Steve, or Jamal. In fact, they never searched Akhan or Brother B, nor did they look in her bag or see whatever Najira might have been packing. The two old men had brought everyone a piece and the last thing she'd seen them hoist into the back of the van was Brother B's box of so-called canned goods.

It seemed as though everyone else made the same connection and a subtle truce was struck. Clearly, if they were being abducted, then their weapons to defend themselves would have been stripped. Conversely, as was the case, if they were being couriered to safety, then there would be no need for that. The only problem was, did Hakim have anywhere one could call safe? The expressions on James and Steve's faces as they took their cell phone calls, which seemed to emanate from the same strangely coincidental source, told her no.

Their driver seemed like he was on pins and needles as his

neck repeatedly craned to look in his rearview and then side mirror; the man who rode beside him followed the same pattern of head-bobbing and glancing over his shoulder out of the window. Akhan and Brother B shook their heads so slowly, as though trying to send a warning without words. James and Steve made a sign with their hands for everyone to slide down and ride low in their seats—just as a precaution against a hail of bullets each time a vehicle passed on the opposite side of the road. Heat and perspiration made everyone's clothes stick to them. Humidity and tension were thick enough to cut with a machete.

Disorienting was the only word for barreling down the thin lanes at breakneck speeds while riding on what felt like the wrong side of the road. Then out of nowhere, Laura saw it from the corner of her eye. A Jeep pulled out of the roadside thicket, swerved onto the blacktop, and gunned the motor. The minibus fishtailed as the driver jumped and stamped down on the accelerator—but the oversize vehicle with so many passengers was no match, speed-wise, for the lighter Jeep.

To her horror, the henchman leaned out the window, produced a nine-millimeter, and began firing at the Jeep that was practically on their bumper. In an angry swerve, the Jeep pulled around to the driver's side of the minibus, came alongside it, and two marksmen shots took out their driver and his soldier. Brains and blood splattered the cab and dashboard. The Jeep passed them, eating up road to get away. Chaos and screams broke out as the minivan careened out of control on the perilous strip of road. James was over the seat and grabbed the wheel, but a bloody body was in the way. Unable to reach the brakes fast enough to avoid oncoming traffic, the best he could do was yank the wheel to pull the minibus off the road into a rain ditch to stop its forward progression.

Coming to a hard, crashing stop that sent everyone tumbling, was far better than a head-on collision or meeting their destiny with the cliff-side drop that had no guardrail.

Working feverishly to attend to the elderly and Najira—James, Steve, and Jamal put shoulders to doors and began getting people out. Unhurt, Laura was also able to assist, and was thankful that it seemed no more than minor bumps and bruises had been sustained by anyone.

But the Jeep was right on them, burning back down the road. Laura watched it all happen in slow motion. James and Steve dropped to one knee in unison, Jamal and his father took up a position behind the mini van with Brother B. The moment the Jeep was in range, they opened fire. Suddenly the Jeep swerved and went over the embankment. A huge explosion rocked the earth and a plume of dark smoke billowed up in the distance.

"We've gotta take the suitcases, because they've got identifying evidence. Throw the box of ammo over the cliff so it looks like it was theirs. We've gotta walk back the way we came while I call for a cab, and we play this like tourists who were in a bus that broke down—serious cash might help a taxi driver turn a blind eye," James said quickly. "Can you walk a little ways, Uncle Akhan?"

Akhan nodded as Steve and Jamal sprung the back of the minibus and quickly ditched the weaponry. Laura was on a cell phone trying to give the resort their coordinates and sweetened the pot by mentioning the thousand dollar reward for a quick pickup—of course due to her elderly uncle's health condition in the sweltering heat. Everyone who could carry something did. Before long three taxis pulled up and came to a brief stop.

"You called da resort, Mum?" one driver asked, glancing at Laura and Najira as though not sure which woman had phoned in the distress.

Laura stepped forward and nodded. "Yes, our minibus broke down, my uncle is ill, and we need to get him—"

"To the American Embassy," James said, cutting her off.

"Dat's all the way to Kingston, mon," one driver protested."

"Here's a thousand, cash, as promised," Laura said.

"Between us all, we can put three grand in your pocket today—no questions."

All three drivers smiled.

"Then, no worries, mon," the first driver said and adjusted his crocheted knit cap as the others began to collect bags to put them in the trunk.

Within minutes, Jamal, Akhan, and Brother B were in one cab, Steve and Najira in another, with Laura and James bringing up the rear. Then their cab pulled out ahead of the other to lead the small convoy. Acid roiled in her stomach as they passed the wrecked minibus, and she held her breath hoping the three taxi drivers couldn't see the dead driver and security henchman on the floor. But their driver's gaze caught the billowing smoke.

"Dat's a bad sign, mon," he said, and then kissed a small leather pouch that he wore around his neck. "Somebody should call that in, could be a brush fire or worse—some tourist not knowin' dese roads could be down dere roasting in a rental car. Appens more than you know . . . people drink, dey tink dey can drive in Jamaica on the opposite side of de road, den boom. They crack up."

"Tragic," Laura said quietly, trying to keep her expression neutral.

"*Irie,*" their driver said, and then pulled over to a small roadside stand in a clearing that allowed cars off-road access.

James and Laura looked at each other but didn't speak.

"All way down to Kingston is a long journey, mon," the taxi driver said, unfazed. "Need sometin' cool for de throat, maybe some bottles of water—you might want to stop and let de lady go to da bathroom? I gotta stop and fill de tank anyway. Long trip. Sure you don't have to go?"

"No, thank you—we're good," Laura said, glancing at James.

James spied the other taxis coming to a stop at the rest area behind them. Obviously understanding that resistance was futile, James got out of the cab. "I'll get some water and make sure Akhan has some water and snacks. All right? I'll be right back."

"Yeah, mon," the taxi driver said, also getting out of the cab. "Dey also got Red Stripe in dere."

Laura sat back for a second and closed her eyes. She dabbed the sweat off her brow and her throat, gently patting it with the back of her hand, and then looked out the window to see Akhan slowly shuffling to her cab. The sight of his bent and tired form made her open the door to meet him in the sun-scorched clearing, but he held up his hand to stop her as though he wanted to talk in private within the cab.

Ready to accommodate his every wish given all he'd endured, she followed his non-verbal cues and simply held the taxi door open for him. He entered her vehicle with a weary sigh, stiffly getting into the backseat with her. Yet, as soon as he did so, their cabbie seemed to return out of nowhere, and he jumped into the front seat brandishing a weapon. He snatched her purse from her and put it in the front seat with him.

"We jus' need you two," the driver said. "Ever'body else can get out at the rest stop. But if you act foolish, you sign da death warrant for dem. Understand?"

Torn between looking down the barrel of the huge gun that was too close to her face and searching out of the window for James, she asked the burning question on a dry swallow. "Where's my husband?"

"Don't worry 'bout 'im." The driver motioned toward the rear window. "You got more family to be concerned 'bout, pretty lady."

She and Akhan glanced back to see luggage and family members being ejected by the taxis—but there was no sign of James. Horrified, her gaze ransacked the landscape of the small roadside watering hole. People native to the country went back behind lean-tos and continued cooking jerk chicken and pork on corrugated tin roof grills. Others went back to shucking conch to prepare conch salad and to sell the gleaming shells to tourists. A man sweated in the heat as he painstakingly shaved a massive block of ice to go in a cooler for colored syrup cones. The lady selling cowry shell and bead necklaces seemed annoyed that with all the Americans that had just piled out of their cabs with expensive luggage, there would be no sales. No one seemed to notice the duress or care. It wasn't their business.

Hard eyes that saw nothing ignored the scene, and stayed out of what clearly appeared to be a fracas between cab drivers and arrogant American tourists. Another driver joined them and slid into the passenger's side of the front seat, taking up the task of holding a gun on them while the driver gunned the engine and pulled away.

"It's taking too long for them to come back," Hakim said, pacing within his office.

"I called the other resort and the bellman said they left over an hour ago."

Hakim stared at Daoud. "It's only a fifteen minute ride from there to here."

"What if they weren't ready when our men got there?" Daoud said, trying to stem his elder brother's panic.

"What if you go over there yourself and check on things—as my top security advisor?"

Again the brothers shared a look, but this time there was malevolence embedded within it.

James struggled to his feet, his vision blurred. Intense pain shot through his skull as he stood, and his hand went to the site of the wound, his fingers sliding against a warm, sticky substance that he knew was his own blood. Reaching for his weapon, he saw that had been stripped. His cell phone was also gone, and his wallet lay on the ground not too far from him, relieved of cash and credit cards. All he had left was his ID.

He stumbled from the side of the building where he'd been dragged and dumped, and squinted against the sun glare, trying to count familiar faces. The family rushed toward him, but something was wrong. Where was Laura? His secondary thought was— and her uncle? If they got rolled in a foreign country for being stupid and desperate enough to tell them they had serious cash on them, that was one thing. But Laura and Akhan should still be there.

"You okay, dude?" Steve asked, catching James under an armpit.

"Where's my wife?"

"They took her and Pop, man," Jamal said, out of breath.

Tears were streaming down Najira's face. "This wasn't some

robbery, James. At least I don't think. Why'd they take Laura and Dad, if it was?"

"It wasn't some highway pirates," Brother B said. "Dis was people who had an objective."

"We need a ride and a cell phone," James said, holding the back of his head. "Gotta get word to Cap, gotta go make a deal with Hakim, who's the only one with enough muscle to find them both alive."

"Hey!" a lanky Rasta called out from the conch shell heap around him. "You need a ride somewhere, mon?"

The group looked at him with blank, angry stares.

"Real cheap, good price." He put down his fish knife and wiped his hands on the thighs of his low slung shorts. With a nod indicating a rusted out pickup truck, he shrugged. "For de right price, mon, I can take you to family, the police station, wherever."

"You might have noticed," Brother B said almost through his teeth, "that we just got robbed and have no cash on us at the present time."

"Yeah, mon, although I didn't see nuthin' 'appen, I know what you mean." He offered a brilliant smile and shook his head in feigned empathy. "Dese dangerous times off road away from de resorts . . . but if you got family dat can send you money, or make a loan, I can wait. No problem, mon, I can give you a ride in good faith."

Hakim tapped the Bluetooth unit in his ear as he walked the resort grounds. He'd amassed over a hundred uniformed guards with heavy weaponry to add to the security measures at his resort. There would be *nothing* to make tourists feel like the grime of the streets beyond their haven had entered to sully their vacation experience. Their good time was his cash cow. He listened to his brother's report and stopped walking. The four henchmen that were with him also stopped moving and waited.

"What do you mean you found the minibus and our men dead inside?" He rubbed the tension away from his neck. "Good. Our men drove theirs off the side of the cliffs?"

Again his brother's voice filled the earpiece. "Three of our taxis? From here?" He looked at his men and also spoke to Daoud. "Find them, and take a small army through here very quietly and bring me the men who were working both sides of the road. Call me back when you find out who's a turncoat."

Hakim disconnected the call and walked away from his henchmen. An incoming call didn't even make him break his stride. He would torture the bastards who had wreaked havoc on his plans. The sound of Terrence's voice, however, made him stop and stand very, very still.

"You've fucked us both up, Hakim—you stupid mother—"

"Me!" Hakim shouted. "You return my goddamned father and cousin!"

"I don't have 'em, you don't have 'em. De outside world has gone to war against us, brother. You'd better wake up and smell de coffee."

"Why should I believe you!" Hakim ranted. "You—"

"No, you are de one, you arrogant bastard!" Terrence hollered. "You said to do Scapolini, and I was your muscle. Now you tink you're better than me and Hector—God have mercy on his soul. But you better make some calls to the United States to see what is 'appenin' to your holdin's and mine over dere. You wanted dem hit hard and strong, well, the price is hard and strong, mon. So, fuck you and your prissy ass ways. You better have soldiers dat can deliver, or you're a dead mon walking—not because of me, either. Holla at me after you talk to some people in your camp who know what time it is. Den we deal when you can stop whining long enough to pick up the spread on the green felt and look at your cards."

They rode in abject silence for over an hour, and neither she nor Akhan said a word as the taxi pulled off the road to a small, nondescript white and aqua house that sat off the road a bit in a quiet, residential enclave.

Clothes at neighboring houses fluttered on the yard lines. A few chickens pecked gravel and scooted out of the way of the taxi's intrusion when it pulled up. Children were visibly absent on this school day, and rough hands opened the cab door and yanked at Laura and Akhan's clothes to make them quickly exit the vehicle.

Shoved forward, Laura and Akhan glared at the men who'd made them stumble up the short walkway and short flight of steps. The men glanced around and then opened the door, pushing them inside.

Not sure what to expect, Laura's eyes adjusted to the dim interior. Sitting on the sofa with a smug expression was the last person in the world she'd expected to see: Bradley.

He stood with a cocky smile and folded his arms over his chest. "Well, as I live and breathe."

"What do you want with us?" Laura said, her fear eclipsed by worry for James. If they'd killed her husband . . .

"To make money on you. Simple." Bradley chuckled and shook his head, addressing Akhan. "You've got the big families on all sides trying to get you to change some paperwork—which won't mean shit once the land is taken by eminent domain. But they don't know that's imminent," he said, laughing at his own bad joke. "In the meanwhile, they all need you alive to sign, or so they think . . . and I bet the way they'd see it is, if they pay the ransom you'd be oh, so willing to sign the problematic region over to them for protecting your lives and making bad guys like me go away." He leered at them from where he stood. "So, we're gonna make some phone calls while one of you screams—you can flip a coin. Gotta make this authentic, you know."

"Don't touch her," Akhan said in a dangerous whisper. "I'm old and already near death. But if you harm my niece, I'll kill you."

Bradley laughed with the two other men in the room, his eyes filled with amused disdain as he looked at Akhan. "I bet when you were buying up all that land and making all those mortgages, you never dreamed of getting your ass in such a sling, did you?"

Akhan didn't answer or blink. His gaze simply burned with years of unspent rage.

"Leave him alone," Laura said in a near hiss. "He's an old man, and he's sick. He needs to eat and sit down, have plenty of water if you're going to make money off us."

"Bitch," Bradley seethed. "You're done running things. He sits and eats and drinks when I say he does—just like you do." He gave her a menacing glare. "There are things I could do to you, even though I'll keep you alive for monetary reasons, which would not be pretty." He looked her up and down as the men behind her and Akhan laughed harder.

"Doubtful," Laura said, looking Bradley up and down. "They might, but you? I just don't see it."

The men behind her hooted; suddenly Bradley lunged and reached for her throat. It all happened in slow motion. Akhan pulled out his Beretta and aimed at Bradley's head—just in time for his gaze to lock with Akhan's. Two stunned henchmen who had underestimated an elderly man, and who'd never patted Akhan down, hesitated for one second too long—the reefer they'd smoked in the cab on the way up was their fatal undoing as Akhan turned and opened a clip in their chests.

Laura was on the bodies instantly, stripping them of weapons and collecting her and Akhan's cell phones out of their pockets. Their eyes met, they knew what they had to do. There was a car in the driveway. This was a quiet, residential neighborhood. Gunshots would bring the police.

"So, you have come to your senses and both want to meet on neutral ground," Terrence said. "*Irie*. Dat can be arranged."

"You're not gonna make any of this bullshit stick," Joey shouted. "You know and I know that I didn't whack Caluzo, Balifoni, or Costanza. I know my fucking rights!"

"Here's what you oughta know," Captain Bennett said close to Joey's ear so no one else could hear. "I know it, you know it, but since you're the only Mob boss left standing after this shit, people in your own organization are starting to wonder. And in their wonderment, they are losing faith that Joey Scapolini is an honorable guy. Family homes blew up, Joey, and now people want amnesty and all sorts of shit. For all these deaths, you will probably get life, maybe even a lethal injection. Your people are squealin' left and right. It's bad in an organization when there's no trust."

Scapolini jerked his head away from the captain's, panic glittering in his eyes. "Those fucking Jamaicans did this shit, and you know it!"

"Uh-huh. But they're in Jamaica, and anybody we wanted you did us a favor and exterminated here. . . . So, thank you. It's been a pleasure doing business with ya, Joey."

A series of almost unintelligible expletives flew from Scapolini's twisted mouth as officers restrained him in the middle of the narrow South Philadelphia street.

Captain Bennett pushed Scapolini's head down hard against the police cruiser as a lieutenant cuffed him. "Read this bastard the Miranda."

SWAT kicked in a hotel room door in Philadelphia. A startled George Townsend rolled off the prostitute he'd hired. She scurried away to huddle against the headboard. Gun barrels trained on a pair of surprised gray eyes.

"Freeze! George Townsend, a.k.a. John McHenry; you are under arrest for extortion, racketeering, being an accessory to kidnapping, attempted murder, and illegal campaign contributions."

"Keep the faith," Brother B said quietly as he sat next to James in the back of the pickup truck on the bumpy ride back into Montego Bay. "Dey took the guns, so we can't be blamed for anyone that got shot with them. It all looks like a tourist robbery, by and large. Once we get to dat girl Megan's shop, we can get cash, money from our banks sent to—"

"Brother B, no disrespect," James muttered, his eyes on the horizon. "I don't want to focus on anything but getting my wife back in one piece."

Najira and Jamal nodded.

"Dad, too," Najira said as Steve pulled her closer under his arm. But they all fell quiet again as they passed the accident scene that made traffic grind to a halt. Police and rescue vehicles closed the road and a fierce, searching roadblock had been established.

Hakim and Daoud looked down from the helicopter at the yacht out in the water. Hakim nodded and the pilot circled the area to prepare to set the chopper down on a deserted strip of beach. Carefully maneuvering it to a soft landing, he began to power down the engine.

Through the large bubble windows, Hakim and Daoud saw Terrence advance with two men—another cousin they recognized and an old friend from the neighborhood from years gone by. Those men, like Daoud and the pilot, were armed. That was as neutral as it could get. Hakim and his brother climbed out of the craft.

Both bosses nodded and walked several feet ahead of their security teams.

"Shame dat blood has to act like dey're strangers," Terrence shouted over the surf and dying chopper whine.

"Shame that family would cut a side deal with strangers," Hakim retorted. "That is what fucked this all up, Terrence—no trust."

"It wasn't 'bout trust," Terrence said with a sneer and then spat on the sand. "It was 'bout respect and money, neither of dat you was ready to share, you greedy bastard."

"Fuck you—where's my father?" Hakim shouted.

"I tol' you, we don' 'ave 'im!"

Someone blinked; a bullet exited a chamber. Terrence fell back in time to see Daoud's hate-filled expression.

"You think you'll be taking my place and my money?" Daoud shouted. "After all the years I waited, bitch!"

Hakim turned, yelling "No!"

Terrence fired from the ground, his grip squeezing off gat rounds more out of reflex than from awareness as he hit the sand. The pilot opened fire on the men who'd been with Terrence.

Bullets riddled Hakim's back, sprawling him out in a bloodied heap. From nowhere a bazooka launched as Daoud jumped from the helicopter screaming for his brother.

Everything on the beach within the dead family circle burned.

"The big mistake he made," Montgomery said, "was going to my daughter's house to case it and plant surveillance equipment in there. That gave us time to put a LoJack in his rental car, follow him around, as well as go behind him, take out the bugs and set them up where Megan could feed him phony transmissions."

Laura and Akhan stood in the driveway numb; neighbors peered at the police cruisers and State Department cars with avid curiosity.

"We've got a man who will clean this up. You were never here, this was just part of organized crime activity," Montgomery said. "Under normal circumstances, I wouldn't have even come here—but after what you did for Megan . . . and seeing them try to harm her again, but still you helped, I wanted to personally escort you to a helicopter so we can get you to the embassy."

"Ma'am," an officer said discreetly, taking the weapons from Laura and her uncle's hands. "Your purse." He gave her back her purse in exchange for a weapon, and she watched the officer begin to wipe away her prints as he walked back to the cruiser.

"Don't worry, we'll have a good media spin on this."

Laura and Akhan looked at Montgomery.

"I have a man on the inside—Rick. Can you help him out by sending the party line through him?"

James sat in the helicopter, his nose almost pressed to the glass. He didn't take a full breath until they touched down at the embassy, disembarked, and walked a short distance through the building, and he saw Laura's blurry face.

Epilogue

Back in Maui . . . a month later

A full family meeting convened in the large living room of Laura and James' winter home. The dead had been laid to rest, police inquiries had been answered, and like Teflon, any hint of involvement didn't stick. They had gone through the worst; now it was time for positive, forward motion.

Laura's mind worked on two plateaus at once as the conversation went on around her unabated. One part of her mind was putting the finishing touches on Najira's wedding.

James would be Steve's best man; she was the matron of honor. Najira's seed pearl–splattered, strapless empire waist gown was beautiful. Her flowers stunning. Her veil just right to dust her shoulders. The cake would be butter cream icing topped with white roses. The guys all had their tuxes. Aqua raw silk, knee-length, strapless sheaths for the women in the wedding party was something she and Andrea could deal with and use again at a cocktail party. Jamal would walk with her attorney, Andrea, who had become very interested in the serious, handsome man ten years her junior. It all worked to the greater good, Laura reasoned. Rick would be there as her media man with his wife; the Montgomerys,

Megan, Kaitland, Sean, Donny Haines, Captain Bennett, Luis, the people who meant something in their lives would be there, the feast would be small, intimate, and lavish—just the way Najira wanted it. Laura's mind riffled through the details to be sure everything was in place. Najira's father would walk her down the aisle and her uncle, Brother B, would say a few words in a poem he wrote himself. They'd honeymoon in Fiji, *not* in Jamaica. The wedding dinner would be later that night, but there was business to attend to.

Laura looked away from the window and shifted gears. "Give it all away and take the tax relief from the charitable donation. At this juncture the holdings are a burden. I have the other money we made along the way set up in trust for future generations, anyhow."

"It makes the most sense, Laura," Akhan said, sipping his ginger tea slowly. "I want everything to go to a nonprofit corporation that deals with preserving poor people's housing—and I want it to be very public with every elected official present. A huge ribbon cutting ceremony. Anyone who defaults on an Xavier loan should be given forbearance, due to the flood, as a stipulation of this generous, tax deductible donation . . . but all these millions turned over should hit the headlines hard enough that any predators still lurking will know that coming after us is of no use." He sighed sadly and took another long sip of tea. "And anyone who was a threat is now dead and buried—God rest their souls in peace."

Laura glimpsed her uncle's somber expression as Rick took notes and her attorney, Andrea McPherson, scribbled furiously on her pad. Everyone in the room knew that Akhan was referring to his and Brother B's sons. Even the primary dangers from the Mob had been wiped out—and no one could come after her or her family, because they didn't have a thing to do with it. Joey Scapolini was behind bars for longer than he'd been alive already, and he had no words of blame for her. It was the Jamaicans. They felt the same way. Bradley's name was mud, no credibility, and he was dead and gone . . . and even Townsend, who'd been sent to prison for a very long time, probably didn't have long to live, once Scapolini's boys or the Jamaican clans figured out how to get to his duplicitous hide. This also meant that any scary politician who was planning to ride on the eminent domain scheme would step away from the whole tainted deal.

Yes, this was a very good exit strategy indeed. As her uncle Akhan had taught her, the universe was efficient. This time it proved itself being the best master of the game by orchestrating a series of events that Laura could only run behind, catch up to, and follow like the adult-child of the world that she was.

She turned to Rick, her tone gentle for the sake of her uncle and brother B's significant losses. "We need to do something symbolic like turn the keys of the kingdom over to Habitat for Humanity, or some analogous organization. Maybe we'll break it up into many pieces for many charities. This way, any politician who attempts to eminent domain the land up and out from under individual families will have the stock media footage that your network takes, as well as the whole community backlash thing to deal with it in a very open forum."

"Sometimes you have to give up something to get something worthwhile," Andrea McPherson said, completely oblivious to all that had occurred.

"*Ashe,*" Akhan murmured. "This is deep wisdom, and I have found in my years that the greatest wealth is peace of mind." He looked at Najira and Steve. "Tomorrow I get to walk my daughter down the aisle when I didn't think I would." He looked at Jamal. "I have a son who makes me proud and who is a warrior. If he hadn't brought certain facts to illumination, we would have perhaps never known how involved this struggle truly was."

"And now that we know," Laura said quietly, "we make sure that they are never, *ever* allowed to put us in a position like this again." She glanced at Andrea, who nodded. "I want a reinforced electrical legal fence around the terms and conditions so tight that if they pick up the papers to read them they'll fry."

"Done," Andrea said and went back to poring over the paperwork.

Rick looked up at James and then shot his gaze to Akhan. "Man, you don't ever want Laura on your bad side, do you—even if this is my favorite girl."

"No, you don't," James said with a half smile, pulling Laura into a loose hug. "But if she's on your side and has your back . . . there's nothing in the world that can stop her."

He watched her undress slowly while he stretched out on the bed, enjoying the sensual view. As much as he loved their family and had been bugging Steve to go hang out for the traditional bachelor's beef and beer, he was actually glad to be home. He'd had enough adventure in the streets for a whole lifetime—so had Steve and Jamal, so they'd called it an early night.

James smiled just thinking about what Jamal had said about having a nervous tic when it even came to chasing foreign tail in a club. Steve was good for two beers, and then kept looking at his watch. That suited him just fine—they were his boys, but damn, what he had waiting at home was beyond compare.

As far as he was concerned, this was the best part of the day. She almost seemed to be peeling off layers in a quiet striptease, but he also knew that was just her way. Laura was so damned sexy sometimes, especially when she wasn't even trying to be. Her natural flow was more than enough for him, and remembering how many times he'd almost lost her, gave him a sense of deep appreciation for everything about her.

The way she tilted her head as she stood by the dresser taking off her earrings in deep contemplation . . . then how she turned over her delicate wrists and dropped the jewelry in the case. Her graceful fingers unhooked her watch and took off her bracelet. The air around her almost felt charged, because she moved with such current building within him as he waited for her to unhook the back of her linen dress.

His eyes followed her slowly lifting, toned arms and the curve of her breasts as they tilted upward, and then his gaze zeroed in on her fingers as they fumbled a bit with the hook before getting it to yield. Watching her do something so simple had made him hard. The sound of the zipper sliding down made his mouth go dry. With her back to him, she pulled the lime fabric away from her toffee-hued skin to reveal a flesh-toned bra made completely of lace.

Anticipation made his breath shallow. He knew when she finally turned around he would be able to see the dark outline of her nipples through the lace, and couldn't wait for her to slip the dress all the way off so he could see which panties she'd worn to match it.

He was rewarded for his patience. She took off the dress and kicked off her little flat sandals. Lace. Nude lace was what she'd chosen. God help him, her smooth behind looked so good peeking through the sheer fabric. His line of vision slid down her shoulder blades, down the supple length of her spine, down the dip in her back that had two small dimples indented in her skin right where her pelvis fanned out to full, round hips. But her ass . . . maaan . . . and her long, toned legs. When she turned around, his breath literally hitched.

"I've been so busy with planning the wedding and tying up all the loose ends . . . Did I tell you today that I love you?" she murmured, watching him watch her with a knowing smile.

"I don't think so," he murmured, too turned on to even smile back as his gaze slid from hers to travel over her beautiful mouth, and down her throat, stopping to linger at her breasts before caressing her navel, and then settling on the dark thatch unconcealed by lace. "But that's okay, baby, you can just show me."

NO TRUST

LESLIE ESDAILE BANKS

ABOUT THIS GUIDE

The suggested questions are intended to
enhance your group's reading of
this book.

DISCUSSION QUESTIONS

1. Do you think it's possible for extreme jealousies to exist between siblings/family the way it played out in *No Trust*?

2. Have you or anyone you know ever experienced "high drama" around potential inheritances or post-funeral arrangements?

3. If you were in Akhan's shoes, with a set of children from a first union who had gone to a life of crime, murder, and drugs—and another set of children who were "doing the right thing," would you have made his choice?

4. What do you think Akhan could have done differently?

5. Do you think that now that the main players in the Philly mob have been killed or jailed, Laura and James will have some semblance of peace?

6. What do you think about the concept of this book—that the most dangerous people, in the end, were the ones closest to them?

7. Was Jamal's tryst with bad girl Safia a good thing (because it opened Pandora's box so the family could find out the truth), or a bad thing (because he shouldn't have been messing with that girl in the first place)? What is your opinion?

8. Do you think the family should have told Najira what was going on from the beginning, given that she nearly had a nervous breakdown worrying about her father in the previous book?

9. What about Steve's role? Are you glad to see him and Najira finally tie the knot, or do you think she should have hooked up with someone else?

10. Do you think all of this will make the family (Laura, James, Jamal, Najira, Steve, and Akhan) tighter, or will there be fall-out later?

GREAT BOOKS, GREAT SAVINGS!

When You Visit Our Website:

www.kensingtonbooks.com

You Can Save Money Off The Retail Price
Of Any Book You Purchase!

- **All Your Favorite Kensington Authors**
- **New Releases & Timeless Classics**
- **Overnight Shipping Available**
- **eBooks Available For Many Titles**
- **All Major Credit Cards Accepted**

Visit Us Today To Start Saving!

www.kensingtonbooks.com

All Orders Are Subject To Availability.
Shipping and Handling Charges Apply.
Offers and Prices Subject To Change Without Notice